Hetta Coffey is a woman with a yacht, and she's not afraid to use it.

A self-employed engineering consultant with a penchant for taking on oddball—read: shady—projects, Hetta has a way of attracting trouble.

With her floating home dry-docked for repairs in Mexico, Hetta needs a place to live, and a job to pay the boatyard. Landing a project at a mining operation not far from her boat, Hetta finds herself on the tumultuous Arizona/Mexico border, where all hell is breaking loose—even *before* she gets there

WHAT READERS ARE SAYING
HETTA COF

Needing cash to get her beloved boat's bottom fixed, Hetta takes a new job at a copper mine close to the Arizona border in Cananea, Mexico. In Hetta's words, "And, presto chango, I was off on another adventure, and this time with a regular old, probably boring job where I couldn't get into any trouble. I heard wings flapping and a pig flew by."

If you've read her other Hetta Coffey books you too will laugh at the pig as he flies by because you know Hetta will soon be neck deep in trouble. Sure enough, Mexican bad guys, International smugglers, a semi-domesticated coyote, a not so domesticated bad-boy who goes by the name of Nacho, some home-grown American terrorists, a love life that threatens, and friends and family who begin to show up, threatening her sanity. It's enough to drive a girl to drink.

There's enough humor to keep you laughing through the book, and enough mystery to keep you turning the pages. Regardless, I guarantee, you won't be bored.—**RP Dahlke, The Dead Red and Sailing mysteries.**

****

For anyone who has not read any of Jinx Schwartz novels, you are missing a masterful storyteller who tells a memorable and enjoyable tale.

JUST DESERTS is the fourth novel in this Hetta Coffey series by author, Jinx Schwarz. She also wrote an outstanding young adult novel, *LAND OF MOUNTAINS,* which was based on her own life growing up in Haiti.—Teri A. Davis

****

Jinx Schwartz makes me laugh. Hetta Coffey books are feel-good reads. We know we're in for it when she observes, "I was off on another adventure, and this time with a regular old, probably *boring* job where I couldn't get into any trouble." Trouble in the mines? Nah. So what's with smugglers, drugs, dirty bombs and terrorists, and what do they have to do with boredom? To say nothing of flying pigs. That's not all. Boat troubles and love troubles jazz up the mystery. This fourth in the series is highly recommended for pure enjoyment.—EGF "Book Nut"

Just Deserts
Published by Jinx Schwartz

Book 4: The Hetta Coffey Series

Second edition print publication Jinx Schwartz 2013

The characters and events in this book are fictional, and any resemblance to persons, whether living or dead, is strictly coincidental

BOOKS BY JINX SCHWARTZ
www.jinxschwartz.com

The Hetta Coffey Series

Just Add Water *(Book1) EPPIE AWARD, Best Mystery*

Just Add Salt ***(Book 2)***

Just Add Trouble *(Book 3) EPIC AWARD FINALIST*

Just Deserts ***(Book 4)***

Just the Pits ***(Book 5)***

Just Needs Killin' ***(Book 6)***

Just Different Devils ***(Book 7)***

Just Pardon My French ***(Book 8)***

Hetta Coffey Boxed Collection 1 (Books 1-4)
Hetta Coffey Boxed Collection 2 (Books 5-8)

Other Books

The Texicans
Troubled Sea
Land of Mountains
(Finalist EPIC AWARD, Best YA)

Just Deserts
by
Jinx Schwartz

Acknowledgments

Thanks once again to my first line of defense, editor Holly Whitman, for her sharp red pencil and keen eye, and Candi Keeney for her input. As always, I owe much to the guy who puts up with this writing thing, my husband, Bob "Mad Dog" Schwartz.

Dedication

In loving memory of my cousin, Clemmie Sue Maul.

As her daughter, Misty Toomey, wrote: She was a little woman with a big heart. A ninth generation Texan, Clemmie was born September 22, 1952 to Beuford Lemoyne and Al Marie Maul in New Braunfels, Texas. Although she was a free spirit, she lived most of her life in the same house she was born in. She was a loyal and hard worker. Marriage was not her strength, but friendship was. She always said that her two girls were her greatest accomplishments in life. She loved fishing, classic cars, live music, campfires, friends and family.

I was so depressed last night I called one of
those suicide hot lines.
I reached a call center in Pakistan.
They got all excited and asked if I could drive a
truck.—Anonymous on the Internet

Just Deserts

Desert: Pronounced dessert; what you justly deserve. "Upon a pillory-that all the world may see, A just desert for such impiety."—Warning Faire Women, 1599

Prologue

Safiyya removed her prayer rug and a water bottle from her rucksack. Then, in preparation for her morning prayer, she washed her face, head, hands, forearms, and feet in the icy water. Checking her compass, she faced Mecca and performed the first of the required five daily salats. For her, though, it might be her last. She would be living with the enemy, and must avoid detection, but her handler had assured her God forgave, for her intent was pure.

Ablution and prayer completed, she returned to her perch. Soon, a fine mist blanketing the fertile valley below yielded to the sun's rays. Rooster crows, dog barks, the smell of cookfires, and human voices wafted upward. She trained her powerful binoculars on a group of workers laughing and chatting as they headed for a day in the fields. Even during winter months, farmers had work to do.

A stream, running clear and low this dry time of the year, meandered through the valley. Come summer, though, southwest monsoon winds carried rains that swelled the river into a muddy rampage, trapping villagers between crossings for days at a time. It is these storms, however inconvenient, that pump life into what would otherwise be a barren, sunburnt valley.

The sun's warmth granted some small relief from yet another miserably cold night spent on surveillance. For almost three weeks she'd kept vigilance day and night. Every few days a runner brought provisions, but otherwise she was alone. She'd had little sleep, for if anything or anyone moved, day or night, she was instantly alert. Her notes grew as trucks groaned and bounced up and down the mountainside from the main road, people walked and rode to work, meals were served, laundry hung out to dry, equipment rolled in and out of hangars and barns. Every action went into her book, one she must soon burn.

She sketched people, noting their habits. This information was to be shared with others at the camp, even though she instinctively disliked these men. They were, after all, of the same class as those who tormented her people, and they remained infidels. However, she needed them for her mission so she would do as told.

A fat tractor driver smoked hand-rolled cigarettes and occasionally nipped from a bottle hidden under his seat.

At eleven each morning a cook threw scraps to four patiently waiting dogs. No matter what else was going on those dogs gathered by the kitchen door like clockwork. No wonder in that, thought Safiyya, the curs eat better than many of my own people.

Horsemen rode fence lines every Monday, checking for breaks and rounding up stray cattle.

Saturdays, around one, the workweek came to an end and many people drifted down the hill, in groups or alone, to shop, or perhaps visit friends and relatives in the nearby village. Some rode horses, some walked, a few drove battered cars or pickups.

She'd easily picked out her target from the description given her. Unfortunately, this individual rarely left the premises, and spent most hours of the day in what she knew to be an office building. Inconvenient to her mission, but Safiyya had figured a way to solve the problem. Even people with seemingly few habits always had at least one.

Snapping off a few last photos, she took pride in the mastery of such a sophisticated camera. Because of her humble beginnings and lack of education, her training on this and so much other high-tech equipment had been slow, but the teachers were quick to praise her sharp mind and dedication to Jihad.

They were also pleased with her chosen appellation: Safiyya. It was a fitting name for a martyr, as Safiyya was Muhammad's aunt who saved Muslims from destruction in the battle of the Trench when she heroically used a pole to kill a Jewish spy.

Accepting Muhammad as her only God, Safiyya now knew the enemy, and would have the satisfaction of avenging the loss of her once proud heritage. It was finally all so clear, thanks to her new family of believers. She would fight so that her people would never again be forced from the sidewalk into the street when meeting a light-skinned person. Her dark skin and small stature, which had once relegated her to near animal status, was now a blessing for her mission; the despised enemy simply ignored her. Her class, her caste really, made her a non-person, no more noticeable than a stray mongrel foraging for scraps at their feet.

A hot wave of hatred surged through her body, warming her. She smiled, shimmied back behind a boulder, pulled a colorful scarf over her head, and headed for the main road, back to base camp. Her stakeout complete, she must prepare for the next step.

With her Glock18 and camera tucked out of sight in her back satchel, she sauntered from a path onto the pavement. Even walking alongside a main highway in broad daylight, Safiyya was as good as invisible.

A truckload of soldiers rumbled past, never giving her a second glance.

She ducked her head, hiding another smile; she was probably better armed and trained than any one of them.

A pickup sped by, purposely passing close enough to force her from the pavement, but skidded to a stop a few yards ahead. She made no move toward the truck, for she knew they had not stopped to give her a ride, but the five men walking ahead of her. The men vaulted over the tailgate and the truck sped away, leaving her to plod along in a cloud of red dust.

Insolent infidels.

Within ten minutes her own ride arrived. She lay in the back seat, covered by a blanket, until thirty minutes later when they left the asphalt and bumped onto a dirt road to their training stronghold. Only then did she sit up and relax, looking forward to the company of her fellow Jihadists, others whose spiritual fire and purpose matched her own.

Oh, she knew liberation of her own people would not come in her lifetime, as she was soon destined for imminent glory in the name of God. Her reward would be with Him, but only after striking the infidels where they least expected it.

When the dinner bell rang, she headed for a small mess hall reserved for her faith. Unlike in the main dining room, a Muslim cook insured that the tortillas were lard free, and the refried beans contained no pork. On her way she whispered lines from the surah known as Al-Anfal, or the Spoils of War: *"Against them make ready your strength to the utmost of your power, including steeds of war, to strike terror into the enemy of Allah and your enemy."*

The steed of war carrying her to glory will be mighty and satisfyingly devastating. The enemy shall feel her wrath, and reap their oh-so-just deserts.

Chapter 1

San Carlos, Sonora, Mexico

Dry dock.

High and dry.

On the hard.

All nautical terms for a vessel out of the water, which is where both *Raymond Johnson* and I were destined after Mario, the guy who takes care of my boat, surfaced.

He hauled himself onto the dock, pushed back his dive mask and said, "You have bleesters, Café," using the Spanish word for my last name, Coffey. Most Mexicans prefer the nickname, as attempting to wrap their mouths around my first name, Hetta, is difficult, and comes out sounding something like I-ate-ta.

"Bleesters," he repeated, "you have them on you bottom."

"Beg your pardon?" As far as I knew this handsome young Mexican had no knowledge of my bottom, but then I had been tippling a tad intemperately of late.

Another boater joined me on the dock and overheard Mario. He pulled a face, shook his head and spat, "Blisters," like an expletive. "Bummer. Looks like you're headed for the hard."

I took a slug of iced tea, which needed something. Like, say, rum.

"Hard should be my middle name, Russ," I whined, hating myself for it. I'd been on a three-week downer after Jenks Jenkins, my long distance sig-other, returned to his job in the Middle East, leaving me on my boat in San Carlos, Mexico, all alone.

Not that I don't like San Carlos. As a matter of fact, the combination of the Sonoran Desert and the Sea of Cortez, both the Baja and mainland sides, appeal to my fascination for desert islands such as Mykonos and Aruba. When fronted by turquoise waters, an otherwise barren landscape of volcanic rock, sand, and cactus take on a surreal quality I equate to boating on the moon. I guess you could say I'm a desert rat, when said desert is surrounded by water.

I'd grown to love the Sea of Cortez, but being left alone, once again, made me cranky. Of course, that was nothing new, either. I've been solo, and cranky, most of my adult life, but too busy working to think much about my aloneness, or maybe I'd simply convinced myself that, with my crappy track record where men are concerned, I was better off as a loner.

Then I met Jenks and all that changed, but now he was gone, off to Kuwait to finish up a project, and I was once more on my own. Nothing to do but throw myself a pity party nonpareil.

I knew I should a gotten another dog instead of a boyfriend.

"Hetta, are you all right? You don't, uh, seem yourself lately," Russ ventured, albeit gingerly. He'd only known me a few months, since I'd rented a slip in Marina Real. Up until recently I'd been on my game, which isn't always a good thing, but at least it's eventful rather than plain pathetic.

"Hey, just because the *federales* haven't been around for a few weeks doesn't mean I'm not having any fun," I growled.

He grinned. "It has been blessedly quiet in this part of the Sea of Cortez. No bodies, no kidnappings. You must be losing your touch."

"Oh, hush and explain to me why I'm headed for the hard. Is this some kind of stupid intervention attempt? Should I expect the guys from rehab to show up, maybe even Doctor Phil?"

Russ—Mad Russ to his friends—threw his hands into defense mode. "Whoa, there. Someone got up on the wrong side of her bunk this morning." He moved behind the dock box, in case I moved to shove him into the water.

Mario, on the other hand, sat tight, grinned, and sluiced fresh water over his face from a water hose. He finds it amusing when I get my dander up, so long as he's not the danderee.

"Did I hear the B-word?" another sailor, Smith, asked. He and Maggie, his sweet-faced West Highland terrier, and her buddy, Marina the ex-dock dog, were returning from their morning constitutional.

I scooped the terrier into my arms and scratched her ears. "Baby dog, they are calling me names. You wanna bite 'em for me?" Maggie wiggled and licked my nose.

"Not you, Hetta, although I have heard folks use another B-word in conjunction with your name. B, as in blisters, is what I meant."

Russ scrunched up his well-tanned face and narrowed his blue eyes in concentration. In his fifties and sporting a graying ponytail, he assumed a stance that had probably served him well as the college professor he'd been before dropping out to cruise. "Water gets past your gelcoat, which is a combination of resin and pigment that makes the boat look all smooth and shiny. Plain old fiberglass ain't cute."

My boat's seemingly seamless, shiny, gelcoat looked fine to me. "Gets past? How?"

Smith, also fiftyish, wore shorts, tee shirt and flip-flops. He pushed back his battered hat to reveal longish hair that might have once been red, but now looked almost pink. Both men, dressed in the uniform of a cruiser, were single-handing their sailboats in search of adventure and, if they got lucky, women. Adventure is easily available in the Mexican cruising world, but single women are rare. As far as I knew, I was the only woman on her own boat in the entire Sea of Cortez.

"Well, Hetta," Smith said, "that's a very good question. How do blisters happen? There are tons of theories out there, but it's probably a microscopic hole in your gelcoat, unseen by we humans, but sneaky little water molecules find them. They enter the hull, mix with the chemicals used in the manufacture of fiberglass, and morph into an acid composed of larger molecules."

"Acid?" I shrilled. "Acid eats stuff."

Mad Russ let loose a Hollywood horror film maniacal laugh and bent into an Igor-like stance. "Eats stuff? Why, yes my dear, and your lovely boat may be the next to die."

Funny, yes, but this was no time for antics. "Russ, get on with it."

"Oh, okay. You are much more fun when you're drinking, you know. Here's what happens. The larger molecules are trapped under the gelcoat, can't find their way out. Pressure builds and forces the gelcoat to separate from the fiberglass, forming a bump, or blister. If the blister breaks while the boat is in the water, you got a hole that allows for greater water intrusion into the fiberglass laminate, and the blistering process spreads to deeper levels. Enough to shiver the timbers of any skipper."

I groaned. "Coming to a marina near you: The Molecule That Ate My Boat."

Russ cackled again, probably because it was my boat, and not his. He patted my shoulder, saying, "But there is some good news. I can get rid of them for you. Unfortunately, though, you'll have to dry out for at least six weeks."

"Hey, I haven't been drinking that much."

"Not you, Hetta," Smith said, "although that's not such a bad idea. Your boat has to dry out. As in, out of the water. If *Raymond Johnson*'s bottom has blisters big enough for Mario to detect underwater, they must be pretty bad." He picked up Maggie, who had squirmed so wildly in my arms when she spotted a seagull that I'd put her down on the dock. She'd immediately hied after the gull and returned empty-mouthed, seemingly satisfied that she'd driven the offending bird to flight with her fearsome barks. "You gotta haul, pop the blisters and let them drain and dry. Then you grind out and refill holes."

I did a quick calculation of my finances. Not good. "Sounds like the expensive microdermabrasion I once had at a snooty San Francisco spa. It hurt like hell and, I have a feeling, so will this."

Russ shook his head. "Not so bad if I do the work. Come on, let's walk over to the boatyard and I'll show you some boats that are in various states of recovery."

He explained what had to be done as we inspected pockmarked victims lined up in what I called the sick bottom ward. Within a few minutes I had the dismal picture.

"Okay, Russ, once we grind, fill, sand, what then?"

"You might consider laying on a barrier coat, a film over the fiberglass that adheres to the hull and sometimes helps prevent blisters from recurring."

All of this was starting to sound very, very, expensive. "What if I, like, pretend the blisters aren't there?"

Russ shrugged. "Worst case? Your hull delaminates."

"Delaminates? As in, falls off? Holy crap."

"I doubt it's all that bad. When was the last time you had the bottom painted?"

I thought about that. "Never."

"And you've had the boat how long?"

"Couple of years."

"Was there an out-of-the-water survey?"

I recalled my forty-five foot powerboat, *Raymond Johnson*, sitting high and dry, with a boat inspector, for some reason called a surveyor, climbing all over, making notes. I worried over every little mark he made on his clipboard, wondering what it meant. In the end, all was well, or so it seemed. Now I have bumps on my hull?

"Earth to Hetta."

"Huh?"

"Did you finance the boat?"

"Uh, sort of. The owner is carrying the paper. And there was a survey. Why?"

"The survey can give us a clue as to how bad the blisters are. If they didn't find any two years ago, that's good news. However, if I were you, I'd get this baby out of the water, pronto, and take care of the problem before it becomes a big one. I'd say you were due for a bottom paint job anyway."

"How long will she have to dry out?"

Russ shrugged. "Depends on how deep the blisters are, but probably a minimum of six weeks, max three months. If I were you, I'd start looking for somewhere to live. The boatyard is a tough place to camp in for any length of time. Can't use your holding tanks because there's no place to pump out, and getting up in the middle of the night, climbing down a ladder and walking all the way to the marina John can get real old, real soon."

Well, fooey. My plan, the one I'd budgeted time and money for, was to wait for Jenks to finish in Kuwait and return to Mexico in a couple of months. Three tops. We'd then cruise up the west coast of Baja and California, take the boat home to Oakland in time for me to get on someone's payroll before I got tossed into debtor's prison. I sighed. "Okay, let's hear the bad news. What do you think I'm looking at, money-wise?"

"Again, depends on the damage. In a way you're lucky, though."

"And that would be how?"

"In the States this job would run into the thousands. Down here, with me as the worker, much less."

"Less than thousands can still be a thou," I growled. "But what's gotta be, will be."

While Mario cleaned up his dive gear, I asked him what came next if I wanted my boat repaired. "Café, you go to the *oficina* and talk with Isabel. I will pull out the boat when you are ready."

I'd watched boats being hauled out daily by an inventive submersible trailer with six hydraulic arms. Pushed to the boat ramp by a large tractor, a trailer is eased under the floating boat, then mechanical arms are maneuvered, embracing the hull like an octopus around a tasty shellfish. Mario then carefully reverses his tractor, pulling the boat and trailer onto land. From there, the whole dripping shebang jounces down the road to dry storage, or *marina seca*, a quarter of a mile away. It seemed like such a smooth operation, but now that it would involve my boat, it suddenly looked iffy. The whole thing made me nervous. Does marine insurance cover your boat if it falls off a trailer? Or gets broadsided by a cement truck speeding toward the new house sites on the hill?

I told the guys I needed to check on a few things and headed for my boat files. And a beer.

Chapter 2

"Ja-yun," I wailed into the phone, Texas-izing Jan's name. We Texans tend to make any one syllable into two when under stress. "My bottom has blisters and I don't know how they got there."

"Well good grief, Hetta, at the rate you've been sucking on a bottle lately, perhaps you've developed diaper rash?" my best friend unkindly remarked.

"Very amusing. You should know about diaper rash. What do you use on Chino?" I couldn't resist a barb that obvious, what with Jan's amour du jour being a dozen years her junior.

"Play nice, or I'll hang up."

"Okay, okay. Anyhow, it's not my butt, it's *Raymond Johnson*'s bottom."

"He always did have an itchy bottom. Remember how he used to scoot it over your loverly peach carpet in your old house?"

Raymond Johnson, my dog, not my boat, was my much beloved, but dearly departed yellow lab. After his death, I sold my house—the one with those dog poop streaks on the peach carpet—and bought a forty-five-foot motor yacht that I named after RJ. He'd gone to doggy heaven over two years before, but it seemed like only yesterday he was happily harassing mailmen and wreaking general mayhem in my old Oakland, California neighborhood. "If he was still with me down here he'd be in butt-drag overdrive, what with all the jalapenos and refried beans. What magnificent farts he'd have."

"Ah, yes. Eau du Dawg. So, what's this crisis of yours all about?"

I told her about the looming bottom job and how I was about to become homeless. "And trust me, Mexico ain't no place to be homeless."

"Tell me about it. Not that I'm totally homeless, just creature comfort deprived. You can come over here to the Baja and stay with me and Chino if you're desperate, and if I'm still here."

Until a few months back, Jan, a CPA and computer whiz, was involved with my boyfriend's brother, Lars. Then she helped me bring my boat down to Mexico, met the handsome Doctor Brigido Comacho Yee, whose nickname is Chino, en route, and jumped ship on poor old Lars.

Now she was beginning to realize that her Latin lover, a world-class expert on whales, might be more devoted to cetaceans than her lovely self.

I tried to picture myself living, like she was, in a little grass shack on a windswept Baja beach facing the cold Pacific Ocean. "What, Miss Jan, would I do there with you and Chino? Count whales all day? I think I'll leave that to you two. I prefer living with some simple basics, like running water and ice. How long will you be on the whale count? And what do you mean, if you're still there? Trouble in paradise?"

She sighed. "The whales'll start migrating north in late February, but we're scheduled to hang around through maybe mid-April. Then Chino wants to go back to the dive boat and continue the hunt for that sunken galleon he's convinced is somewhere in Magdalena Bay. As for me, I'm getting a little homesick."

"As for me, I'm still waiting for my cut of that treasure. After all, my boat anchor snagged the astrolabe." Not that I knew what an astrolabe was at the time, but Chino did: a circa 1590 navigational tool used by the Spaniards for their Manila Galleon route. He not only knew what it was, he was certain the ship it came from was the San Carlos, a galleon that sank and stranded his ancestors on the Baja. Valued at a cool million or so, the astrolabe now resided in a Mexican museum.

"And I've told you a hundred times, when Chino finds that galleon, you'll get credit in the history books."

"I want credit at the bank."

"Forget it, everything belongs to the Mexican government. So, what are you going to do with yourself for the next several months? Drink yourself silly? Ya know, Hetta, maybe it's time for you to dry out, right along with your boat. After all, you are pushing fort—"

"Don't say that word!" I yelled into the phone. "I'm still in my thirties."

"Late thirties. I know you miss Jenks, but every time I've talked to you for the last few weeks you had that, well, sound."

"What sound?"

"Like you had a hangover."

"Hangovers have sound?"

"Yours do. After all these long, long, really long years, I know when you're on a bender, and this one has gone on far too long. Don't make me come over there."

"Jeez, you sound like my Mama."

"Let me rephrase that last statement. Don't make me call your Mama. Matter of fact, maybe you should go home to Texas and stay there until you, and your boat, are rehabilitated."

"My parents aren't even home. They're out RVing somewhere."

"In that case they'd probably be thrilled to have you house sit."

"Jan, Aunt Lillian lives a half mile away from them. Without Mother there to intervene between me and her crappy sister, I'd probably off the old broad in no time. Lillian ain't worth going to jail for."

"She is a handful."

"She's a miserable, mean old sot."

"So that's where you get it."

"I am neither mean nor old," I protested, leaving *miserable* and *sot* unanswered.

She let it slide, satisfied, I guess, with a fifty-percent insult. "So, like, what are you gonna do?"

I sighed. "I thought I could skate by down here on the boat until Jenks gets back, but since that's no longer an option, I guess I'll call the Trob."

"Atta girl. Think positive. Get a job. Clean up your act. Have your roots touched up."

How does Jan know when I need a root job? And for that matter, why doesn't she ever have dark roots in that blond hair of hers? Life ain't fair. "Hey, how do you know when I need a root job? You haven't seen me since Christmas, and now it's February."

"Because I know you, and the way you operate when you're feeling sorry for yourself. I'll bet your hair has faded to orange by now, right?"

"None of your bidness," I growled, but a glance at my reflection in the sundeck window confirmed her suspicions. My normally thick red hair was flat and lifeless with dark roots and orangish tips flaming the lank spikes of my outgrown pixie cut. Add a puffy face and blood-shot eyes, and any sign of the perkiness that usually gets me over with guys is history. Just as well I'd stayed out of the local cantinas, for the lack of male attention, welcome or not, would thrust a coup de grace unto my suffering self-worth.

The woman's a freakin' psychic, I thought as Jan went in for the kill. "I'll bet you look like crap, and you know what to do about it. Drag out those exercise DVDs, do some Pilates. Yoga. Tai Chi. Something. No more booze. Get your hair done, take two aspirins, and call me in the morning."

"Thank you, Doctor Killfun."

I hung up and dialed a number in San Francisco. "Yo, Wontrobski, how's it hanging?" I chirped into the phone, trying to sound more chipper than I felt. Not that the Trob was as attuned to my moods as Jan, but when looking for meaningful employment, one needs to project a modicum of enthusiasm, so I chirped. After all, I was talking to the guy who, by giving me projects, keeps me one bare step ahead of bankruptcy.

"Hetta, where are you?" He didn't have to ask who it was because few people have his private number: me, my what-ever-he-is, Jenks, and Allison, his wife. I have the number because Wontrobski and I are friends, and Jenks has it because at the moment he was working on contract for Baxter Brothers, and therefore, The Trob.

"I'm on the boat, in Mexico."

Silence followed on his end, as the Trob is the Ebenezer Scrooge of small talk, so I got right to the point. "You got any jobs that no one else wants?"

Fidel Wontrobski—his father was a Polish communist, thus the name—didn't answer, but I heard him tapping the keys of his humongous laptop, an oxymoron unless you have a lap the size of Michael Moore's.

When folded closed, his so-called laptop was the size of a large suitcase. It fit well on his massive desk, in his massive penthouse office, atop the massive headquarters of the massive engineering firm, San Francisco's Baxter Brothers.

From experience, I knew to shut my massive mouth while the master worked. For all his brilliance, neither multitasking nor sociability is his strong suit.

With his hooked beak of a nose, black frizzy topknot, stooped posture and dark, baggy clothes that flap as he stalks the halls of his aerie, he closely resembles a turkey vulture. When he somehow captured the heart of my friend, the petite, black, gorgeous, and politically ambitious Allison Cuthbert, you could have knocked me over with one of those black tail feathers. It must be true that there is someone for everyone, but this oil and water combo still had me puzzled.

While Wontrobski attacked his keyboard at the speed of sound, I jotted down a list of stuff I had to do before leaving the boat. After all, *Raymond Johnson* is my home, and everything I own, except for some stuff stashed in Jenks's Oakland apartment, is onboard. I'd load up my old Volkswagen with work clothes, my computer, and all of my—

"Detroit."

"Excuse me?"

"Detroit," he repeated. "A job there."

"Gee, couldn't you come up with something a tad more fashionable? Like, say, Bangladesh or Darfur?"

Silence. Sarcasm is lost on the Trob, as is most humor. He flat doesn't get it, but knows enough to be annoyed that he doesn't get it. Rather than nettle him further with any clever repartee, I clammed up. As my mentor, the Trob is the one who keeps me out of the poorhouse. We'd remained fast friends although I was rudely dropkicked from the Baxter Brothers' payroll a few years back after being told by no less than a past Secretary of State that I wasn't a team player.

Since then, with the aide of the Trob, I have established a reputation for taking on jobs that might be kindly described as marginally legal. They pay well, but land me in hot water more often than not. My friend Jan, a preteen when Charlie's Angels was a big TV hit, teases that I am the devil to the Trob's Charlie.

If it weren't for those Wontrobski moneymakers, Hetta Coffey, SI, LLC, would be out of business. The SI is my little phonetic joke for Civil Engineer. As the sole owner, employee, Chief Executive Officer and Chief Financial Officer of my own engineering consulting firm specializing in materials management, I don't mess with the Bank of Trob, lest he quit tossing those lucrative scraps in my direction.

So far, even though I've been known to occasionally consort with those of questionable character, I have never been jailed, thanks in part to my old friend, Allison Cuthbert Wontrobski, who along with being married to Fidel, is also another best friend and, when required, my lawyer. The two Wontrobskis, to paraphrase Jack Nicholson's Melvin Udall in *As Good as it Gets*, sometimes make me wish I was a better gal.

"Sorry, Wontrobski, I'm a little cranky today. I just found out my boat has to go into dry dock for repairs, so I need a job. If I have to go to Detroit in the dead of winter, so be it."

"Okay."

"Okay? Does that mean I have to get out my mukluks, or that you'll look for something else?"

"Something else."

"Great, thanks. My options are running thin down here."

"Bye."

After I hung up, I realized I hadn't asked about Allison, who somehow became pregnant. I say somehow, because my mind simply cannot wrap around those two doing IT. The former Allison Cuthbert, a radical black lawyer lady from Houston, married to Fidel Wontrobski, a brilliant engineer and driving force of one of the most conservative firms in the whole world is mystifying enough, but trying to imagine them actually making a baby is downright incomprehensible.

And to think, I introduced them.

Chapter 3

Since I figured it would be awhile before I heard back from Wontrobski, I walked to the marina office, made arrangements to haul my boat, then took a hike up a series of stepped terraces leading to the fancy new homes on the hill. Most of the houses were empty, their million dollar views left to lizards lounging on elaborate decks above sparkling infinity pools.

Gasping for air after the one hundred and fiftieth stair—yes, I counted—I semi-jogged downhill via the road, back to the boat. After downing a quart of water, I stretched my aching calf muscles and took a hot shower. Feeling downright virtuous that I might be on the way to losing some of those pesky extra pounds I haul around, I ate a bowl of low sugar oatmeal laced with mango slices before going to town in search of a haircut.

By late afternoon, my hair was both red and perky again, and I sported a French manicure. I fired up a DVD and struggled through all twenty-four forms of Tai Chi while pelicans dove for the bait fish boiling around the boat. They refused to share their catch, so I ate a salad, no wine, popped those two aspirins prescribed by Jan, and slept like a baby, except I didn't toss and turn, pee in my pants, or cry every two hours.

Early the next morning I scaled the dreaded terraces again, downed more water instead of my usual pot of coffee, ate an egg white omelet, and geared myself to tackle the world's evils. I started by calling Jan, my parents, and Jenks. Not that they are evil, mind you, but superwomen have to warm up, too.

Jan was delighted I'd taken her advice, and would be leaving Mexico.

Mother and Daddy were relieved I was leaving Mexico.

Jenks was delighted I was leaving Mexico.

Call me perceptive, but I detected a pattern here. Was I the only one on the planet who thought I belonged in Mexico?

Evidently not, for the phone rang shortly after noon. "Cananea."

"Good day to you, too, Wontrobski. Can I buy a vowel?"

"What?"

Not a Wheel fan, I gather. "Never mind. What about Cananea?"

"A job."

"You're sh...kidding me. Cananea? That's only three hours from here." Actually, more like five if one does the speed limit, which one never does. I had actually driven through Cananea. Of course, I was kidnapped at the time and therefore slightly preoccupied with the status of my future, but I recall it as a dusty little mining town only a few miles south of the U.S. border. In Mexico. "I'll take it."

"The job doesn't pay like your usual ones. It's legitimate."

Drat. "Oh, well, at least I'll make enough to rent a place and buy a tamale or two, right? I have enough in the bank from the last two projects to pay for my boat repairs."

"You'll be fine, so long as you don't live at the Cananea Four Seasons."

Wow, was that a joke? "I seriously doubt that's an option. Best I remember, it's a pretty small town. What will I be doing?"

"Something you do well. Their whole system is old, brinking on hazardous, and they are taking heat from labor unions, which effectively shut them down three years ago. Now they've gotten a legal nod to break with the unions and feel this is the time to modernize in anticipation of a rise in copper prices. All of the old as-built drawings and equipment manuals are in their files. All you gotta do is put together a cost estimate for a fast-track repair or replace schedule, what it will take to get them fixed up and operational. I had a guy lined up to go down there, but his wife got sick and he backed out."

Double wow. The Trob managed an entire paragraph, but of course, it was work related and that he can talk about.

"Sign me up. Do I have to come to San Fransicko for paperwork and the like?"

"Monday."

"You want me at your office on Monday?"

"No."

"You'll take care of everything on Monday?"

"No, you have to be in Cananea on Monday."

Yikes. Today was Thursday. I'd have to get the boat hauled, secure her, pack, and drive north, all in record time. "Send me an email with details. I'll be there."

And, presto chango, I was off on another adventure, and this time with a regular old, probably boring job where I couldn't get into any trouble.

I heard wings flapping and a pig flew by.

In whirling dervish mode, I prepared to leave. Only once during the day did a soupçon of self-indulgent pathos creep into my elated attitude.

While packing I mistakenly pulled out one of Jenks's shirts, caught a whiff of him, felt a sting in the back of my eyes. Right before he boarded his flight in Hermosillo, he'd told me, "Honey, I'll be back in two or three months. Meanwhile, you really, really need to stay out of trouble, because I've had to leave Kuwait, and the project, twice, to fly into Mexico. I can't keep doing it. It's not fair to my client, or my brother." He didn't add, or me, but it was implied.

At the time, I promised to be good, kissed him goodbye, watched his tall lanky form head for the runway, trudged back to my car, and sat in the parking lot, waiting until his plane took to the air. Driving to Walmart for supplies, my spirits plummeted, and by the time I was back on the road to San Carlos, his parting shot had taken on, in my mind at least, less of a request and more of a warning. Maybe even a threat. I do not like being warned or threatened.

Even so, with my crappy track record where men are concerned, the thought of losing the only good guy I'd ever been with was devastating, and when I'm devastated I tend to hole up and drink wine, or worse, hit the bar scene looking for a distraction. Those distractions have brought me a world of hurt in the past, so, on the sunny side, this boat bottom thing came along in the nick of time to save me from my miserable self; the one who'd been replaying Willie Nelson's soulful version of "Am I Blue" ad nauseam while drinking myself blue in the face.

Being forced back into the work world greatly reduced my odds of messing up with Jenks, but his admonishment, which I took as ominous, set my bleach-enhanced teeth on edge. I despise being in a position of vulnerability, and that's how I felt: vulnerable. With most sensible people, fragility might instill caution, but in my case it can spin me into a foolhardy spiral that bodes badly for me and everyone around me.

Maybe a case of bleesters is someone's way of letting me know I need an attitudinal correction?

Chapter 4

It only took one night aboard the boat in dry dock to convince me this was no way to live.

Monday morning, after a restless night high and dry, I was more than ready to jump ship. Even though I made two preemptive after-dinner trips to the marina loo, I feared I'd have to trek over during the night, which, of course, made it so.

Not only did I lose sleep, I was exhausted from the drudgery of putting the boat to bed for a prolonged period. I gave all the packaged and perishable food to the gate guards and other boaters, shut the sea cocks on the through-hulls to keep out bugs and critters. Wrote myself notes on everything I'd done that would need undoing when I went back into the water—open all sea cocks, for instance—covered the windows with aluminum foil, removed canvas, tarped what I could.

To ensure my boat didn't flood on dry land, I arranged for Mario to keep an eye on the batteries so the bilge pumps remained operational during rainstorms. My solar panels keep a trickle charge on the batteries, but one cannot be too cautious. Then there was *Se Vende*, my panga. I had been fortunate to get a small enough slip so as not to share with another boat, leaving ample room for my skiff. Now I had to find a place to put her, as the slip would be rented to someone else. It became apparent that the only thing to do was haul her as well, so now I was paying storage on two boats.

The list went on and on, and so did I, until I was too tired to even go out for dinner. I ate a bag of potato chips instead and skipped the beer in light of the distance to the bathroom, for all the good that did.

By the time I got behind the wheel of my old Volkswagen Fox Monday morning, I was sick to death of my boat and ready to move on. I didn't look back, not that if I did look back I could see anything; every square inch of the car, with exception of the driver's seat, was crammed with my stuff. Jed Clampet *et famille* might come to mind, were it not for the fact that my VW Fox was totally restored and therefore quite respectable looking for her age.

While I merrily cruised around in Mexican waters, a dastardly old enemy of mine rudely pushed my Fox into the Oakland Estuary, which should have been it's demise, but the VW held sentimental value; it had belonged to my dog, RJ. Okay, so he didn't actually drive it, but in the old days before I bought the boat, I drove a dandy little BMW convertible, and dog slobber upon my leather upholstery was verboten, so I bought the VW for dog outings.

Call me overly schmaltzy, or perhaps a dullard, but when the little station wagon was pulled from the estuary, I coughed up eight grand to a car restorer, and now I had it back, all brand spanking new. Since her restoration, I have dubbed her Holle, after an ancient woman who, depending on whose mythology you choose, is either a Goddess of renewal and transformation, or a mean old crone. Holle has elements of both and can be a cranky starter at times. I guess those automobile outfits can only do so much with a car that's spent several days under salt water.

All packed and ready for a new adventure, I gave *Raymond Johnson* a fond goodbye pat and wound my way over to San Carlos Bay during the morning so-called rush hour. Hundreds of worker bees in buses, cars, flatbeds, and on foot, headed for myriad construction projects springing up along the beaches and mountains to assuage Gringo baby boomers' and retirees' quests to own waterfront property, even during an economic downturn.

Not even the twin-peaked Tetakawi's, San Carlos's famed landmark, were spared the building boom. A new façade marked the entrance to a road cutting between the goat teats, where one can, for a mere million or so bucks, live in what I've dubbed the Casas de Cleavage. Or perhaps Domiciles de Décolletage.

I stopped by Barracuda Bob's for breakfast, got a sandwich to go. I had a two o'clock appointment in Cananea, and the coffee-swigging regulars at Barracuda Bob's Table of Knowledge and Wisdom informed me that that last seventy-seven kilometers, a sinuous two-laner on Mex 2 from Imuris to Cananea, could easily eat up two hours.

My handy conversion card revealed that seventy-seven kilometers is only 47.8455 miles, and divided by two hours is a whopping 23.9 miles per hour. I headed northward, knowing that getting stuck behind an overloaded, fume-belching truck on that treacherous piece of road plays hell with one's driving schedule, unless, like me, you know the Mexican rules of the road.

Creeping truckers traditionally turn on their left-hand turn blinkers, an indication for a following car to stomp the gas and pass, even though the passer can't see past his front bumper. Overtaking in this manner, usually on a blind curve with a solid stripe, is not for sissies.

Lucky for me, the VW Fox is a peppy little model. Made in Brazil in 1987, she had a four-cylinder fuel-injected engine that for some reason handles like a sports car. When jammed down a gear, and the accelerator stomped to the floorboard, this car is capable of whipping around a truck in time to avoid a head-on with an oncoming semi.

Of course, while I'm doing this, I hope like hell the trucker who gave me the go-ahead blinker really isn't meaning to turn left. Judging by the number of five-cross curves, many a driver failed to wait for the okay. This little game of turn-signal roulette leads many an unsuspecting Gringo to being T-boned when they foolishly turn on the blinker to indicate an intention to turn left. Silly buggers.

Hoping against all odds that I wouldn't end up with my own little white cross, I white-knuckled my way northeast, toward horsemeat.

Chapter 5

An online search garnered the following on Wikipedia:

Cananea, from the Apache term for "horsemeat," is a city in the northern Mexican state of Sonora. The population of the town was 30,515 as recorded by the 2000 census. The population of the municipality, which includes rural areas, was 32,061. The total area of the municipality is 4,141.1 square kilometers.

This is the location where the company The Cananea Consolidated Copper Company was founded in 1899 and was the protagonist in the Cananea Strike of 1906 that resulted in the death of 23 people in a fight between strikers and a posse led by Arizona Rangers.

A corrido titled La carcel de Cananea—the Cananea Jail—written in 1917 became famous in Mexico.

Sounds like my kind of town.

Why it was named Horsemeat I never learned, but since the first mining registry in 1760, Cananea has been a lightning rod for conflict. Some say the mining strike there in 1906 fomented the Mexican Revolution of 1910, and as I soon found out, little had changed. Not that anything like a little civil strife stops me from tackling a new project. My entire life I've always looked forward to fresh horizons and any new turn in the road promising adventure, usually because of some debacle I'd left in the ditch behind me.

As I wound my way into the mountains, my spirits soared despite a small, dark suspicion that Wontrobski's first candidate for the job didn't really have a sick wife. Caught up in the euphoria of tackling a new undertaking, I drove to my date with Destiny. Luckily, Destiny was on a Mexican time clock, for a string of ten-mile an hour trucks that even I couldn't pass put me behind schedule for my two o'clock meeting.

Lunch, siesta, or both had emptied the mining office. Not a mouse in the house when I arrived at two-twenty, but someone had conveniently left a computer online, so I picked up my email, and then, under the auspices of furthering my Spanish skills, tried, fairly unsuccessfully, reading a few in-house memos, which were as boring as those in any language. I was checking out file names when two men walked in. Caught red-handed behind the desk, I closed out the file and said, "*Buenas tardes.*"

"Do you speak English?" one of them asked. I nodded.

"Oh, good. We have a three o'clock appointment with the director."

"Yeah, well good freakin' luck. I had a two o'clock and haven't seen a soul."

"Let me guess, you gotta be Hetta Coffey."

"Guilty as charged. Who are you?"

He produced a card with a logo I knew and loathed: Baxter Brothers Engineering, San Francisco, California.

"Mining and Metals Division, huh? If you guys are here, why am I?"

"Oh, we're here on another matter, but Mr. Wontrobski asked us to look you up."

"You mean the Trob wanted you to make sure I showed up sober, right?"

The Gringo looked genuinely perplexed by my question, or maybe it was that I called Fidel Wontrobski, a Baxter Brothers heavyweight, by a nickname. He was saved from answering by the arrival of a giggly flock of young women in ubiquitous Mexican secretarial uniforms, and two well-dressed men. As I was still ensconced in someone's chair, I quickly rose and joined the Baxter guys. If anyone took exception to me being behind the desk, they certainly didn't show it. Or maybe any concern was tempered by what I surmised were tequila fumes.

The short Mexican, only slightly taller than my five four, stepped forward, grabbed a Baxter man's hand and pumped it as he gave the rest of us a gander at his mouthful of yellow, malposed teeth. "Our apologies for being late. It is Maria's birthday, so we took the *señoritas* to lunch." His upper lip twitched as he gave the other men a beady-eyed wink that implied more than lunch was served.

Something about this guy set my own perfectly straight and bleached teeth on edge. Perhaps it was my past experience with some short men who overcompensated their lack of stature with exaggerated swagger, or maybe it was his uncanny resemblance to that little rat-faced president of Iran,

Mahmoud Ahmadinejad. Whatever it was, he gave me the creeps.

Creep boy didn't do himself any favors, either, when he totally ignored me while fawning over Baxter boy. Twice, within a three-minute conversation, he managed to intimate he was somehow related to Carlos Slim, the richest man in Mexico, probably the world. The name-dropping further inflamed my already tweaking last nerve almost as much as his discounting the presence of my precious self.

That just will not do.

I took a giant MAY I? step forward, hoping to menace his personal comfort zone at least as much as he was pissing off mine. "Well, golly gee," I said, grabbing his damp little hand and giving it a wrist-snapping yank, "it's just too bad I didn't arrive in time for lunch. I'm a barrel of laughs with a bottle or two of tequila under my belt."

His smarmy smirk uncurled. "Excuse me, Miss uh...."

"Hetta Coffey, *a su servico*. I guess you're the big cheese around here?"

Totally discombobulated, he squeaked, "You are *engineer* Coffey?"

"In the flesh."

"But, you are—"

"Very welcome," interrupted the other Mexican man, smoothly recovering Shorty's fumble and running with the ball slicker than Jerry Rice in his heyday. "I am Juan Orozco," the handsome man said, "and *Señor* Racón here and I have looked forward to your arrival."

"*Mucho gusto, Señor* Orozco. And you too, *Señor* Ratón," I said with what I hoped was a sincere look on my face while using the Spanish word for mouse. Mouse, rat, what's the diff?

His eyes narrowed. "It is Racón, not Ratón."

"Oops, sorry." I turned back to Juan Orozco, and since I'm a sucker for Julio Igesias types, granted him a million peso smile. "It is *señorita, señor. Por favor,* call me Hetta, or if you prefer, *Café*."

"Oh, I like *café*, very sweet."

I guffawed. This Mexican I was going to get along with. He flirted fair.

On the other hand, if Rat Boy had to work within a mile of me for the next few weeks he might as well gnaw D-con and get it over with. I continued exchanging pleasantries with Juan Orozco until he excused himself to usher the Baxter types into a meeting room somewhere, leaving me with Racón.

His beady little eyes darted about the room, as though seeking a hole in the wall through which to make his escape from mean old me. I really wanted to bat him around a little longer, but perhaps I had overreacted? Maybe, shocked that I turned out to be a woman, he was simply flustered and just kept stepping into it? So, in the name of working relations, and being the charmer that I am, I gave him a shot at a fresh start. Sort of.

"So, Señor Ratón, looks like we will be working together."

He sniffed the air. "Engineer Coffey, since you seem to have a problem remembering my mother's last name, perhaps you would prefer my father's: Hayat."

"Oh, yeah, I've stayed in his hotels."

He gave me a pained look. "H-A-Y-A-T. And, I do not work. I hold a position."

That's *it*. "Doggy hide the bone?"

"Excuse me?"

"Never mind. What position would that be?"

"I am liaison to the mine."

"Oh. What do you liaise, exactly?"

"The Hayat family have vast holdings in the mining industry. I am here to watch over our interests."

"Ah, I get it. Happened to me, once, so I feel your pain. I screwed up so badly the company banished me to Mogadishu. That's okay, I'll try to get things running smoothly around here so you can get out of this hell hole, back on the old polo grounds."

His cheeks bloomed purple and he developed a bad case of guppy mouth. He finally got it; he'd been saddled with Überbitch from Hell. He quickly fobbed me off on Maria and fled.

Maria's English was excellent, and she made it clear she was delighted and fascinated that a mere woman sent Racón scampering for cover.

Now that I was her hero she'd be a wealth of info as to where they kept the skeletons. As always, if you really want to know what's going on in a company, make friends with the gals who assist.

Maria steered me into a dimly lit back room where faded drawings, manuals, spare parts lists and the like were crammed into wooden file drawers, then gave me a quick rundown on the so-called filing system. I pulled out a folder, and with it a plume of dust. Maria apologized and handed me a tissue. What I needed was a gas mask. Hadn't these people heard of Valley Fever?

A sneezing fit sent me back into the front office. "What are the chances of getting that place vacuumed?"

She looked doubtful, but said she would try to get something done.

"Also, Maria, I'd like a jobsite tour, get my bearings. Oh, and do I need a pass, or sticker, or something to come and go at the main gate?" I didn't add, *Just in case the old guard and his dog should regain consciousness.*

"I will have the operations manager give you the tour in about an hour, and I shall arrange a pass for your car window. You have a car, yes?"

"Oh, yes," I beamed. Most folks might not think much of my twenty-year-old VW, but I love her.

"*Bueno*. Now, if you will excuse me, I must take refreshments into the men of your company."

"Not my company. I own my own consulting firm and contract myself out to Baxter. Oh, before you go, can you give me a key to the office? I tend to work odd hours."

She looked a little perplexed, but shrugged. "As you wish, but we never lock the door. No need, for everyone must pass through the main gate."

"Oh, of course. Security." I hid a grin.

She made to leave, then turned back. "I have made a reservation for a room tonight, but, well, perhaps we should change it?"

"I definitely need a room."

"Miss Café, Cananea is a working town, with limited accommodations. The good hotels are both full and when I booked your room, I did not know you were...alone."

"You did not know I was a woman."

"Well, yes."

"What, they don't allow lone women in the hotels here?"

"Yes, of course they do. It's only that the hotel I was able to put you in is not so...good."

"So, what do you suggest?"

"Perhaps you would prefer to go to Douglas, or Bisbee, for the night?"

"I'm pretty tired. You don't think I'll be safe at the hotel here?"

"Oh, you will be very safe. It is just not the best hotel in town."

"I'm beat. I'd settle for a couch tonight."

She smiled uncertainly, then left to get the guys some coffee, which evidently they were incapable of doing themselves. Was I gonna have fun here, or what?

The hotel thing reminded me that unless I'm working in a very large city I don't blend in. Even if I scored the best room in town I'd still be relegated to a crappy social life. I can't hang out with the guys without raising eyebrows and it was plainly clear that

I wasn't gonna be bosom buddies with the women working at the mine. I'd need a house and even then I'd be a curiosity not to be trusted with the male population, and inaccessible to the female. Dang, why can't they build mines in places like downtown Paris?

Sighing at remembrances of past outposts like this one, I ventured once again into that back room and surveyed with dismay what would be my office as soon as the HAZMAT team moved out. Gingerly unrolling a curl of drawings marked PLOT PLAN, I walked outside to orient myself. Off in an azure sky to the north, some kind of blimp glinted white above a mountain range. At least ten or twenty thousand feet high in the deep blue sky, I reckoned.

Sweeping vistas lay in all directions, some marred by old strip mining scars. Didn't look like much mining going on now, though. On the way into town, I got the definite impression of a fading economy. Maybe the results of my little job here would give the place a much-needed shot in the old pocketbook.

North, under that blimp, mountain ranges flanked a wide valley, itself dissected by a stand of huge leafless trees that I'd bet my bottom dollar were cottonwoods. From a previous project I did back in San Carlos, I remembered the San Pedro River, the only river running north from Mexico into the States. And one of the last free-running rivers in the U.S.

"*Señorita* Café," a timid voice called out from the office. One of the other secretaries stuck her head out the door.

"Yes?"

"Do you wish for some, uh, *café*?" She giggled at her inadvertent joke.

"No, gracias." I pointed at the blimp."What is that?"

Misunderstanding me, she said, "Sierra Vista, Arizona. She is our sister city and," she got this dreamy look, "they have a mall."

Ah, the ever-popular shopping mall. The way she said it, she could have been talking about Disneyland. I'd ask someone else about the blimp later. I motioned her outside, walked to the side of the building and pointed south, toward another valley.

"And that?"

"The valley of the Rio Sonora."

"A big river?"

"Oh, yes. It is in a beautiful valley, with much vegetables. I am from the village of Arizpe, near the river."

"Maybe I'll drive down that way one of these days, check it out."

Her face clouded. I've learned that Mexicans, who can be almost childlike in their honesty, do not like to give out bad news, or contradict you, so I asked, "Is that a problem?"

"No, but you should not go alone. It is a very...solitary road."

"But you go home to visit, right?"

"Yes, but I take the bus. It is safer."

The phone rang and I didn't get to ask, "Safer than what?"

What I should have asked was, "Safer *from* what?"

Chapter 6

Hotel Afrodita had the appearance of a drive-thru fast food joint, but at the frosted window, instead of taking my order, they handed me a drawing with my room and parking place Xed in. My parking space turned out to be a garage, and as soon as I eased the car inside, the door slid down. A dim light marked an unlocked door into a room decorated in early ugly.

It was a fairly large room, as motels go, and ornamented entirely in whorehouse red. Even the ceiling was red, except for the portion covered by a huge round mirror. Dusty velvets covered the bed and windows. Sliding open what I thought was a closet door, I found a whirlpool tub. The decorator had evidently tired of vermilion, for the heart-shaped tub was bright fuchsia.

Hearing a knock, I opened the door to the garage, found no one there, then followed the rapping sound to a wooden slide-up window where, once opened, only the chest of a man was visible. A hand appeared with an invoice, and what looked like a menu. I took the menu, set it aside for later, handed over a five-hundred peso note, got two hundred back, and the window slid shut.

I put a six-pack of Tecate I'd purchased, along with some ham and cheese, into the mini-fridge, then dug out a pair of disposable rubber gloves, and the bug and disinfectant sprays I never travel without. I stripped off the ratty bedspread and a suspicious looking blanket to find clean sheets, which I covered with my own linens and the blanket I also travel with. I'm no Howard Hughes, but when I can, I take my own stuff.

Chores done, I sat on the bed, flipped on the TV, and grabbed the menu. Maybe I wouldn't have to settle for a cold sandwich, after all.

The first page indeed offered food and booze available for delivery through that sliding window, after placing an order on the—what else?—red phone. I was trying to decide between cheese enchiladas and *carne asada* when a moan caught my attention.

On the fuzzy television screen, two hairy beings, genus and sex indecipherable, groaned and panted while performing indeterminable things on one another. Then the camera panned out and my mouth fell open. Diving for the remote, I quickly surfed through at least eight more porn channels before finding the nightly news from Mexico City. The commentator, a buxom blonde in a low cut sweater, spoke slowly enough so I caught important details. A commercial boomed on after yet another curvy gal gave the weather, so I turned the menu's page, and lost all interest in world events.

At first I was confused by what I saw, but then I'm sure my eyes bugged when it became apparent what I was looking at. Photos of sex enhancement devices, along with instructions for their use, were available from room service, through that same sliding window. I'd heard many a dildo joke, but never actually seen one, and certainly not a dozen configurations. Who knew they came in colors? This called for a beer and some serious reading. Getting my Spanish/English dictionary from the car, I worked my way through the confusing contraptions, ointments, and potions never covered in your average high school Sex Ed class.

Deciding on a ham and cheese sandwich after all, I briefly considered the whirlpool, but thought better of it. Considering this room obviously normally rented by the hour, Lord only knows what was in the water. I took a shower instead.

I'd had a long day and dozed off just after eight. Good thing, for I managed only a couple of hours sleep before business picked up. The bang of garage doors and sliding windows, creaking bedsprings, and vocally satisfied clients passed through the paper thin walls all night. I finally grabbed a few Z's toward dawn, when the passionate returned to their dispassionate wives.

I later learned that love hotels in Mexico are designed for maximum discretion and security. One's car is hidden from the street, and a back exit affords the ever-changing clientele's undetected egress, safe from prying eyes of wives, husbands, boyfriends, and the local clergy.

Sleep deprivation does not set well with me, and I was on my second day. This, coupled with that long drive and an exhausting few days of putting the boat in the yard, took its toll. When the morning cadre of lovers catching a quickie before work arrived, I gave up on any more rest, packed up, and drove to the mine.

The same old man and dog snoozed at the gate. I was beginning to suspect they were dead, stuffed, and placed there for effect.

As Maria told me the day before, the office door was unlocked. I grabbed a pillow and blankie from the car, threw on a Mexican poncho to ward off the chilled office air, and curled up on a dusty leather sofa. I was dead to the world when Maria showed up at nine. I sat up and blinked, startling her.

"Oh," she gasped, then realized the poncho-clad person in her office wasn't some kind of bandito. "Café, you are here."

"What, you didn't expect me to live through the night?"

"Your hotel was so bad?"

"It depends on your definition of bad. Believe it or not, I've been in worse. Once in Sumatra, for instance."

Not getting my sarcasm, she smiled. "Oh, I am so glad. *Señor* Orozco was very upset with me when he found out where you were staying. He has instructed that I ask you to take today, and tomorrow if necessary, and find a place to live across the border. He feels you will be happier there, even if you have to drive thirty miles each morning."

Who was I to argue, especially since I had already reached the same conclusion?

I rifled through a few file cabinets, took a couple of plot plans, packed up my gear, told Maria I'd call her, and drove to the Naco, Arizona, border crossing. At the U.S. checkpoint, I handed over my passport and asked the customs guy where I could get some decent food. He directed me to Turquoise Valley Golf Course, less than a mile away.

Expecting a snobby atmosphere and exorbitant prices, I was delighted to find a clubhouse with cheap food and the ambiance of an old bay area yacht club, like the ones Jenks and I haunted. Even better, cowboys bellied up to the bar, half the early lunch crowd chatted in Spanish, and everyone was friendly.

Had I taken a wrong turn and ended up back in Texas?

Chapter 7

Seated at a table with a golf course view, I practically chugged one ice-cold mug of beer, then ordered another to wash down all five million calories of enchiladas, *chiles rellenos,* refried beans smothered in melted cheese, and tortillas. As stuffed as the *rellenos* I'd devoured, I waddled to the bar for a dessert beer, and to check out the local classified ads for rentals.

Engrossed in marking mostly dubious possibilities—in my book buzzwords like cozy and charming are euphemisms for tiny and full of spiders—I was startled when the bartender asked, "Looking for a place to live?"

"Yep, something preferably without black widow spiders?"

"You've obviously rented here before."

I laughed. "No, but I've lived in other so-called historic abodes and had my share of shacks. I'd like something built during, say, this half of the century?"

She grinned. "That could be a tall order. Heck, even the golf course is over the century mark. And this clubhouse? A 1936 WPA project. If you want new, you'll probably have to head for Sierra Vista."

I shook my head. "Nope, I need something right here, and right now. I'll be working in Cananea, driving down there a few days a week."

Her eyebrows shot up. "What? Why?"

Pleased I could surprise a bartender, most of whom have heard it all, I sized her up. My age or thereabouts, dark hair and eyes, pretty face with startling green eyes. Her slight southern drawl matched her nametag: Georgia Lou.

"Georgia Lou, if I tell you, I'll have to kill you."

That comment drew a snigger from a few eavesdropping bar dwellers. The cowboys had moseyed off, replaced by golfers. Georgia drew me another beer. "Sorry if I seem nosy. The reason I asked is—" She halted mid-sentence, looking past me. I followed her gaze. Two nattily dressed black men glided by. Young, maybe under thirty, sporting those nifty short haircuts I associate with Denzel Washington.

Both men wore dark suits, brilliant white dress shirts adorned with blue bow ties, and very hip dark glasses. Something about them struck a familiar note with me, but one thing for sure, they stood out in this setting like proverbial turds in a punch bowl. Passing behind me, they headed for a table in the dining room.

Georgia stared after them, then checked her watch. "Like clockwork," she muttered.

"What?"

"Oh, nothing. Sorry, where was I?"

"You mean before," I jerked my head towards the dining room, "the men in blue?"

She had the good grace to chuckle. "They're new around here. Pulled in with a fancy RV, California plates, a week ago. I heard they'd reserved the space since last summer, paying all along, but just arrived. Not what you'd call real social, stick to themselves."

She shrugged, "I guess I wonder why they're here. Don't play golf, but rent a cart. Eat breakfast and lunch in our restaurant every day, take something to go for dinner."

"Jeez, you got 'em under surveillance?" I asked, impressed with her nosiness, which rivaled my own. This was a very small town, so I wondered what the locals would think when they got wind of *me*.

"Naw, they're parked across from my RV, and after a week you'd at least expect a howdy. Just a little…strange."

"Don't get a lot of black people down here, I guess?"

"Oh, no, it's not that. We're a pretty diverse population, what with a military base in Sierra Vista and all the feds around."

"Think they're G-men?" I whispered in my best James Cagney imitation.

Georgia's face lit with delight. "Ooh, I loved Cagney in "G-Men". They just don't make 'em like that anymore. Anyhow, anything and anyone is possible around here. Being right on the border, we have government types galore. See, hunks, three o'clock."

Sure enough, three uniformed border patrol agents, one black, one white, one Hispanic, all burly, strode through the door. They greeted Georgia by name, then noisily scraped back chairs at a table next to the black men. I watched all this in the bar-back mirror and drawled, "Makes me downright warm and fuzzy, just knowing there are armed men about."

Georgia nodded and winked. "Trust me, ninety percent of the people in here are packin'. Cochise

County's citizens take their guns right serious-like, and are some of the most heavily armed in the United States."

"I knew I was gonna like it here." She gave me a high five and went to wait on the other end of the bar.

I watched for any interaction between the BP guys and the men in blue, but they made no eye contact. One of the border agents gave the pair a once over, but since the bow ties did not look as though they'd recently vaulted the fence, his glance was cursory.

Georgia returned. "What I was going to tell you is, there are a few winter rentals around here. One of them is a new house, and I think it's available. Owners live in Mexico this time of year."

"Who do I talk to?"

"Hang on, I'll find out." She called someone from the phone behind the bar, and thirty minutes later I was on a guided tour of a fully furnished, all bills paid, hacienda-style home with mountain and golf course views to die for. The gourmet kitchen was right up my alley, but the pièce de résistance had to be the twelve-foot wide wraparound verandah. Taken as I was with the place, I was pretty darned certain it carried a price tag way over my budget.

However, hope springs eternal, so I continued ogling the house while the manager parleyed with the owner who was, indeed, in Mexico. When he shut his cell phone he told me the house was available for the next four months. I crossed my fingers in hope and asked, "How much?"

He told me, and added, "When you do the math, cheaper by the day than a local hotel."

There is a God, and She's on my side today. "When can I move in?"

"Got references?"

I gave him my business card and the Trob's phone number, not his private one, but the main switchboard that routes calls to the big wigs through a long line of minions at Baxter Brothers. These folks' jobs seem to be weeding out unworthy callers, so I figured the agent would be duly impressed. He was, but also exasperated with being switched through line after front line. I could have cut through all the crap for him, but wasn't about to give him the Trob's private number, and my own American cell was not activated as yet.

I took the phone from him and gave the next annoying foot soldier Wontrobski's direct extension. My mentor clinched the deal for me by giving the property manager a name and number in Bisbee, assuring him that within ten minutes I'd be vouched for. Sure enough, a word from the local office of one of the biggest mining companies in the world, and quicker than one can say greased wheels I was no longer homeless.

Because I am a single woman, a non-smoker with no pets, and had corporate backing, they'd settled for a month-to-month rental, plus a thousand dollar deposit. The Trob even agreed to foot the grand, and thanks to the wonders of electronic age banking, the deal was done, I had a key, and was left to unpack. Hot damn.

Unloading my meager belongings into what seemed palatial digs after living on a boat took only a few minutes. I set up my computer, connected to the home's high speed Internet service, added five hundred minutes to my old prepay cell phone, emailed the marina office with that number, and called the Trob back to thank him.

"Blue," he said.

Sigh. "Like to elaborate on that?"

"Bisbee blue. You can send me some for my rock collection."

"They have blue rocks here?"

"Bisbee blue turquoise. Has chocolate brown veining."

"You've got it. Thanks again for the job, and the neat house. Bye."

"Bye."

My new home, although built in the middle of a cow pasture bordering a golf course, had everything I could ask for. Unlike most golfing community tract homes, this one sat alone, on a private, unpaved road. Peace and quiet reigned.

Five miles up the main highway, at a small shopping plaza, I opened a bank account, then headed for Safeway. Gawking like a starving cat in a seafood store, I cruised the aisles. So many choices. More than one brand of bread; what a concept. My cart soon runnethed over, crammed to the gunwales with stuff I didn't realize I'd missed in Mexico.

Feta cheese, sourdough bread still warm from the oven, ice cream, and several other items that would not meet the approval of my diet conscious friend, Ms. Jan. However, my best friend, with her meddlesome calorie counting ways, was still in the Baja and I was here, surrounded by a king's ransom of refined sugar, processed foods, and empty calories. Yippee.

Anxious to get home and tear into my cornucopia of goodies, I was at first puzzled, then annoyed, to find the little dirt road leading to my new abode blocked by a large black van. Although facing me, its darkly tinted windows prevented my seeing the interior, so I sat a minute or two before my patience, never on the long side, ran out. Backing up a few feet, I was cutting through the desert, around the annoying vehicle when, out of a deep arroyo fifty feet to my left, at least a dozen people, dressed in dark clothes and holding hands, bolted in front of me.

Jamming on my brakes, I barely avoided colliding with the group. They ran past me toward the van. In my rearview mirror I watched as the back doors of the vehicle sprang open and runners leaped in. The last one was pulled roughly inside, the doors slammed shut and the truck took off, hell bent for leather, toward the main highway.

I sat, taken aback by what I'd witnessed.

On one hand, I am sympathetic to people who are so desperate for work they risk all to get it. On the other, when that van's rear doors flew open, I caught a brief glimpse of a large automatic weapon. It happened in a flash, but I was convinced there was a moment, just before the doors closed, when that barrel was aimed directly at me.

Had I just escaped becoming collateral damage in the drug and human smuggling war plaguing both sides of the border?

I dialed 9-1-1.

Welcome to Arizona, I told myself as I unpacked my groceries.

Here only one day and I'd had a close encounter with a dozen obvious illegals, and a gun-toting smuggler. When reading reports of the border struggles, I hadn't envisioned myself as being affected, but how wrong I was.

By late afternoon, despite a chill in the air, I sat on the verandah, sipping a rum and coke and wondering where that van was by now. And how in the hell had those illegals crossed the border, right here, not in some isolated no man's land?

A golf cart swished by, clubs clanking. The driver waved.

As the sun set behind the snow-capped Huachuca—pronounced Wah-choo-kah—Mountains to the west, another hilly range to my north glowed pink and orange.

The San Jose Mountains, in Mexico to the south, and between me and Cananea, took on deep purple tones. The only sour note was a rusted iron, butt-ugly, evidently ineffectual, fence running as far as I could see in both directions. Behind it, a huge Mexican flag flapped in the breeze.

Sounds from Mexico wafted north. A loudspeaker-equipped car announced either a carnival coming to town, or a sale on chicken, by the few words I caught. Dogs on both sides barked sporadically at each other, probably discussing how much noise they could generate by teaming up around midnight.

Soaring over the snowcapped Huachucas, the blimpy thing I'd seen from Cananea glowed white in a coloring sky. My view was a panorama of sand, yuccas, cactus, and mountains, all contrasting with the vivid green of the golf course.

I mixed another rum and coke and threw on sweats and a heavy sweater, determined to stay outside until the cold drove me in. Tomorrow night, I decided, I'd fire up the outdoor fireplace to kill the chill. I'd already learned that my new digs were at near five thousand feet and air temps dropped into the thirties almost every night in February, even sometimes diving into the teens. As I'd witnessed at lunch, though, by noon snowbirds in shorts chased that little white ball, and their dream of shooting their age. Later in the afternoon, locals in tee shirts and baseball caps and even cowboy hats showed up, getting in a few holes after work. Evidently they never heard of a dress code down here. Good.

Tired but content, I watched a sky streaked with ever more intense peach, that fleeting beauty of an Arizona sunset. The tranquility of the late afternoon was occasionally broken by the distant whack of a golf ball, followed by a cheer or curse.

Then, something out there moved.

And it wasn't a golf cart.

Chapter 8

My legendary peripheral vision, a gift when practicing my legendary snoopiness, had picked up a motion in the fast-fading light, and after my smuggler encounter earlier that afternoon, I was instantly on the alert, ready to make a dash into the house.

Snapping my head left, it took a moment or two to differentiate what had moved from the brown brush and red dirt where the verdant fairway ended. A dog?

Sitting up straighter, my brown eyes locked onto glowing blue ones. My heart did a little trip as my mouth cottoned up. I had chanced upon critters like this one before, in Mexico, but for the most part they were skinny, scraggly, skittish, and had yellow eyes. This coyote, easily the size of a medium German shepherd, was sleek and not at all cowed by my presence. Matter of fact, he sat very still, staring me down with those weird blue eyes.

Logically, I reasoned, he was a full six feet away, and we were separated by a three-foot high wall and a two-foot slope. Unless he could fly, there was nothing to fear, but, unnerved, I inched backward for safety behind the double French doors. Reaching behind me, opening a door, I never took my eyes from the creature. Just as I slipped into the living room—and I swear this on a stack of Texas Monthlies—he stood and wagged his tail.

I bolted the door and headed for the phone.

My friend Craig, Craigosaurus by nickname, answered on the second ring. "Noah's Bark."

"Yo Craig, Hetta here."

"Hetta!" he roared. I pulled the phone from my ear about three inches. "Where are you? We miss you."

I wondered who the *we* was. Dr. Craig Washington, a gentle giant of a veterinarian, hauls around a hundred extra pounds and wears his heart on his sleeve. Black and shy, he closely resembles his dog, a redbone hound named Coondoggie. Doc Washington is one of my best friends and confidants, and I never call him Craigosaurus to his face, even though others do. I know about weight jokes.

Craig is the only person I know who is worse at keeping a man than I am. His insecurities over his weight, and a natural good nature, make him a target for pretty boys looking for a free ride, so to speak. I've long hoped he'll find a nice, fat, rich, ugly, boyfriend. Heck, I wouldn't mind one myself.

He'd made a small fortune in canine plastic surgery, specializing in the implantation of fake balls on neutered dogs to give 'em that macho look. Big in the gay community for some reason. His latest venture is a Global Positioning System locator implant for tracking stolen or lost pets.

He'd already co-patented the chips and, once final testing is approved, stands to make a large fortune to go with his other small fortune. As for his vet business, he operates a fleet of mobile veterinary clinics credited with saving many an animal life by bringing the operating room to the almost-roadkilled.

"I'm in Arizona," I said, peering out the window at the critter, who wagged his tail again. "We can catch up in a minute, but first tell me what you know about coyotes."

"*Canis latrans*. Prairie wolf. Indians called them song dogs. Native to all of the north American continent, as I remember it. Species—"

"I don't want a biology lesson. Are they dangerous?"

"Depends."

"On what?"

"In packs, they've been known to take down a cow. Attacks on people are rare, but they do happen. Out here in California they prey on domestic pets where we've built in their natural habitat, which is everywhere. Heard one story of them grabbing a baby right out of a backyard. Why?"

"One of them, the size of Coondoggie, is sitting outside my porch, staring at me with these funny blue eyes."

"That's not good. Can he get to you?"

"No."

"Wait a minute, did you say blue eyes?"

"Yep."

"Coyotes don't have blue eyes. Throw something at him. If he doesn't run, you might have a problem."

"What kind of problem?"

"Rabies."

"He's not foaming at the mouth or anything, he's just sitting there grinning and wagging his tail."

"Have you been drinking?"

"Really, Craig, it *is* after five. However, I am not drunk, or blind. This guy actually looks friendly. Well, except for those weird eyes."

"Does that wagging tail have a bush at the end?"

"Yep."

"Then it's a coyote, or more likely a coydog. Coyote got mixed up with a dog. Can you see his paws?"

"I ain't gonna get that close, why?"

"Real coyotes have no white on their toes. That's the way furriers know for sure it's a genuine pelt."

Furriers? In all my travels I had never, ever, met anyone wearing a coyote skin. Mink, chinchilla, fox, yes. Coyote?

"You are kidding me about their fur, right?"

"Nope. Actually, they make really nice warm coats, but it just ain't PC anymore." There was a momentary silence, then he repeated, "Throw something at him."

"Like what? A rock?"

"Anything. See how he reacts."

I looked around the kitchen for ammo, but all I found was a glass decanter filled with cookies. I wasn't about to start launching the family crystal, so I grabbed a handful of the cookies.

Opening a French door enough to stick my arm out, I lobbed a cookie. The coyote snagged it in mid-air like a Frisbee, finished it off in two bites, sat down, and waited for seconds. Laughing, I tossed another to him and went back to the phone. Craig's voice crackled from the receiver. "Hetta? Hetta? Where are you?"

"I'm back. And guess what?" my eyes lit on the glass container's label: Blue. "Not only did the coyote, whose name seems to be Blue, catch the treats I threw at him, he is evidently a regular." I told him about the jar and what I now suspected were actually dog biscuits.

"As a veterinarian, I have to advise you that feeding the wildlife is a really bad idea. Where in Arizona are you?"

"It depends on who you talk to."

"What does that mean? Don't you know where you are?"

"I thought I was in Naco, but I'm actually in Bisbee. I'm on a golf course that is half in Naco and half in Bisbee, so someone said, and I'm on the Bisbee end."

"But you are close to Naco?"

"Yes. There's a Naco, Arizona, and a Naco, Sonora."

"I know. Want company? I'd like to check on Pancho Villa."

"Er, didn't he like bump into several speeding bullets a while back?"

"I meant, do research on the whole Pancho Villa thing. You see, my great grandfather, Jedediah Washington, was eighteen when he was wounded in the Battle of Naco in 1914. My parents have a photo taken there when he was a buffalo soldier. Story goes the Villa forces clashed with federal troops led by General Benjamin Hill on the Sonora side, and our guys were in trenches, making sure the battle didn't spill over into the States."

"Neat. I love family history. I haven't been there yet, but I saw on the Internet that there's a museum at Fort Huachuca in Sierra Vista, thirty or so miles from me, dedicated to the buffalo soldiers. But if your grandpa wasn't fighting, how was he wounded?"

"Once in awhile, the two Mexican armies got tired of fighting each other and lobbed a shell at our guys. And during the battle, people came from all over the county, brought picnic lunches and watched the action like some play. He was trying to move them away from harm when a shell exploded nearby and he got nailed by shrapnel. My mother remembers him showing her the scars."

I am a big history buff, and this kind of thing is something I can sink my teeth into. I had studied, as well I could, all nine generations of my Texas heritage, along with the political events that made them who they were, so this was right up my alley. "You want me to check this out for you?"

"Maybe. You know, I've also heard of Bisbee. Matter of fact, several of my friends have moved there recently."

"Artsy types, I presume?"

"Yes, and Bisbee's supposed to be the new Lesbian and gay hot spot. What are you doing there? You're straight."

I told him about my job.

"You found a place to stay? If not, I can make a couple of calls."

"Oh, I have a house already. After living on the boat for so long, I feel like I'm in the Taj Majal."

"You live in a mausoleum?"

"Smart assed banter, my man. Craig, you are not going to believe this, but that four legged creature ain't the only coyote I ran into today." I told him about the van.

"You've been in Arizona one day and you're already profiling?" he teased.

"Oh, golly gee, I must have jumped to conclusions," I drawled. "They're probably just a bunch of innocent legal citizens who hide in draws, and run, holding hands, to jump into dark vans manned by gun-toting goons. Surely some sort of local ritual I misread. Silly me, what was I thinking?"

He laughed. "According to some here in Oakland, your thinking makes you a racist. What did Jenks say?"

"Well, uh, he's not exactly here."

"Uh-oh. I think I need to get out of California weirdness for awhile, so maybe I'll trade it in for some Arizona weirdness. Want company?"

"Oh, yes," I practically yelled.

"Let's see, one day to Laughlin...this Friday okay?"

"You can up and leave, just like that? What about your patients?"

"Actually, I've lightened my load. I have a new partner. Business, that is. As usual, my love life is in the dumper."

"Misery loves company, so come on down. Sorry though, Coondoggie ain't on the invite list. My lease says no pets. I guess Blue doesn't count."

"No problem. Coondoggie hates traveling anyway."

"If I overnight a key to Jenks's apartment in Oakland, can you pick up a few things for me? I'll send a list of stuff I'd like to have, and where to find them."

"I'll do 'er, and be there by the end of the week. Weekend at the latest. Stay away from that Blue feller until we can figure out exactly what he is. No petting, no matter how friendly he seems, or how much you drink. And Hetta, be careful. It sounds like you're in bad guy territory."

Chapter 9

I hung up after my talk with Craig, and tossed Blue another cookie before locking up for the evening. Setting the security system, I made a mental note not to open any doors or windows during the night lest I scare the crap out of myself with a raucous alarm.

Flipping on the TV I learned that little had changed in the five months I'd been without television. Threats of gang killings, dope deals, political unrest, weirded-out celebs, and that was just in Tucson. No mention of a dark van full of illegals being stopped in Cochise County. I wondered if that kind of news was even newsworthy here.

A touch on a nifty remote, *et voila*, flames sprang to life in the fireplace. Channel surfing, I landed on a shark feeding frenzy on Animal Planet. Not to be outdone by a bunch of toothy critters, I harpooned an entire round of creamy French Brie, backed up with a loaf of San Francisco sourdough bread, and a bottle of cold, crisp, Pinot Grigio. Life doesn't get much better for a dry-docked damsel.

Dinner done, I snuggled down into the big couch and called Jenks in Kuwait City.

Already at work, he answered on the second ring. "Jenkins."

"Hi, it's me."

"Hi, honey, it's good to hear your voice this morning."

"Evening here. I'm sitting on a big old cushy couch, in front of a blazing fire, getting ready to watch a movie on my forty-two inch high def."

"I take it you are not on the boat, unless you've upgraded."

"Nope, I'm in Arizona."

"Now, there's some good news for Mexico," he teased, then added, "and for me. I've heard some disturbing news about the escalating violence south of the border."

And north of the border, I thought, but I said, "You know how the press is. They exaggerate."

"So you say. Does this move mean you'll stay in Arizona until I get back?"

"Uh, not exactly."

"What does that mean, exactly?"

Evidently the Trob hadn't shared my latest with him, so I told Jenks about my job, and that I would be commuting into Mexico on a daily basis. He didn't like the sound of the commute part and said so.

"Jenks, it's only thirty-five miles to the mine, and the road is good." I didn't mention that it is also pretty much deserted. However, since I was on my own clock, I hoped to find a bus that ran in the mornings, drive ahead of it all the way to Cananea so it covered my backside, and do the reverse each afternoon. When I told him of my plan, he seemed to relax. He also liked it that Craig was coming to stay with me.

"You rented a house right on the border?"

"Practically. In Bisbee, and it is a beauty."

"Bisbee is a beauty?"

"Depends on where you look, according to the locals. There's historic Bisbee, where Jan and I stayed last December. It's chock full of what I call New Age cliff dwellers, who, according to Doctor Craig, consist of a big gay population. Old mining town turned artsy. I love it, you would hate it.

"Then there is Warren, where old miners retired, and worker types find affordable housing. Lots of cottage style homes in need of beautification, only a few really brought into this century, but pretty cool in a blue collar kind of way. The house I've rented is new, and according to my mailing address, is in Bisbee, so I call it cowboy Bisbee. Whatever, it's built in a cow pasture, but smack dab on an eighteen-hole golf course. Go figure."

"You're on a golf course?" He sounded intrigued, so I tossed a lure.

Picking up a brochure I read the course's bragging points. "They have a par six, which means nothing to me, but it's called the Rattler, and is the longest golf hole in the Southwest."

"I definitely gotta play that one."

"How about, say, next week?"

"Sorry, I would love to, but no can do. Craig'll keep you company."

"Not like you do," I purred, trying to sound sexy instead of downright desperate.

"I hope to hell not. Honey, I hate to do this, but I've got to get going. Already late for a meeting. I'm really glad you're living in Arizona and found a nice house. I know how rentals can be. I'll call you tomor— You know what? I have this old friend, Ted Burns, who lives south of you somewhere, in Mexico. Guy I worked with in Desert Storm. He married a Mexican and moved down there to farm. I'll email him, find out exactly where they are. Maybe you can visit them."

"A farm? What do they grow, cactus?"

"Her family has been farming that land for several generations, so they must have some kind of cash crop. He's retired Navy, so I guess they can live pretty good south of the border. Might be a fun trip for you and Craig if they're nearby."

"You know me, have car, will travel."

He chuckled. "Boy, are you easy."

"Come home, and I'll show you how incredibly easy I can be."

"Promises, promises. Sorry Hetta, you know I have to stay here until we wrap this thing up, and this time I don't want anything to interfere."

I almost sniped, *Anything, meaning me*? but bit that back. Instead I tried inveiglement. "Oh, did I mention that this house is on the sixteenth green, and a golf cart comes with the rental?"

"Why didn't you say so? Screw the project, I'll be right there."

"Talk about easy."

"Golf course or no, I wish I was there with you, right this moment, but it can't be. Only a couple of months longer. Sorry."

I sighed. "Me, too."

We said our goodbyes and I checked out my email before crashing for the night.

According to my inbox, I'd won the lottery in three countries, someone from Liberia wanted to deposit several million dollars into my bank account, and my penis is too small. I deleted everything but the one from the marina office in San Carlos.

I read it once, sucked air, read it again. A man came looking for me, they said, but when the office people wouldn't give him my email address or phone number, he left a message: Mind your own business and stay away! Lamont.

"Lamont?" I yelled into the empty house. "That's Nacho!"

A rush of fear, mixed with excitement and, okay, call me fickle, a slight shiver of lust, sent me scrambling for wine. I hadn't seen Nacho since Christmas eve on that Baja beach, when he shot at me. I'm a sentimentalist, I guess.

I returned with a large glass of red, and reread the message. Mind my own business? That'll be the day, but what does he mean. Stay away? From where? The boat, or him? Both? He'd used his a.k.a.: Lamont, as in, Lamont Cranston, The Shadow.

Answering the email, I instructed the marina office personnel not to, under any circumstances, tell anyone where I was, hoping I wasn't too late. Okay, that felt better, but who had I told about the job in Cananea? Only half the regulars at Barracuda Bob's, and the guys on the dock. Hell, why hadn't I just taken out an ad during the Super Bowl?

Thinking about it some more, though, I realized not any of them knew I was living in Arizona. Not even the harbormaster knew. All they had was my email address and my prepaid cell number. Relieved, I double-checked the door locks, and found a romantic comedy on STARZ. Of course, I promptly fell asleep on the couch, finally dragged myself to bed after midnight, where I tossed and turned in restless frustration.

Flashbacks of what I call Fun With Nacho and the Thugs came flooding back. I first saw him in a panga, a small fishing skiff, in the company of Paco, who turned out to be a member of one of the most dangerous gangs in the world, Mara Salvatrucha 13, commonly known as MS-13. As if that wasn't bad enough, Paco was not only a methhead, but a deranged psychopath who preyed on just about anyone who got in his way.

What I didn't know, until much later, was that Nacho probably saved Jenks and me that day, when he prevented Paco from killing us on the spot, for a can of gas.

Thanks to Nacho, Paco was no more. I figured Nacho, who vanished after the shootout on the beach, was long gone from my life, but evidently not. What on earth, though, did his message to stay away *mean*? From what? Whom? Where? Crap.

I was, at long last, soundly sleeping when my alarm clock chirped "The Yellow Rose of Texas".

Doble crap.

Chapter 10

La cárcel de Cananea Está situada en una Mesa Y en ella fui procesado Por causa de mi torpeza.

(The jail of Cananea Is situated on a plateau And in it I was processed on account of my stupidity.)— Corrido (folk song) by Rubén Fuentes Written during the Revolution of 1910

I've dealt with commute nightmares in Tokyo, San Francisco, Brussels, and Paris, but nothing topped my first day on the road from Naco to Cananea.

Something, an accident I suspected, blocked the main highway, creating a backup comparable to a Los Angeles freeway. After two hours I finally realized the problem wasn't the wreck I'd suspected, but a Mexican military checkpoint that sprang up since I'd passed this way yesterday. I dug out my passport, my Mexican tourist card, and car registration, the things they normally check. I didn't have a work permit, but it would never occur to them that I needed one. After all, I am a Gringa.

Nearing a huge ALTO sign, I rolled down my window. When he spotted me, the uniformed inspector's mouth fell open. With a look that said, what in the hell is this red-haired Gringa doing out here by herself, he gave me a flat-palmed stay right here sign, whirled, and strode to a nearby tent. I sat tight while another man waved others around me.

Within two minutes the first one was back, with another officer on his heels. Neither looked amused.

Number two soldier leaned down, peered into the window, chuffed his cheeks, and demanded, "Why are you on this road?"

My first response would have been, "Because I prefer driving on pavement?" or some other smartassed comeback, but for once common sense prevailed. "I am on my way to Cananea."

"Why?"

I didn't think, because it's there, would win friends, so I blurted, "To visit the mine."

He did a double take. "Excuse me?"

"I consult at the mine," I explained, then remembered I didn't a have work permit. "Temporarily."

Obviously having a problem wrapping his mind around the concept, he didn't know what to say, so I explained further. "I am an engineer, and I was just hired by the mine." I handed him *Señor* Pretty One's business card. "You can call my *jefe, Señor* Orozco."

He snatched the card and went back to his tent. I was sleep-deprived, hungry, and needed to pee, so the ten minutes he was gone seemed interminable. Finally, as I was eyeing a nearby bush as a possible *pissoir*, he strode back, gave me my business card, actually smiled, and said, "You may pass, but you must be careful on this road."

"Can I ask what the trouble is?"

"Please, you go."

"Okay, thanks, I think."

I made a pit stop at the next Pemex station, paying their exorbitant five-peso bathroom fee. The military presence on the road was heavy, but no one messed with me again until I reached the mine's main gate. The old man and dog who normally slept there were gone, replaced by soldiers.

Once again, I went through my song and dance as to why they should let me pass—don't these people talk to each other?—and was told to wait. If this was the kind of commute I faced every day, the Trob and I were in for some serious renegotiations on my contract.

I waited, sandwiched between a line of what looked liked sullen fourteen-year-olds packing automatic weapons, and glowering miners hopefully packing nothing but attitude. Both groups eyed me suspiciously, making me feel guilty of something. By the time a bedraggled Maria arrived on foot fifteen minutes later, I'd broken into a light sweat despite the almost freezing temperature.

Maria convinced the military dudes that I wasn't some kind of *norteamericana* subversive, and as we headed for the office in my car, she clued me in.

"When the troubles started yesterday afternoon, *Señor* Orosco told me to call you not to come here today, but you did not answer. I left a message."

"Sorry, my Mexican cell phone doesn't work in Arizona. I'll give you my new US number. Did you call Mr. Wontrobski?"

"Yes, he said he would tell you. He did not?"

Crap, I'd turned off my cell after talking with Jenks and was so groggy this morning I flat forgot to turn it on. "He probably tried, Maria, but I missed his call. Oh, well, here I am. What is going on?"

"After the judge in Mexico City ruled this strike illegal, the strikers are very angry because they can now lose their jobs and be replaced. They have control of some facilities, and would not allow us to leave last night. We slept here, but the soldiers have arrived to stop...*el alboroto*.

I grabbed my Spanish-English dictionary. *Alboroto*: uproar. "Why are they, uh, uproaring now? Haven't they all quit work anyway?"

"Oh, yes, they do not work, but most still receive pay from the union. Now, they might never work here again. They have homes and family. Some have lived here for many years. And now there is a problem with the union. The leader left for Canada with all the money. It is very complicated." She looked about nervously, moved closer, and whispered, "Poison."

"Poison?"

"They say bad things are in this air, and maybe the water. We are not to speak of it."

Poison? I looked around for a facemask and oxygen cylinder, but finding neither, went online to see what she was talking about. Between a Mexican newspaper article and the handy dandy Spanish translator program in my laptop, it didn't take long to find out why I was hired to put together a list of equipment required for a quick revamp.

A volunteer group of occupational health professionals wrote a scathing condemnation, alleging the mine was deliberately run into the ground, with no effort made toward maintenance, repairs, or safe mining practices. I made a note to myself to ask for a copy of any purchase orders for items, like basic filters, that would at least denote someone tried, but one look at the dusty offices told another story. The health professionals claimed, as a result of gross negligence and downright greed on the part of the owners, workers were being exposed to high levels of toxic dust and acid mist.

Lighting the flame under an already volatile situation, a three-year wildcat strike, which shut down the mine, was deemed illegal by a court in Mexico City. Over seven hundred Mexican troops, with the assistance of the local, federal, and state police, arrived to quell the union uprising. Nevertheless, miners still blockaded the gates, a riot ensued, tear gas and pellets were fired, trucks burned, and some facilities on the other side of the mine were damaged by Molotov cocktails. About fifty miners were now holed up in key locations on site. What we had here was a true Mexican standoff.

And I thought this job was going to be boring. Gee, thanks, Wontrobski.

I checked the US news for reports of this situation. Mama would pitch a hissy if she flipped on the news and saw her daughter, once again, in the middle of a controversy, especially one that involved Molotov cocktails. And Jenks? I didn't even want to think about what he'd say.

Maria, after whispering poisonous news in my ear, added, "Please let me know it you need anything," and left the room.

My Net search garnered good news, not so good news, and extremely bad news.

Although the strike and escalating tensions were mentioned in some Arizona papers, it wasn't important or catastrophic enough to catch the attention of big networks. They needed something bigger like, Hetta Coffey and Thousands Others Massacred by Mexican Police, details at five. So, in this case, no news was good news.

The Mexican press gave mention that one of their own had, several weeks before, written an article on the overall situation in Cananea. He reported that, exacerbating the loss of over two million dollars a day by the mine and a corresponding economic disaster in the area, drug activity and gang crime were on an alarming rise. Just weeks before two gangs clashed and dozens of *drogistas* were killed, but not before they kidnapped, tortured and murdered several ranchers and policemen. Again, the US news networks let it slide, probably because in Phoenix or just about any other city large in the US, this kind of story is daily fodder.

However, as I read the next article, I whispered, "Oh, boy," to myself. Just yesterday, the reporter in the last article was murdered, along with his entire family. Shot in their home, execution-style. AP was on the story, it was flashing on the home page of most every Internet user in the world, and would, of course, be news at five. It was probably all over FOX and CNN already. Sigh.

Oh, yeah, my parents and Jenks were gonna be mighty riled when news of riots and murder in Cananea hit the American media. I didn't think it would warrant more than a blip, certainly not a crawler, but the word, MEXICO, catches Mom's attention now like PIZZA does mine.

They'd all demand I quit this job immediately. It would do no good arguing that Dad dragged his family all over the world, into some fairly unhealthy climates, both weather-wise and political, or that Jenks was now in Jihadist territory. Nope, they'd focus on the dangers of my situation, but I've never been a quitter.

Turning from the computer, I decided since I was probably going to be out of a job one way or another, I'd rack up some billable time. I compiled a master equipment and operating spares list. Maria brought me a boxed lunch a little after noon. I thought this was great service until I realized the delivery meant we still couldn't leave the premises. She did, however, assure me that by quitting time everything would be under control, and we could go home. I was not assured.

On the bright side, my lunch included the best carne asada burrito I'd had in a long time, served with—and this was totally foreign to any office I'd ever worked in—two ice cold beers. How could anyone be expected to quit a job with those perks?

I was happily munching away, proving once again that good food and booze can temporarily take my mind off anything, when a harried, but still handsome *Señor* Orozco strode in and caught me in mid-bite. He was flanked by two burly uniformed men, both sporting flattop haircuts and swarthy scowls. Arm patches indicated they were something federal. Now what?

"Miss Café, I must ask you to leave at once."

"Gee, *Señor* Orozco, I've been bounced off better sites, but you haven't even given me a chance to screw things up yet."

His frown softened, then he grinned. "Ah, a joke. I am not dismissing you, it is that we simply cannot have you crossing the strike line again."

I pointed to the files and drawings I was working on. "So, then, how do you expect me to do the job you hired me for?"

"You may take what you need home with you. Maria will help pack as many records as you can carry today, then these officers will escort you to the border. When you need more files, fax a list and we will bring them to you. And please, call me Juan."

"As in Don Juan?" My flirt made them all smile, so I added, "In that case, Juan, you can drop the Miss and just call me Café. Can I get more of these burritos thrown in with those files you'll send?"

"Café, I will deliver them personally, if that is what you wish."

¡Carumba! Burritos and Don Juan?

A deal like that could turn a girl's head.

Chapter 11

By three in the afternoon the day I was dropkicked out of the mine's offices, my car resembled a college prank scenario from the sixties, as in, how many people can you get into a Volkswagen? Except this time it was how much paperwork.

My escort, the two *federales* driving an unmarked, slightly battered, Crown Victoria, instructed me to stay close on their tail as they led the way off the mine premises. Even knowing the Crown Vic's propensity for bursting into flames when rear-ended, I hugged my bodyguards' bumper as they threaded us through a vociferous mob on the other side of the gate. We bogged down occasionally, coming to a halt until men in combat gear pushed back the throng. A couple of times I heard something bounce off my roof, but once through the line of scrimmage, a black and white with flashing lights fell in behind me and my convoy picked up speed.

The entourage made me feel downright presidential until an innate paranoia set in.

What if this was all a ruse, and I was on my way to the Cananea jail? Had the authorities somehow linked me to at least one of those drug cartel types involved in a shootout in their fair city only weeks before? Nacho's cryptic message to mind my own beeswax and to stay away still rankled. If he meant I was to stay away from the mine, I was golden.

Jan and I were never certain just who Nacho worked for, but we suspected he was either a drug lord, DEA, or both. I was fairly certain he was somehow a part of a showdown between the cops in Cananea and unruly gang members just weeks before. Many gang members died, but accounts were sketchy on the who, what, where, when, and why details. I'd pored over online articles, looking for clues to someone who might be Nacho, but found nothing.

Other than kidnapping Jan and me, threatening to shoot me, then actually aiming in my direction and pulling the trigger, Nacho was an okay guy in a handsome, criminal sort of way. As one might surmise, my expectations of men are abysmally modest.

A sharp pain shot across my shoulders. Lighten up, I told myself, there is no way this cop escort can make any connection between Hetta Coffey, engineer, and a cabal of methed-out gangsters. I relaxed my death grip on the steering wheel and shrugged my shoulders, but minutes later found myself once again performing a strangle hold. After what seemed an eternity, but was probably only forty minutes, my escort turned around, and I was in line at the border. I exhaled long and loud.

Only two cars, and bare minutes stood between me, the good old US of A, and a cold beer on my verandah. Or so I thought.

Although my two-car escort had turned around, they'd stopped a short distance away and continued to watch my back. The black and white left his lights flashing, just in case no one had noticed him.

This, quite naturally, piqued the interest of several uniformed types at the border crossing, who were more than a little curious as to why I was escorted out of Mexico in the first place, and what all those papers were in my vehicle.

I have to admit that what sounded like a perfectly logical explanation to me might not have been so clear to Customs. I was waved into secondary by a polite but firm young woman. She took my car keys and passport, then escorted me into a small room. As she was shutting the door, I saw a canine officer trotting toward my VW.

Resigned to a long wait while my car got ransacked, I plopped down in one of the two plastic chairs in my jail cell. Okay, so it wasn't really a cell, but I was locked in, and worse than that, I had been here before. I knew my car was clean, unless you count a dusting of toxic materials, but were these folks savvy to my previous pissing off of their precious officialdom, and were now getting even by taking my car apart for spite?

My friend Marty Martinez, a retired Oakland Police Department officer who has bailed me out more than once when the caca hit the prop, assured me last month that I was no longer a fugitive from US justice, but being tossed in a holding tank had put me a lit-tle on edge.

Should they get around to my past alleged crimes, I'd explain that I did not steal Trouble, my parrot, they had deemed an illegal avian and condemned to death. Poor Trouble was awaiting execution in this very room when he miraculously escaped his cage and flew to freedom in Mexico. Of course, this was shortly after a visit from me, so there could possibly be suspicion of cage tampering on my part, but prove it, copper. Maybe I needed to reword that defense.

Hopefully the men and women now crawling all over my VW simply didn't like the looks of my cargo, and held no personal grudge against me. As far as I could remember, none of these officers were on duty the day of Trouble's escape, but who knew for sure? I've really got to learn not to return to the scene of my alleged crimes.

I was released after almost an hour of fretting. Judging by the disappointed looks and grumpy behavior, the officials had come up empty. A half-eaten burrito lay on my car seat, and the dog-in-training, a German shepherd the size of a small pony, strained his sniffer fondly in that direction, but the search had produced only a pile of moldy old blueprints, none of which was a schematic for building a nuclear bomb. I was free to go, but as a parting shot the frustrated fido peed on my tire.

Probably a good thing I'd be working from home in Arizona, because these customs guys could make a daily commute a nightmare if they wanted to. I vowed to get to know a few of them. Maybe make them cookies?

Back at the house after the border shakedown, I couldn't rid myself of a niggling disquietude over events at the mine. As much as I liked the idea of working from home, I suspected my expulsion from the jobsite had something to do with being female.

Having fought the good fight in a historically man's profession for years, my hackles rise at any hint of sexism in the workplace. Being dispatched to safety in the States roused suspicion. I called the Trob.

"Hetta, where are you?"

"Back in Arizona, as if you didn't know." Silence.

"So, lemme ask you this," I snapped, "if I were a man, would they have sent me away from the front lines?"

"Yes."

That man really knows how to fizzle my fuse. "Oh, well, then," I mumbled. Properly defused, I added, "I'll need a bunch of office equipment."

"Okay."

"A copier, fax, scanner combo."

"Okay."

"I have to upgrade the house phone service to long distance."

"Okay."

"And a Xerox 2510 drawing copier."

"Okay."

This was too easy, so I added, "And a new BMW."

"Nope."

"Just making sure you're listening."

"Call Allison."

"Oh, crap, I forgot. I will. Give her my phone numbers, will you?"

"Yes."

"Gosh, it's been grand having this little chat. Ta ta, Chatty Cathy."

"Bye."

Chapter 12

Feeling sheepish about practically accusing the Trob of sexual discrimination, I made a note to get him some Bisbee Blue. I mean, how expensive can a little piece of turquoise be?

Mulling over my day, I realized that as crappy as it started, I'd now landed in tall cotton.

In celebration of this turn of good fortune, I gave Blue extra treats as I told him that I no longer faced a daily commute across the border, and I didn't have to work in a dusty, possibly deadly, mining compound surrounded by armed guards and disgruntled strikers. He congratulated me with a wag.

Now I could honestly tell the parents and Jenks the good news without the bad should they ask. No use stirring up things when they were already settled, *n'est-ce pas*?

The seemingly endless tasks required for setting up a working office filled the next couple of days. Equipment leasing, signing up for myriad services, reconnecting lines of communication—schmoozing, actually—with engineering contacts I'd later tap for info. I made lists of lists, color-coded on Post-it notes, which I consider one of the best inventions *ev*er. Walls, windows, and the refrigerator door were aflutter with an informational Post-it snowstorm.

The Safeway items, which I cleverly dubbed Craig's list, grew large. Dr. Craig isn't much of a drinker, but I bought a case of Tecate, just in case. He eats beef, so two whopping filets waited in the fridge for our first night's dinner, along with all the fixings for twice-baked potatoes, and a Caesar's salad. For lunch on the day he arrived, I planned on serving grilled eggplant, feta cheese, and sun-dried tomato paninis, his favorite.

He called on his way in, so I was out front when he pulled up, not in his van, but in a brand new candy apple red Porsche. As he unfolded from the snazzy car, that was not the only surprise of the day. "Okay," I called out, "whoever you are, what have you done with the rest of my friend Craig?"

He grabbed me in a bear hug. At six-four to my five-four he hoisted me off my feet to do so, then he set me down and did a twirl. "So, what do you think?"

I used my best Billy Crystal accent from a Saturday Night Live skit. "Dahling, you look mahvelous."

"So do you."

"Liar."

We put his fancy new wheels in the garage, then spent half an hour unloading it. "Ya know, Craig, if you'da told me you weren't bringing the van I wouldn't have given you such a big list of stuff to get me from Jenks's apartment."

"I wanted to surprise you with my new wheels. Besides, I got it all in somehow."

With everything stashed in his room and my closet, we retired to the verandah for an iced tea. The day was warm and golfers were out in force.

"Wow, Hetta," Craig said, "this house looks like something you'd design and decorate. It's fantastic. I'd say this equals that great place you had in Oakland."

"That was a nice home, wasn't it? It seems like a lifetime ago since I sold it and moved onto the boat. I had put my heart, soul, and a ton of money into renovating that old mini-mansion, but after RJ died, it wasn't the same."

"I know. I sure miss that dog. But you've found a new way of life on the water, and you met Jenks, so things have a way of working out."

"Um-hum," I said, unwilling to dampen our reunion with my insecurities. "Okay, Craig, let's hear it. Were you a candidate on one of those extreme weight loss shows?"

He shook his head and looked sad. My heart froze. "You aren't sick, are you?"

Reaching over, he patted my hand. "I'm fine, far as I know."

"Oh, thank God."

"Truth is, I had an epiphany. One of those Oprah, oh, I get it, moments. That little shit Pierre, the guy I was seeing when you left Oakland, did me a big favor in a nasty kind of way. Barely six months into our relationship, he wanted me to buy him a, get this, Porsche."

"Why on earth would he think you'd do that? You, of the old vans?"

He shook his head sadly. “Because, I guess, he thought he had me where he wanted me. You know, I never really trusted him. Too cute and needy. Anyhow, I say no, he pitches a little queer-boy hissy, telling me he’d already gone to the dealership and picked out his car. He also told me he’d assured the salesman I’d be down to pay for it. The fight got nasty, and ended up with him screaming that I was so fat and ugly that if I wasn’t rich, no one would want me.”

“Oh, Craig, I’m so sorry.”

“I’m not. I did exactly what he wanted me to do.”

“What? Are you nuts?”

“Probably. I went right on down to that car dealership and bought the Porsche. For myself.” He beamed with satisfaction.

“My hero. So, where did you bury Pierre?”

Craig laughed softly. “I admit I was cut to the quick. The truth hurts. Instead of curling up and licking my wounds, I removed Pierre from my life and hired your personal trainer, Pamela.”

“The Paminator?”

“Yep, she’s fantastic. Unlike you, I let her train me. It works if you actually do what she says.”

“You mean just hiring her doesn’t count? Go figure.”

“I’ve lost over seventy pounds in five months, more to go. Because she’s worked me so hard, my muscle tone is good, and I now run five miles every day. She couldn’t do much about my face.”

“There is nothing wrong with your face. It has...character.”

"I know. I look like my dog, Coondoggie."

"Coondoggie's cute, in a hang dawg kinda way. Besides, now that you're so svelte, your face is downright handsome. Okay, maybe in a puppy dog kind of way, but trust me, sweetie, if you were straight, you'd be fighting women off with a bat by now."

He brightened. "Really?"

"Would I lie to you, Craig?"

"Yes, but thanks anyway."

"Okay, what's the secret, other than the Paminator?"

"No white stuff."

"You're only dating black guys now?"

"Cute. Not dating anyone anymore. No white stuff is my diet regime: no sugar, rice, pasta, starch, flour. Period."

"That's it?"

"That and exercise."

"Uh-oh," I said, then gave him the day's menu. "I'll sign on for your diet, but not until tomorrow, right around two."

"I'll splurge today," Craig said, "and have a panini, but why put off your diet until mid-day tomorrow?"

"Because the golf course restaurant serves menudo on Saturdays, and I believe hominy qualifies as white stuff."

Menudo is a spicy Mexican soup touted as a hangover cure, and is traditionally served on weekends and during the Christmas season. Its ingredients include tripe, hominy, lime juice, dried chile flakes, onion, and epazote, a Mexican spice they make tea with. Topped with chopped fresh cilantro, basil, and onion, it's this Texan's idea of comfort food.

Craig wrinkled his nose when he heard the recipe, and opted instead for a vegetarian omelet topped with salsa. He didn't touch the tortillas. Too white.

We'd already walked two miles before brunch, so we were pushing the lunch hour by the time we sat down at the club restaurant. Half the people ate a late breakfast, others were into luncheon fare. We took our time, enjoying several glasses of iced tea while watching golfers frustrate themselves on the practice putting green out front.

We were leaving the dining room when the two black dudes from the RV park sauntered in. Craig stiffened visibly as they passed. The men didn't acknowledge our presence, even though you'd think they'd give a nod to the only other black guy in the place.

Outside, Craig muttered a curse. "What?" I asked.

"Those brothers. Didn't think I'd see them in these parts."

"You know them?"

"Not *them*, personally, but Oakland has a bunch of these thugs operating under the auspices of friendly neighborhood Black Muslim groups."

Now I realized why those two looked familiar. Bay Area newspapers and television stations had featured photos and videos of men dressed like Louis Farrakhan, the Nation of Islam leader, when a story broke they'd been mixed up in alleged nefarious activities. The cops had raided at least one bakery, whose owners were suspected of ties to a murder, extortion, and kidnapping for hire plots.

I nodded. "I remember the news."

"Mark my words, there will be a day of reckoning. I had a friend who was gunned down in broad daylight while jogging around Lake Merritt. No one was ever charged, but I know who did it, and so do the police. My friend was working on an exposé related to a renegade offshoot group of the Black Muslims, and he got too close to the truth."

"That's awful, Craig. You think they'll ever nail the jerks that did it?"

"Oh, yes. The bastards are getting bolder and bolder. As I said, their day of reckoning is coming."

"I don't know much about them, but what I've heard wasn't especially good. I know Farrakhan has been accused of anti-Semitism and homophobia."

"He is, no matter how much he says he's misquoted. Trust me, I know. When I was an undergraduate, they tried to recruit me. They didn't know I was gay. Hell, I didn't know I was gay."

"Little slow on the learning curve there?"

"Total denial. Anyhow, I was raised in an all white neighborhood, the son of two doctors, and the grandson of a state senator. I was the fat fly in the buttermilk and one lonely dude. Guess what the other students called me behind my back."

"No idea," I said, but of course I was thinking, *Craigosaurus*.

As if reading my mind, he said, "No, not Craigosaurus, neegarosaurus."

I barked totally inappropriate laughter, then clapped my hand over my mouth, but another guffaw escaped. I finally gasped, "I'm sorry, Craig. I know it's not funny."

He grinned. "Actually, it is. If it wasn't aimed at me, I would've laughed, too. You gotta give cleverness, even when it's vicious, it's due. I was an overweight nerd and believe me, kids know how to spot a loser when they see one."

"You are not a loser."

He shrugged. "I'm working on that. Anyhow, I guess I thought once I got away from my high school tormentors I could start anew, but hate groups prey on loners, so I was a prime target. At first the Muslim brothers at Berkeley who befriended me pushed the black pride thing, my African roots, all the stuff that I hadn't learned much about in predominately lily-white Atherton. I have to admit, I was flattered by the attention but, little by little, their malevolence surfaced. By then, though, I realized I didn't fit well at Berkeley and transferred to UC Davis, since I already planned to attend Vet school there. Not many militants hanging out at Davis, so I graduated a virgin, non-militant, closet dweller. By the time I had my first fling, AIDS was a well-known killer, so my refusal to admit the truth may have saved my life."

I reached over and gave his shoulder a squeeze, and teased, "And look how far you've come on the high school social scale. I mean, here you are, friends with an ex-cheerleader."

That made him chuckle. "Oh, yeah, I'll bet you were class sweetheart, as well."

"Hardly. I was odd gal out, sent to live with my grandmother in a very small, Baptist, Texas town while my parents finished up a job overseas. I might as well have stepped off the bus from Mars. Yes, I was a cheerleader, but only because I knew what one was. I had one close friend, but trust me, the others thought I had a secret tail."

"So, we have that in common. Maybe that's why we get along so well. One thing, though, your parents seem to accept you for the rebel you are. I'm still in the closet, parent-wise."

"Surely your folks know you're gay by now."

"Nope, or at least we're in a don't ask, don't tell mode. I think they suspect, because they never, ever, drop by my house uninvited, and I don't invite them if someone is there."

"That must be so hard on you."

"Not really. Not yet. But if I ever meet someone really important to me, I don't know what I'll do. As they say, we'll cross that bridge if we have to."

I tilted my head back toward the clubhouse. "So, what do you figure those two bow-tied types are doing down here in the Arizona desert?"

He glowered in that direction. "I have no damned idea, but I'd bet it ain't to take a tour of Tombstone, watch the shootout at the OK Corral."

Chapter 13

In his first full day in town, Craig and I drove into Historic Bisbee so he could check out what a national organization named one of the quirkiest places to retire in the United States.

"Quirky is a pretty good description, but those retirees better have some serious legs on them," I chuffed when I finally caught up with Craig on the top step of a tier of the famed Bisbee stairs. Craig was mounting two at a time and then jogging in place with the faked nonchalance of an exercise nut. I bade scourges upon him as I labored upward in the five thousand foot altitude.

Already light-headed, gasping like a guppy who'd escaped his bowl, I ultimately made it up the first one hundred and fifty steps of the one thousand he wanted to climb and shooed him on, wheezing I'd meet him at the car. Oddly enough though, I pushed through, got a second wind, and made it to step five hundred before packing it in. Afraid my wobbly legs might trip me up should I try descending via the stairs, I slowly walked the winding road down to town, stopping often to inspect charming old miner's shacks.

Or what used to be old miners' shacks. Some looked to be completely renovated, others new, but built to look old. I'd been told that the town hit on tough times in 1975, when the mine closed. At that time, you could buy almost any house in town for a few hundred dollars. Of course, once word of cheap housing in a scenic setting got out, artists, mostly from California, flocked in. Little by little, Bisbee became a tourist attraction. Its cool temperatures in summer months draw folks from Phoenix and Tucson, and the mountainside perches are being snapped up and restored as fast as the historical society can approve plans. Even now, some are still only accessible by those dastardly stairs. Quaint, and when I was younger and feeling artsy, I'd have bought one. No more. Been there, done that.

Craig was smitten, however, and was already checking out real estate listings when I met him at the car. While I headed to the Bisbee Coffee Bar for a latte, he hit several more offices and returned with a handful of flyers touting possibilities, all of which I deemed way overpriced and much too much work. I gave him three words of advice: foundations, plumbing, and electrical. I'd renovated a 1906 Italianate in the Oakland Hills and knew well the pitfalls of a money-sucking real estate black hole. But then, I own a boat, so who am I to talk?

We drank our coffee while he read up on Bisbee's history, marveling that, in the early 1900's, it was the largest city between St. Louis and San Francisco. Then came 1975, and the bustling city turned ghost town, albeit one with appeal. Miners' shacks sold for a song, more and more people were drawn to the town, renovations began, and the rest is now history.

Meanwhile, the stairs the miners built to access their hillside abodes fell into disrepair, so a group named Save our Stairs was born. The Bisbee 1000 Stair Climb has grown from two hundred intrepid stairistas in 1991 to nearly fifteen hundred climbers from all over the world who attend the yearly October event.

"No more talk of stairs," I groaned. "I need an aspirin and a nap."

"Wimp."

We bundled up and sat on the verandah that afternoon, despite a growing chill. Watching the sun sink beneath ominous clouds, I filled him in on the romantic saga of my friend, Jan, and Craig's old schoolmate Doctor Brigido Yee, also known as Chino. It was Craig who first put me in touch with the acclaimed marine biologist, whom I'd hired for his expertise in whales when I needed one for a project on the Pacific side of the Baja peninsula. Now Jan and the doc were an item, even though Jan had serious reservations about their age difference. When they met she had no idea she was twelve years older than he. After all, he had all those degrees.

I told Craig of Jan's shock when she found out she was cradle-robbing and asked, "Hey, since you are my age, how is it that you and Chino were in school together? He's at least a decade younger than any of us."

"Guy's a genius of some kind. Finished college at sixteen. I met him at UC Davis Vet School while he was taking on a second doctorate."

"That 'splains it, but he seems so...normal."

"He's a great guy, and was way mature for his age when I met him. He wasn't raised rich, that's for sure. He told me that when he was a kid, he was hired to drive a boat for some British marine biologists doing a study at Magadalena Bay. Chino was an autodidact, self-taught in English, French, and German, and had read every book available to him on whales. Hell, he knew about as much as the scientists did, plus some, because he'd lived with the whales all his life."

"So they mentored him?"

"I'd say. They sent him to special schools in the UK, then on to Imperial College, near Hyde Park in the heart of London, which focuses on science, engineering, and medicine."

"Oh, yeah, I know it well. Not that I could have gotten in. Great school."

"After graduating with an education equal to that of a British royal, he returned to Mexico and was back to running whale tour boats when UC Davis Vet school got wind of him and brought him up here."

"And now he's back in the Baja, once again communing with whales."

"He prefers the simple life, so how did he end up with Miss Jan? Or rather, she with him? I always considered her high maintenance."

"Love conquers all?"

"I guess so. Maybe I'll go down for a visit. I haven't seen Chino in years. Tell me about Mexico. I've never been there."

I had to think for a minute. How does one describe Mexico? "Everything south of the border is more, and less," I told him.

"What does that mean?"

"More rules than you can shake a stick at, but no one seems to really know what they are, and are not inclined to enforce them, except when you don't expect them to. Everything takes more time, but generally costs less money, except when you don't expect it to. Stuff like that."

"So, Hetta, what do you like most?"

"The excitement, I guess. It's like living in a casino. Every move you make, there's a chance you'll win, or lose. The Mexicans seem to make a game of everything. For instance, they set up speed traps, but when a friend of mine was caught in one, and then inadvertently backed his van into the cop's car, they only shrugged and let him go. Didn't even give him a speeding ticket.

"Another friend was taking a lit-tle more goods across the border than Mexican law allows, and by the way, we never know exactly what that is, and got stopped for inspection. They glanced inside the van, and waved him on, but his car wouldn't start. Thinking he was royally screwed when a customs pickup with two big guys rolled up, he figured on a big fine for smuggling, but what did they do? Helped him jumpstart his van. And on another day, other people have had their boats, cars and everything in them confiscated for not having the proper paperwork, even though other officials told them they didn't need it. It's a crap shoot."

"I don't think most Americans want to live with that kind of uncertainty. We hear horror stories."

I shrugged a fairly good Mexican shrug. "Oh, ca-ca occurs. Cops looking for payoffs, or *mordida*, the bite. There's much less of that now, but the escalating cartel wars and human smuggling are far more dangerous. Many Americans won't cross the border. Folks in Nogales, Arizona, used to walk over to the Mexican side for dinner, but no more. Drug thugs peppering your enchiladas with automatic weapons fire is crappy for tourism. Here, at this border though, no problem. So far."

"Except that you've already seen armed smugglers. As for random gunfire, people have been shot at in Oakland restaurants. And speaking of, those bow tie dudes at the golf course this morning? The more I think about it, the more convinced I am that they are up to something, and it ain't good. Stay away from them."

"Gee, and here I was, thinking of asking them over for cocktails."

He grinned. "Muslims don't drink, and by the way, after you finish that glass of wine, neither do you. Cocktails are curtailed for at least ten days."

"Ten days? Are you nuts?"

"Nope. Ten days, then you can have a glass now and again."

I mulled that over, changed the subject back to Mexico. "I hope the Mexicans get this drug war thing under control soon. I'll be driving back and forth to San Carlos and, when I can, the mine. I have to admit that I'm a little on edge, and you know I ain't no scaredy cat. If I can get spooked, it is no wonder tourists are staying away in droves."

"America is a country of laws, even if we do grouse about too much government interference. We know what is expected of us, and what the consequences are when we decide to break the rules. Unfortunately, the bad guys use those very laws to get away with just about everything. What do they care if they get a few days in the clink, make bail, get a sleazy lawyer and return to the streets to break more laws? Other than a little speeding or tax evasion, most of us manage to stay out of jail, and like to know where we stand at all times."

"True, but Gringos who live in Mexico are different. For starters, they've taken a step away from the ordinary by moving to another country. Some do it for economic reasons, some for romance, others for the beaches and culture. Expats are a breed unto their own."

Craig looked thoughtful. "You think I'd like it there?"

"Absotively. You'd be a natural. Well, except for the fact that Mexicans hate Blacks and Gays, you'll fit right in."

Craig brayed just as Blue, who for some reason hadn't shown up the night before, trotted up for a treat. The coyote, startled by the laugh, skittered away, then returned and sat, waiting. Now that they'd met, my two buddies engaged in a stare-down, Craig's a look of curiosity, Blue's wily, as he carefully checked out the large black human on my porch.

Craig whistled softly. "Whoa, Hetta, you weren't justa wolfin', that is one big old handsome coyote. Gimme a biscuit."

I grabbed a handful of dog treats from the kitchen and Craig lobbed them, each one a little closer. Blue seemed to have no qualms about moving near, and got within two feet of the pony wall. He now snagged his biscuits in mid-air, and with each catch, Craig's grin widened. "I, of all people, should know better than to mess with wild animals, but I gotta admit this is a kick in the ass. I'm having trouble building up guilt here. This guy is a hoot."

"I enjoy him. He is a little hairy, but he's all I got in the here and now. Pitiful, ain't it?"

Craig's smile vanished. "Beats having nothing."

"Wanna go cry together over spilt beer?"

"We can't have beer."

"We'll give it up tomorrow."

"Oh, what the hell. Where?"

"St. Elmo, where we're sure to find trouble."

"Super."

St. Elmo bar, in Bisbee's famed Brewery Gulch, shows every year of its hundred, and is my kind of joint. Dive, actually.

When we bellied up to the bar, it was still early, so we were not the only tourists. A few locals were about, looking as though they'd been there since their first breakfast beer. The famed jukebox played at a decibel level a tad lower than that of a sonic boom. We could barely hear each other as I recounted the adventures of Hetta and Jan on our trip down the Baja, and the messes we got into.

"I knew you two were headed for trouble when you left with that dishy Mexican boat captain."

"Fabio. Yep, he's a looker, all right. A happily married looker, so no trouble there, darn it."

"You talk a good game, but I don't think Jenks has a thing to worry about with you. And now Jan has hooked up with Chino. You know," he turned up his beer bottle, finished it off and signaled for another. "I think I *will* go to the Baja for a visit with them." The Craig I know and love rarely drinks more than one beer, and he sure as hell doesn't take off on trips on a whim, like I do. I fixed him with the evil eye. "Okay, that's it. What happened?"

"Like I said, I had an epiphany. I want to change my life, and I'm starting with actual free time. I've worked my ass off ever since I started my business, and now it is time to smell the roses."

"Oh, God, you're not going to take off for Nepal to contemplate your navel, are you?"

That got a grin. "Nope, but I am doing a lot of thinking while I'm out on those walks and runs. Losing weight has to be for the right reason: me. If I do it just to attract a partner, I have failed myself."

"Dang, that's deep. You know, I set out to change my life a couple of years ago when I bought the boat, and in a way, of course, I have. But what started out as a manhunt ended up with a new life. I did meet Jenks, but only after I let go of some of my own demons. Jenks finds me refreshing, or so he says. I'm so glad I didn't meet him a few years back. Don't think he'd have found me refreshing at all. More like a ball breaking feminist hell-bent on self-destruct."

"You did have a distinctive chip on your shoulder, and very bad taste in men."

"You can talk. However, you're right about my history, and you know what worries me the most?"

He shook his head.

"That if I lose Jenks I'll revert to type."

"No, I don't think so, Hetta. You've mellowed."

"Must be the age, because my bad habits still lurk, they just have to go to bed earlier."

For some reason, probably the beer, Craig found this hilarious, and our laughter drew the company of one very good looking gay guy and a rugged cowboy, who bought me a beer. Tempted to stay awhile and flirt, we soon parted company with our admirers, lest those past devils messed with our good intentions.

On the drive home, snowflakes hit the windshield, which I thought was neat because I hadn't seen snow in years.

While I was loading the coffee pot, Craig came into the kitchen for a glass of water.

"Thanks, Craig, for coming. I needed company and yours is just the ticket. I miss Jenks so much, and I'm terrified I'll lose him if I keep screwing up."

"So," Craig said with a lopsided grin, "here's a new concept for you. Stop. Screwing. Up."

Chapter 14

Nothing puts a hush over the land like a blanket of snow.

The golf course was a winter wonderland of white, dotted with yucca stalks standing stark against a brilliant blue sky. Excited, I jumped from bed and into the warmest clothes and shoes I had.

Set back from neighbors and traffic, the house was normally quiet, but this morning all sound seemed absorbed. The verandah's half inch of snow was just too tempting to pass up. Scooping up two handfuls, I crept back into the house, over to Craig's room, eased open the door and nailed him with a snowball.

Instantly awake, he launched a pillow at me, but not fast enough.

"You'd better have coffee ready, Hetta," he yelled from the bedroom, "or prepare for a roll in the snow."

I poured him a cup, handed it to him as he grumped into the living room in his Bugs Bunny flannel jammies. I'd already turned on the fireplace, so the lure of steaming coffee and a cheery fire diverted him from his threatened retaliation. "I'll get the paper," I offered, "just in case someone should drive by and witness those pajamas. I do have reputation to uphold, you know."

"Yeah, a bad one."

I shot him the finger and headed for the front door, threw it open, and my heart and feet stopped at the same time on the threshold. Inside the gated courtyard, footprints led to the front door, then out again. I slammed the door, which brought Craig to his feet.

"What is it?" he asked.

Pulling up the side window blinds, I pointed. "Look. We've had company."

He got dressed, then together we reopened the door, crossed the courtyard and opened the gate. The Rottweiler across the road was silent, so we knew whoever had been there was long gone. Loca keeps close, vociferous, track of anyone she doesn't know, and is the best guard dog I never owned.

"Did you hear Loca barking during the night?"

Craig, who sleeps like the dead, contemplated my question. "Maybe, but I'm a veterinarian. Dog barks are like white noise for me."

"I think I heard her, but probably figured it was the paper guy punching her buttons."

Two sets of tire tracks marred the fluffy snow. I grabbed the newspaper and we went back inside.

"Okay," I said as we drank our coffee, "one set of tires belongs to the paper deliverer, but who walked to the door? It wasn't him, or the paper would have been inside the courtyard."

"I agree, Sherlock."

"So, someone came to the door, but didn't ring the bell, and it was after we went to bed because the snow just began falling in earnest when we got home."

"Brilliant, my dear Watson."

"Oh, hush. You didn't see the security lights come on?"

"No, but then I sleep the sleep of the righteous."

"Crap. Think I should call the cops?"

"And tell them what?"

He was right, what would I tell them?

The snow was gone by noon, and golfers emerged. The whole thing seemed a little schizophrenic.

A FedEx shipment from Craig's parents arrived. In it were letters, photos, birth certificates, and all manner of family memorabilia, as well as a fairly pointed note saying if he was determined to vacation in Arizona so long, he might as well delve into his roots. Doctors Washington, the elders, were obviously none too thrilled with their up-until-now responsible and predictable son, Doctor Washington Junior, taking off on a lark.

Man, oh, man, were they in for a rude awakening some day.

We sifted through the stuff and found a family tree leading back to one Abraham Lincoln Washington, born 1899, died 1949. A photo, with an inscription on the back identifying the man as A.L. Washington in Huachuca Arizona with Blackjack Pershing, showed a jaunty young black soldier leaning casually on his rifle stock, campaign hat tipped rakishly, jodhpur-like pants ballooning from his knee-high riding boots.

"Wow, did you know your grandfather served under General Pershing?"

"Great-grandfather. No, I just knew he was a Buffalo Soldier."

"What's that mean, exactly? They were good buffalo hunters?"

"Nope, the Indians thought a black soldier's hair looked like a buffalo's curly top knot, thus the name."

"Boy, howdy. Can you imagine what your Black Muslims over at the RV park would do to those Indians these days for an assessment like that?"

"They are not my Black Muslims," he growled.

"Testy, testy." I picked up another photo, one of a tent camp. When I flipped it over, I let out a whoop. It read, Camp Naco, 1914, during the Battle of Naco. For someone like me, a ninth-generation Texan fascinated with my own genealogy, this was like mining into a mother lode of information.

All thoughts of my own work vanished as we dug deeper, finding out more and more about Craig's ancestor. Grabbing the tent photo, I dragged Craig out onto the verandah, held up the picture, and pointed. "Look right there, at the hills behind the camp."

"This is amazing. That camp could have been right here where we stand. My great-granddad might have been wounded in this very spot. He said he was on his way to Fort Huachuca when they diverted to Naco, and he caught that piece of shrapnel in the leg. History, right in our faces."

"Well, now," I drawled, "I guess we'd better prepare to duck for cover, just in case history repeats itself and the Mexicans start lobbing explosives into our future."

Sometimes the joke is on the joker. Albert Einstein was dead-on when he said, "I never think about the future—it comes soon enough."

That box of memorabilia created a monster, one I can fully relate to, since I have spent countless hours in musty Texas libraries, and on the Internet, searching out clues into my own family history.

Craig became a genealogy junkie. Daily he took off for some local historical center, either at Fort Huachuca—touted as Home of the Buffalo Soldier—Bisbee, Douglas, or even Tucson.

We settled into a routine. Early each morning, we walked the two miles to Fort Newell, or what's left of it, and back. Also known as Camp Naco and Fort Naco, the wooden buildings of the camp still stand, albeit in bad shape. Georgia Lou, the bartender at the golf club—and who turned out to be a gold mine of info—said it was bought by a neighboring city and slated for renovation, but it looked to me like they'd better hurry up. No signs told us to keep off the premises, so we snooped through those buildings not fenced off, and a couple that were.

With our daily exercise and lack of white stuff in my diet, I felt invigorated. Gone was the maudlin gal back on the boat, and it showed in both my work and attitude. Craig was down another five pounds but I, unwilling to give up my glass of wine before and with dinner, lost a measly two. Better than nuttin'.

We got to know regulars at the golf club, now that we were habitués. Duffers and pros alike mixed with business types, cowboys, construction workers, retirees, and border patrol agents for meals, drinks and golf. Boasting the only large event hall in the immediate area, the club hosted weddings, *Quinceañeras*—a Mexican girl's celebration of her fifteenth birthday—golf tournament award dinners, community meetings and the like for people on both sides of the border. All in all, there was something for everyone. I'd feared isolation in some podunk border town and instead found a friendly community.

Sipping our morning coffee at the bar, we chatted with others, caught up on local gossip, and eavesdropped on conversations we found of interest. Snoopery being my favorite sport, I learned a lot.

"It just chaps my ass," I overheard from a table of border patrol agents. Needless to say, my natural nosiness surfaced and I perked my ears.

Another man shook his head and sipped coffee. "Yeah, well the bastards can just bring it on."

I wanted to yell, "What? Bring what on?" but held my tongue.

Another man shrugged. "You got that right. Who in the hell do they think they are? This is America, last I heard."

"Maybe the politicians will think twice, now, about putting one of us in jail for shooting some dope dealer in the ass."

I waited for them to finish their meals, then, as they dispersed, I headed for the ladies' room and took a detour out the back door to ambush one of them, a fellow Texan named Tim Ramos I'd previously met at the club.

"Hey, Tim, how you doing?"

"Oh, hi, Hetta. All settled in the new house?"

"Yep, and as you've seen, I have company already."

He cut his eyes back toward the building. "I noticed. Boyfriend?" His disapproval was obvious, but I didn't confront it. Not a good idea to annoy a source.

"No, Doctor Washington is only a friend. You know, Tim, I overheard the guys saying something strange is going on around here. Anything you can share? You know how nosy we Texans are."

He hesitated, mulling over an answer. "Well, I guess you'll hear it on the news tonight anyhow, so I'm not speakin' outta turn. We've been warned to back off from UDAs."

"Would that be anything like ET?" I teased.

He rolled his eyes. "Undocumented Aliens. Like that's actually gonna happen. Look, let me give you this, since you live so close to the border." He took a card from his shirt pocket, wrote a number on the back while telling me the latest. Handing me the card, he hitched his gun holster and sauntered off to his green-striped truck, not noticing I was stunned into silence by his news. I zombie-walked back to the bar.

Craig, still sipping coffee, asked, "Line in the loo?"

I swallowed the lump in my throat and tried to answer casually. "Nope, I sneaked out the back way to ambush ole Agent Tim."

"Why?"

"Oh, he tells me stuff."

"That explains it, oh nosy one."

On our walk home, my mind swirled and paranoia descended. What I didn't tell Craig was what the officer told me, something that made my blood run cold; a drug cartel had issued a death threat to anyone who reports drug or human smugglers, be they police, border patrol, or your average Joe Blow.

That would be me.

Chapter 15

Craig left for some archive diving right after our morning walk. After the footprints in the snow, and that little talk with Border Patrol Agent Tim Ramos still fresh in my mind, I set the security alarm even though it was broad daylight and the doors were locked. Cowardice runs right smartly through my veins.

I entered Tim's number into my cell and house phone memories, and was soon lost in my work.

While grateful for the job, and the ability to work from home, I was still mildly annoyed that not once had anyone given me any direction or priorities for what I was supposed to actually do. I'd bounced this lack of guidance off Wontrobski, but he said to just follow my nose.

What the mine management types didn't know was, given no other guidance, my nose was deeply buried in a scathing exposé I'd found on the Internet. Since worker safety wasn't something the owners mentioned as any priority, I figured I might as well make it so. I zeroed in on the most dastardly of their long list of misdeeds, the negligence involving a dilapidated and dangerous concentrator.

A concentrator is actually a processing plant where large boulders are reduced to a fine dust. Fine, deadly, powder that is supposed to be captured. The dust collection system was kaput, dismantled several years before. This alone was enough to give a stateside OSHA inspector apoplexy. Lack of a collection system had not only allowed the release of high levels of silica and other life-threatening substances into the air, these same hazards were now piled in visible heaps. Every time the wind blew, the entire area received a toxic dusting. Just rereading my own report had me holding my breath.

I went online and ordered several face masks with charcoal and HEPA filtration. Next time I was at the jobsite I'd closely resemble Jason, from the Friday the thirteenth movies.

My first whack at a revamp list was extensive. I'd faxed it to the mine office, along with a huge dollar figure required to make the changes, a week ago. I waited for an, "*Aye, Chihuahua*, you're killing us here," response, but got nothing. Maybe their peso conversion calculator shorted out over all those zeroes, but hell, a couple of hundred million to fix stuff up was chump change. They were capable of producing a hundred-and-eighty thousand tons annually, and even with copper under three bucks a pound, we're talking ten billion, less operating expenses.

I called Maria.

"*Buenos dias*, Café. How are you?"

"Good, Maria, and you?"

"I am fine."

Prerequisite social inanities out of the way, I got to the reason for my call. "Did you receive my fax last week?"

"Oh, yes."

"And did you give it to *Señor* Orozco?"

"*Señor* Orozco is in Mexico. I gave it to Señor Racón." I knew when she said Mexico, she meant Mexico City.

"Oh? And how is *Señor* Ratón?"

She giggled. "Do you wish to speak with him, Café?"

"I'd rather eat scorpions, but I guess I have to."

Another titter, then dead air, then the big cheese himself, squeaked, "Yes?"

I cut to the chase. "Did you receive the report I sent last Friday?"

"Yes."

"And?" My impatience with this jerk sent my voice up a couple of octaves, despite my resolve to give ulcers, not get them.

"And, yes, I received it."

"Let's try a harder question, if you are up to it, that is. Did you read it?"

A labored sigh, indicating his unwillingness to trade spars with lesser humans. "Of course I read it. What is it you want from me?"

Eat shitpie and die? Take a long walk off a short plank? Unwilling to let his hauteur ruin my day, I inhaled a deep, cleansing, Yoga breath and, with all the coolness I could muster, answered. "Perhaps you could let me know if I am headed in the direction the mine operators expect?"

"Miss Coffey, you are the expert. That is why we hired you. We have no intention of telling you what to do."

I'm an expert? News to me. "Oh, well, then," I said lamely. Shoot, I was spoiling for a fight. This was way too easy. One might wonder why.

Señor Rat added, "Tomorrow, I will bring you the drawings you requested. Do you wish to meet me at the border?"

"Can't get across?"

"Excuse me?"

"Never mind. Yes, I will meet you, just call me when you get near Naco."

I hung up, not looking forward to a face-to-muzzle, however brief, with the little shit. I was still puzzled with mine management's lack of concern as to what I was up to. I'm used to working on my own, but I usually have some kind of direction other than, *We want to fix it, you tell us how*. I generally like to know what IT is.

But then again, why look a gift rodent in the mouth?

I took Craig with me for my meeting with El Ratón.

Of course, since I'd warned my friend of the Mexican's ratty personality, the little creep was all sweetness and smarmy light when I introduced him. Possibly because I presented the huge and menacing Craig as my bodyguard? Okay, so I didn't exactly say that in so many words, but it was strongly intimated.

Racón gave me my files and skittered away. Craig and I walked back across the border, both carrying rolled drawings and a few file folders. The border guys, despite their past undisguised desire to nail me for something, checked our passports and sent us home. Back at the car, I commented that maybe they'd decided I wasn't a threat to national security after all, but Craig said that was because they didn't know me.

We were in high spirits as we entered the golf course restaurant to catch lunch. Greeting regulars, nodding to strangers, we made our way to a table. As luck would have it we ended up near the pair I'd dubbed the Malcolms X.

They actually acknowledged our presence as we passed them. Not much of an acknowledgement, mind you, but they did nod. For some reason, I didn't think this was a good thing, and the scowl on Craig's face confirmed it. As long as the two had ignored him, Craig did likewise. Now, however, that nod gave Craig an opening. Only a quick, sharp jab to his ribcage preempted what I feared would be a smart-assed remark.

"Ouch," he yelped. "What was that for?"

"Be nice."

"I wasn't gonna—"

"Yes you were," I hissed. "Now, what are we gonna eat?"

What I wanted was the Mexican combination plate, piled high with enchiladas, refrieds, rice, and a chile relleno, all topped with greasy melted cheese and chased with a cold beer. What I got, at Craig's insistence, was a shrimp salad and iced tea.

After lunch, since we'd missed our walk that morning due to the meet with Rat Face, we headed for Fort Newell, snooped around, then circled back for the car at the golf club.

As we passed the RV park, I caught a glimpse of something that stopped me in my tracks.

I grabbed Craig's arm. "I swear to God, I just saw that little shit, Racón, going into an RV. Don't look, keep walking. I'll show you which one later. Why would he meet us on the other side of the border if he was coming over here anyway?"

"Got me. Maybe he has a girlfriend stashed over here."

"Could be. I'll do some snoopery, find out who lives in that RV."

"Or, Hetta, here's an idea: mind your own business!"

"Silly boy."

What do you get when you throw one creepy little Lebanese-Mexican and two shadowy Black Muslims into a million dollar RV? Hell, I don't know, but it can't be good.

Craig and I were mulling this over while tossing Blue his late afternoon treats. "Ya think it has something to do with the mine? Like the Xer's are hired goons? Maybe to terrify the miners back to work or something?"

"Doubt it. From what you said, the mine owners are bullying the miners, legally, all by themselves. My guess is, there's dope involved."

"That's logical, what with their proximity to the border. Think we should drop a dime on 'em? I have Tim's phone number, the border patrol guy I told you about."

Craig grinned. "And tell Ramos what?"

"I don't know. How about, 'Say, it might behoove you to take your drug dog for a stroll in the RV park?'"

"That'll give the feds a giggle, what with that hotbed of Canadian retirees over there. You gotta keep a sharp eye on those Canucks, you know."

"Good point. You got any better ideas?"

"None."

"You know Georgia Lou, the bartender? She's the one who told me which RV belongs to our bow-tied buds. She lives only a few spaces from them. She was too busy this morning for details, but I'll brace her at coffee tomorrow."

"Brace her? You read too many cop books, but—phone, Hetta."

It was Jenks.

"Hi, Honey," he said, sounding like he was next door instead of a bajillion miles away. I did a quick calculation. It was four in the morning in Kuwait City, but then Jenks is an early riser.

"Let me guess, you're calling to tell me you'll be home tomorrow."

"Nice try, but no, I just wanted to hear your voice. I do, however, have some information for you."

I was determined not to whine. "You've got my voice, and I'm all ears," I said, hoping I sounded upbeat, "so give me the info." Upbeat, no. Prickly, yes.

Craig gave me a look under his eyebrows, shook his head, and went back inside. Blue watched him in anticipation, hoping for more goodies on his return.

"Hetta, you there?"

"Oh, sorry, Sweetheart, Craig distracted me for moment." I thought the *sweetheart* was a nice touch.

"For a minute there, I thought you were mad at me or something."

Mad? No. Lonely, mistreated, and abandoned? Yes. I didn't say so, though. "Must be the connection."

"Maybe so." He then told me what he was going to be doing over there, sort of. I didn't like the sound of it.

"Jenks—"

He cut me off before I could protest. "Anyhow," he said, "remember that friend I told you about who lives south of you? I got an email and he's invited you, and Craig, to come down for a visit. I've forwarded the message to you, so maybe you guys can get together. Might make a nice little trip, take your mind off work."

Take my mind off Jenks's stubborn insistence at working in a war zone, more likely. I started to say something about just that, then remembered that I was living on the Mexican border, subbed out to an outfit rife with political unrest and riots. Pots must beware of calling the kettle black.

"And why, Jenks, do you think I'd enjoy a visit with some friend of yours, and his wife?"

"They own a winery."

"Well, crap, why didn't you say so? We'll go down this weekend."

Jenks laughed. "That's my girl. I miss you so much."

Not enough to come home. I bit that back. "I miss you, too."

"Gotta run, have a meeting later that I'm not ready for. I'll call when I can. Like I said, Lars and I are traveling this week."

"Jenks, you're supposed to stay safe and sound in Kuwait City, not traipsing around in a war zone."

"We will not be traipsing, as you call it. Don't worry, we'll be perfectly safe, just out of touch. It may be more than a week, so don't worry if you don't hear from me."

"Well, I will worry."

"I'll call as soon as we get back to the hotel. I promise. Gotta run. Love you."

Click.

"Love you, too," I said into dead air.

"I love you, too," Craig crooned. He walked to the pony wall, tossed Blue a treat, and cheered when the coyote snagged it in midair. Turning to me, he shook his head. "That Jenks must be a glutton for punishment. He calls, you give him crap. Here's a little professional advice, in case you ever get another dog. If a dog comes when you call, don't bite him, praise him."

"I thought I was pretty danged nice, considering the circumstances. He told me he and his brother are leaving Kuwait City, but not where they're going. Probably out into the desert, if I know him. When he took this job he said they'd be working in the city, safe and sound. He promised not to go into Iraq under any circumstances, but now this. I'm worried and pissed off."

"Look, Missy Control, you've gotta lighten up. First off, how do you figure he's going to Iraq? I suggest you call the man back, wish him luck on his trip, and tell him you'll be thinking about him. What he doesn't need, in addition to the stress of working in the middle-damned-east, is crap from afar."

I started to protest, but Craig was right. I grabbed the phone and speed dialed, but only got voice mail. Damn. I left a properly sweet as pie message, and felt better for it. "Satisfied?" I asked Craig when I finished.

"Whoa, someone call channel thirteen so we can make the ten o'clock broadcast. Breaking News! Hetta Coffey actually took advice."

"Oh, hush. Wanna go on a field trip this weekend?"

"Sure, where?"

"I'll let you know after I read my email."

"Oooh, mystery trip. Cool."

Chapter 16

Turns out Jenks's old friend, Ted Burns, and his wife, Nanci, operate a ranch and winery north of Arizpe, under a hundred miles south of Naco.

I Googled their label, Vinas Estrellas, and learned their high-altitude Cabernet Sauvignon had beat out both Chile and Argentina in an international competition. That alone was worth the trip.

I emailed them, they e'd back, confirming their invite for Craig and me to come on down. They gave me a phone number, I called, and arrangements were made. I mean, we are talking wine, here. Award-winning wine, at that.

Craig and I pored over a map of Sonora, figured we wouldn't get too lost, packed, and headed across the border early Friday morning. We planned on a leisurely trip, stopping to check out whatever caught our interest.

As we approached the border crossing, Craig commented on the number of children, walking in groups of threes and fours, crossing into Arizona from Mexico. "Are those kids Mexicans headed for American schools?"

"Yep. I was curious about that myself, so I asked one of the border patrol guys at the golf club. He says some have dual citizenship, others are Mexican nationals who live on the other side, but come over to Arizona for school because their parents or legal guardians own property in the state. They qualify to attend because the family pays county property and school taxes. However, I also heard that no one really checks."

"So they walk across."

"Some probably have a ride, or catch buses once they cross, but the elementary school is only a couple of blocks away." I pointed at a brightly painted, new looking building. "They teach kindergarten through eighth grade, so I guess after that they either have to go to a Mexican school or, like I said, catch a bus or a ride into another part of Bisbee. Maybe even charter schools in Sierra Vista. It's a controversial subject around here, as you might imagine."

We rolled through the Mexican crossing, caught a green PASE light telling us we wouldn't undergo inspection. I slowed anyway, having learned that the green light wasn't always a free pass. Like I'd told Craig, in Mexico, you just never know. Since I was ignored by the customs agent, we drove through town, out to Mex 2, and on toward Cananea with no further stops. The soldiers from the previous trip had folded their tents and left.

Craig, as *copiloto* and navigator, guided us to a left turn just before entering Cananea and we were on our way down the Rio Sonora Valley on a narrow, but paved, two-lane road. Somewhere in the back of my mind lingered a half-remembered conversation with one of the mine secretaries on my first day there. Faint warning bells jangled about traveling this road, but I couldn't quite recall what she'd said. It didn't take long to find out.

We passed through tiny communities from a time long past, and were it not for the occasional satellite dish, beater pickup, or a microwave tower, we might have expected to meet with a caravan of Spanish soldiers and priests headed north to establish missions, convert the locals, and steal their gold and silver.

Craig, who downloaded all sorts of information about our route before we left, kept up a running commentary on the history of the valley, the names of villages and the like. If he ever wanted to quit being a veterinarian, he'd make a passable tour guide.

South of the Cananea turnoff, we rolled into Bacoachi, with, according to my guide, a population of two thousand. Downtown consisted of a standard church square and a few small stores. "That church," Craig pointed, "the San Miguel Arcángel Temple, was founded in 1670, remodeled in the early 1900's. Their big claim to fame is the nearby ninety-year-old Rancho Sierra Coronado, with twenty rooms on eight thousand acres. Some kind of dude ranch, I guess. Ronald Reagan slept there. Wanna go check it out?"

"Why not? How far off the main road is it?"

"Only a mile or so, according to the Internet." He gave me the kilometer marker for our turnoff, which led us onto a sandy desert road that was surprisingly well maintained. A half-mile toward the dude ranch, though, a locked gate stopped our progress, as did a big sign telling us to get lost in two languages.

"I thought this was some kind of resort."

"Well, it was in Ronnie Reagan's time. Guess they've closed, or it could be one of the super exclusive places where you can't just show up. I thought it might be nice to check out the old hotel, but looks like we're out of luck."

We turned around and were headed back for the main road when I spotted, in my rearview mirror, a white vehicle partially obscured by the gate. No one got out that I could see. It just sat there.

"Someone's back there now, Craig, on the other side of the gate. We could hook a U, but I'm not getting a warm and fuzzy feeling here. I mean, no one knows where we are, and it is my experience that leaving perfectly good pavement in Mexico might be hazardous to one's health. I'll leave it up to you."

"I bow to cognitive content, especially when it belongs to Hetta Coffey, Master of Disaster," he teased.

I picked up speed while nervously checking the rearview mirror through our dust. When we hit pavement, I hogged the centerline, rolling along at a good clip. I was in the process of bragging about what good time we were making when we sailed over a rise, rounded a sharp curve, and hurtled downward into a foot or so of water. The ford, originally concrete, had washed out over time, leaving rocks, sand, and mud.

A tsunami of sandy water hit our windshield, blinding me and drawing an, "Oh, shit," from Craig. Tires and shocks threatened to implode. I barely controlled the car as we careened wildly, until the tires grabbed pavement on the other side. The car stabilized and I jammed on the brakes, throwing us against our seatbelts.

For a moment we sat there, both panting, until Craig said dryly, "The Rio Sonora, I presume."

Realizing we'd survived the near-calamity ourselves, we climbed out to inspect my VW for obvious damage. Everything looked intact. With the engine off, the incredible quiet of remoteness was broken only by trickling water and bird songs. Oh, and the pounding in my chest. What if we'd rolled over? We hadn't seen another vehicle or a single house on the main road since leaving Bacoachi.

I shot the low water crossing the finger. Silly, I know, but sometimes taking out anger on an inanimate object just feels good. Assessing our situation, I said, "I'd say we're pretty lucky, my man, but from now on I plan to slow—" I spotted something that gave my tummy a little hiccup of concern.

Sitting on the other side of the crossing, partially obscured by bushes, sat a white vehicle, probably some kind of SUV. It wasn't moving, just sitting there. I could barely hear the engine idling above the water's gurgle. I couldn't see the whole car, or truck, or who was driving it, but a sting of stomach acid stirred my natural paranoia. Had someone followed us from the Rancho's locked gate?

Trying to look casual, I took a glug of water and commented loudly upon the bucolic countryside, with its tree-lined, lazy riverbanks where goats and cattle grazed. Craig, who evidently had not spotted our company, was busy snapping photos. Where, oh where, were people when you needed them?

As if in answer, a rattletrap truck laden with farm implements of some kind crested the hill, rumbled past the white vehicle, down to the ford, and crept over to our side of the river. The driver stopped, eyed my muddied VW, and asked if we needed help. I glanced back at what I now dubbed the Idling Ghost, but it had vanished.

Sighing in relief, I told the farmer where we were headed, he said he was going that way, and if we'd follow him he'd make sure we didn't miss our turn. What he was much too polite to say was, "Or get surprised by another ford, you silly Gringa." He didn't know I would have followed him anywhere just then. I was spooked, probably without cause, but unsettled nonetheless.

For the next stultifying, but safe, two hours, we followed him at under twenty miles an hour. Craig dug out a Clive Cussler audio book adventure and we whiled the miles away, lost in someone else's fantasy.

A couple of pickups charged our bumper, then shot by with seeming attitude that in Arizona would qualify as road rage. In Mexico? Just common passing practice. We dogged the farmer's bumper, having had all the excitement we needed for one day. When we finally crept to our turnoff, the old man coasted his truck to a stop next to a woman and child standing by the roadside.

Dressed in almost identical traditional outfits more often seen in southern Mexico than in Sonora—loose fitting embroidered blouses, long skirts bound at the waist with a cummerbund-like wrap, brightly colored shawls, and needlework backpacks—the two dark skinned females with shiny black braids made for a National Geographic moment. A tethered burro grazing in the background rounded out the picturesque tableau, which was too good to pass up. I grabbed my camera and snapped off a couple of shots.

The farmer talked briefly with the woman, confirmed this was indeed the winery road, bid us *que le vaya bien*, waved *adios*, and clattered away. After he left the woman told us, in very good English, they would appreciate a ride up the hill. Sweet and friendly, she explained they were waiting for a winery staff van, but it was evidently delayed.

The two climbed into the rear seat, settled their skirts and shawls tidily, ignoring the seat belts. After a short distance, I longed for a Range Rover. Twenty rib-jarring, tooth-rattling minutes later, we passed under a massive stucco arch welcoming us to Viña de las Estrellas, Vineyard of the Stars. A quarter mile farther, after bumping along a cobblestone drive flanked by lush, flowering vegetation and towering Eucalyptus trees, we reached Hacienda de las Estrellas, the main house.

The two-storied building was straight out of a coffee table book featuring Spanish colonial design. Stuccoed columns supported a deep red-tiled gallery spanning the first floor. Upstairs, balconies ran the entire length of the building, with French doors and windows flanked by blue shutters. Planter boxes on the balcony rails overflowed with geraniums, and shocking pink bougainvillea vines that also climbed the walls, up onto the roof, then tumbled down the columns in a shower of color.

Craig whistled in appreciation. “Doesn’t anyone around here know it's winter?”

The home’s walls, painted the exact color of the surrounding earth, looked to be hundreds of years old, but in good repair. In the front courtyard, next to where we parked, was a hitching post complete with saddled horse. I felt as though we’d taken a long step back in time.

“Wow,” was my take. The woman in the backseat tittered, the first sound she’d made since climbing into the car. She was either shy, or perhaps terrified with my struggles to keep us tires-side down on the rough road. Now, though, she was obviously amused by my vast command of the English language.

Ornately carved double doors, also painted Colonial blue, swung open to reveal two people I recognized from photos on their website. Nanci, a tiny blonde, and Ted, olive skinned and dark haired, made a handsome couple. Ted looked much more like we Gringos expect a Mexican to look than the fair Nanci, but she was the one with Mexican nationality. From their fit physiques and clear eyes, it was pretty obvious they didn’t overly imbibe their own product.

“You two must be bushed,” Ted said after introductions and handshakes. “By the way, thanks for bringing the gals up. I got a call that our van blew a tire, so the lift was appreciated, although they have the stamina of mountain climbers. I’ve walked that hill with Rosa a couple of times. She breezed up, I wheezed up.”

My two passengers had scurried off behind the house as soon as we stopped. One turned to say *gracias*, but the kid kept going as if she couldn't get away from us fast enough.

"Shy little things, aren't they?" I commented.

"Rosa's been with us for years, but Sophia, or Sonrisa, as we call her, joined us only recently. They both come from down south, Chiapas."

"They aren't mother and daughter?"

"Oh, no. I know, Sonrisa doesn't look much past twelve, but she's actually over twenty. Bet she doesn't top four-five. She's only recently learned to speak Spanish, but with Rosa's help we get along okay."

Craig looked puzzled. "Mexicans who don't speak Spanish?"

Nanci took over. "Rosa is a Quiche speaking native from southern Mexico, as is Sonrisa. They are Indians, or Indios, as we call them, and the true indigenous people of Mexico, unlike we interlopers, even though we interloped a few centuries ago. Many in that region are very poor. Rosa came to us through an ailing aunt of mine. Poor little thing, as a small child, arrived on Tia Laura's doorstep, ragged and hungry. She was only ten, but had wandered alone for a long while before my aunt took her in. Rosa said her parents were killed during one of the conflicts down there. Anyway, Tia Laura took her in, raised her, gave her a good education, and now Rosa is part of our family."

"Such a sad story, but with a good ending," I said. "Good for your aunt. Rosa can thank her lucky stars she didn't land on my aunt's porch."

Ted gave me a quizzical look.

"I have this aunt from hell," I told them. "My Aunt Lillian? You ever see the movie, *Whatever Happened to Baby Jane*? My aunt is the Bette Davis character, only worse. Anyhow, Rosa is one lucky girl."

"Rosa was luck for us," Ted said. "She practically runs the irradiation operation of the winery. She seems shy to strangers, but just wait until you see her in action. Hell, most of the men here are scared to death of her, especially if they screw up. Woman has a vicious streak."

Nanci gave him a look. "Okay, Ted, no more shop talk until we get these folks a welcoming drink. I want to hear more about Hetta's Aunt Lillian."

I laughed. "Trust me, you do not, but I'll sure take that drink."

Ted gave us an apologetic half-smile. "Sorry, we don't get many visitors up here. Enough about the winery for now. I'll get my chance to brag tomorrow, during your tour. Let's hit the verandah, I have a bar set up."

I opted for a glass of their house bubbly, which, because of France's death grip on the label, cannot be called Champagne, but sparkling wine made in the method Champagnoise. "Hey," I said after the first sip, "this is really good, and trust me, I know my Champagne."

"In vino est veritas," Craig quipped. "And trust me on this one, Hetta has vast wine experience."

I gave his shoulder a gentle slap with the back of my hand. "Let these fine people find out about my bad habits on their own. Do you sell this wonderful stuff in the States?"

"No, we make it for in-house consumption only. It ain't, as they say, rocket science. Nor is it made in the so-called champagne method. We cheat."

"Fooled me."

"It's simple, really. We take white wine, add yeast and sugar, re-cork it so carbon dioxide builds up, forcing bubbles into the wine. We only make enough for a summer treat, but since you're here, we broke out a bottle early."

"You might want to lock the cellar until we leave," Craig said, tipping his head in my direction.

"Speaking of summer, Ted," I cut in, ignoring Craig lest he make me out for some kind of wino, "what's with the climate here? It feels and looks like spring has sprung."

"Microclimate, or macroclimate some would call it," Nanci explained. "That's why we can grow good grapes and make great wine here, but in our own method. In the Mediterranean region they have rains and a dry spring and summer. We have a dry winter and wet summer, and because of that, we can grow high altitude grapes, then irradiate them."

"Irradiate?"

"It's part of our special process. That building over there," Ted pointed to a large barn-like structure that looked a couple of centuries old, "houses a well-disguised high-tech laboratory and irradiator system. We use spectroscopy and chromatography to evaluate aroma, color, taste and mouthfeel of grapes, then when they reach their peak, we quickly pick them and put the skids to the natural bacterial process by lightly nuking them."

I was somewhat familiar with irradiated food. "Like they do milk in Europe?"

"Pretty much the same, but less is more. We've found that low-level irradiation and refrigeration of grapes before they're made into wine magnifies the healthful aspects of drinking red wine, making it a good source of antioxidants two or three times more potent than regular reds."

"Aha!" I pumped my fist in the air. "Wine as health food. There is a god."

"Please," Craig pleaded dramatically, "don't encourage her, Ted."

We all laughed, then Nanci said, "Unfortunately, most Americans freak out when they hear the I-word, thinking they'll glow in the dark if they consume irradiated products, but lots of countries, including Mexico, use the process to ensure a bacteria-free food source. Works especially well with poultry and dairy."

"I guess too many Americans remember Three Mile Island," Craig said, "I know I do. I was a teenager and very impressionable. California already had San Onofre on line and it was scary to think we'd all be zapped by Gamma rays. Set nuclear power back a hundred years." He faked a frightened look at the barn.

Nanci patted his hand. "Trust me, you're safe here. The food irradiation facilities themselves do not become radioactive, and don't create radioactive waste." She went on to explain that Cobalt 60, which is what they use, is manufactured in a commercial nuclear reactor. The small radioactive pencils, which have a shelf-life of five years, get re-activated, and that's done by shipping them back in special hardened steel canisters that are designed to survive the worst roads without breaking.

"Designed to survive even your road?" I quipped.

Ted faked indignity. "Keeps the riffraff out."

Craig smiled. "Evidently not, Hetta made it."

"Yeah," I scoffed, "but I could have used a Hummer." Revisiting Nanci's lesson on transporting the steel canisters, I added, "What if the truck carrying the pencils crashes into something?"

"No danger. Even if they did break open, which is doubtful, Cobalt is a solid metal and will not spread through the environment under normal circumstances. However, I would not advise picking one up with your bare hands."

I rolled my eyes. "No worries there."

"Tomorrow we'll give you the Viña Estrella grand tour, but for now, let's get you two into your rooms so you can freshen up for dinner. Hope you're hungry, because we serve fantastic meals around here to go with our fabulous wine. Not to brag, of course."

On the way upstairs, I muttered under my breath, "Craig, there will be no counting of calories, nor glasses of wine tonight. We are on vacation."

He held up his hands in surrender. "Who me?"

Chapter 17

We gathered for dinner at eight, each of us dressed in our own version of casual chic.

I'd draped myself in a long, loose, gauzy, rust-colored number that set off my hair color and covered a multitude of sins. Craig wore a sports jacket and jeans, Nanci was elegantly attired in basic black, and Ted sported a black linen Mexican guayabera wedding shirt, as did his two ranch foremen. Rosa, in a stunningly colorful huipil—pronounced wee-peel—a traditional, richly embroidered top from her homeland, added a splash of Mayan chic.

Soft candlelight bathed the room, strains of classical Spanish guitar set the mood.

I felt ever so urbane, which, after living on a boat for so long, awakened fond memories. There was a time when I jet-setted with the fast crowd thanks to a big fat expense account and the company of men with murky backgrounds, panache, and endless wallets. The ambiance at Hacienda de las Estrellas was reminiscent of starry nights in Aix-en-Provence, a villa in Italy, or a seaside balcony on Mallorca.

Before serving their prize-winning 2002 Cabernet Sauvignon, Estrella Sirius, named after the brightest star in the heavens, Ted, with hammy flair, repeated one wine connoisseur's review. He swirled the wine in his glass and held it to the candelabra. "Brilliant ruby color." Sniffing loudly he declared,

"Forward, fragrant aroma of spice and berry." He took a sip. "Ah, firm tannin laced with," he paused dramatically, "flavors of spicy oak." He swallowed and announced, "Impressively lengthy."

We applauded his act, then Craig said, "So, what does that all mean in English?"

Nanci smiled. "It's wine snob speak for looks good, smells good, tastes good. Hey, it works for us. This wine retails for fifty bucks a bottle, and beats others twice the price."

"Bravo," I said, raising my glass. "To good wine and good company." The wine was, as advertised, fantastic.

Ted stood again. "To Jenks. Wish that rascal was here, but at least he's sent us new friends."

"To Jenks," we toasted, which gave me a moment's fleeting sadness, quickly banished when I dove into savory roasted lamb, freshly dug and boiled fingerling potatoes, salad laced with local goat cheese and, for the grand finale, flan to die for. Call me two-faced, but old Jenks just faded into the background.

A fabulous Cabernet Sauvignon complemented the main course, and for dessert they broke out a bright blue bottle of ice wine they named, Estrella EV Lacertae, after a cold star. I was not only getting a lesson in wine here, they also dispensed a dollop of astronomy.

During dinner I asked Nanci. "How long has your family been making wine?"

"The original vines arrived with my great-grandfather in the 1850's. We've made wine for our own consumption for generations, but I was the first family member to actually get a degree in both viticulture and enology with intent to sell our product."

"My turn to buy a vowel," I quipped, getting a laugh.

"The culture of growing grapes, and the art of wine making," she explained.

"Where does one go to learn such stuff?"

"UC Davis."

"There's a wine school? Where do I sign up?" I asked. "Heck, I've already done my lab work."

Craig shook his head at me and smiled, then turned his attention to Nanci. "You were a Caggie too? I was in Vet Meds."

They talked about their mutual university, we drank more, discussed our backgrounds, the usual chitchat. It was my kind of meal: long, delicious, good conversation, great wine.

Rosa and other management employees sat with us at an ancient hand-hewn dining table that probably decimated a goodly portion of a cedar forest. The employees didn't add much to the conversation until asked a direct question, but it was obvious they all spoke English, which, in deference to our presence, was the only language spoken. On another night, I suspected they stuck with Spanish.

Kitchen help came and went, the diminutive Sonrisa among them. Dressed in the simple white blouse and skirt favored by campesinos, or country folk, for eons, she wore her jet black hair in two shiny braids that reached past her waist. She glided in and out with various dishes and, at one point, while filling my water glass, raised her head and, for the first time I made eye contact with her. I opened my mouth to say thanks, but was shocked by pure hatred in those cold, black eyes.

Rattled, I quickly turned toward Nanci, who was recounting the story of an ancestor, a Prussian mercenary hired by the Emperor of Mexico, Maximilian I.

France's Emperor, Napoleon III, sent Maximilian I to rule over Mexico when the Mexican government refused to pay up on debts. The whole venture was ill fated, certainly for old Max, who was put to the firing squad by Benito Juarez. Nanci's ancestor, however, was a little more far-sighted than the ill-fated Austrian archduke, for he deserted the Emperor's army and beat feet for the Texas border in time to save his own hide.

"Thus, Cinco de Mayo," I said, "the holiday commemorating the liberation of Mexico from France."

"Mostly celebrated in East LA," Nanci quipped. "In Mexico we don't pay it much attention."

"So then, your ancestor hit Texas around 1867, if memory serves me. What was his name, and where did he end up?" I asked, my interest piqued. As a member of the Daughters of the Republic of Texas, and a tenth-generation Texan, I'm always on the lookout for new potential relatives, no matter how many cousins removed.

"His name was Paul Reineke. He married into another Prussian family who had immigrated to Texas in the early 1850's. It was their daughter, also named

Nanci, who scandalized the family by marrying a Spaniard. They ran off to Mexico, to the Spaniard's ancestral land, where we sit today. So, here I am, all these years later, making wine."

I love stories like this, but have to admit I'm green-eyed jealous. If my family had held onto even a smidgen of what they owned during the Republic, I'd hold the deed to most of downtown Austin.

We chatted on about history and the fates left us by our ancestors. After dinner, Nanci, Ted, Craig, and I sat on their verandah, finishing off the ice wine. Ted lit up a Cuban cigar and, to my amazement, Craig accepted one as well. Once Ted found out Craig was a veterinarian they talked horses, cattle, and all manner of farm animals.

When Craig talked about the pet tracking chip he was working on, Ted wanted to know, "Where can I get some? We have a lot of acreage here and hundreds of livestock to track. I could save countless man hours—" he caught a look from Nanci, "uh, person hours, hunting down stray animals."

"Actually, I have a few chips and a tracker back at Hetta's house, but they aren't really approved for use as yet."

"Approved in the United States, right? Hell, man, we're in Mexico. Sell me a few, I'll be your test ranch."

"Deal. I can let you have five chips and a radio tracker unit, but I have to hang onto my more sophisticated toy, the one that uses satellite tracking, to show off to potential investors."

"I'll take what I can get. What do you say, Nanci? Let's cyber-brand some cattle, especially Booger Red, that badassed longhorn of yours. Knowing where he is might save someone from a having a really crappy day."

I perked up. "You have longhorns? We Texans love longhorns."

"Not this one," Ted told me, "he's meaner'n a fire ant."

Now, that is *mean*. I hate fire ants, having stepped into the little bastards' nests and had them swarm up my legs. First they bite, just to get a good hold on you, then they sting. Not only do they attack en masse, every sting leaves a festering reminder for weeks. "Uh, just in case, what do we do if we run into this Booger Red? Kiss our butts *adios*?"

"Actually, once he's introduced to you everything is okay, but until then, if you see a big ugly dude with a six-foot horn span, sit tight. You'll be riding one of our horses and so long as you stay in the saddle you'll be fine. Not that he won't threaten, but he knows our stock and, so far as he's concerned, you are the company you keep. Whatever you do, though, don't dismount."

"Don't worry, I'll hang on like a fly on a fresh bull patty."

Ted grinned. "Jenks said you had tenacity."

"Oh, yeah? What else did he say about me?"

He threw his hands up. "Nothing. Honest."

"I'll just bet. Did he by any chance tell you where and what he's doing that sent him out on a secretive mission to God knows where?"

"No, but knowing him, he's probably somewhere no one else will go. We left a few unsettled scores in that desert. Why, when we were in Desert Storm we forayed into enemy—" he stopped dead when Nanci shot him a searing side glance. Caught mid-sentence he tried backpedaling. "I'm sure things have changed a lot since we were there," he said weakly.

Not to be deterred, I demanded. "Scores to settle? And you forayed into enemy what? Or more importantly, what enemy? He's supposed to be installing software, for God's sake."

"Oh, that's just me, reminiscing about the bad old days like old military farts do. Forget it. Times change, and software guys like Jenks probably don't go out on clandestine missions anymore." If he was trying to redeem himself, he failed miserably by putting in that *probably*.

Nanci chuffed in disgust. "Ted, do yourself a favor and just shut up. And don't ever go into politics."

Ted gave her a *what'd I do*? look and tried once again to weasel out. "I was just telling war stories. You know how we old vets love to relive the so-called glory." He was almost home free until he added, "Like I said, I'm almost sure Jenks isn't doing that stuff anymore," earning him, once again, the hot seat.

I pushed. "What stuff?"

Nanci, done with the direction of this conversation, stepped in. "Hetta, why don't we leave it to Jenks to share his and Ted's military adventures with you. More wine?"

Nice diversionary tactic, Nan. I accepted the wine and the not-so-subtle suggestion to drop the Jenks subject, but my mind flew thousands of miles away, where I pictured Jenks, dressed like Lawrence of Arabia, under attack by keening terrorists dead set on a beheading. For some reason this conjured up the white SUV we'd seen earlier in the day, first at the ranch gate and, to my mind, by the river. Was it the same vehicle?

"Hetta?"

I realized everyone was staring at me. "Uh, you were saying?" I asked to cover my embarrassment. I hadn't heard a word.

Craig waved his hand in front of my face. "Ted was telling me they make a commissary run to Fort Huachuca in Sierra Vista occasionally, and maybe they'll drop in for a visit. We can pick them up at the Bisbee Airport."

Brought back to this continent, I asked, "They have flights into the Bisbee Airport?"

"Not hardly," Ted said. "I have a couple of aircraft. When we go grocery shopping in the States, or down to Hermosillo, we take the Baron. Around here, for running down livestock, I have a nifty ultralight."

"Great. Just let us know when you're coming. Bring your clubs if you'd like to play golf."

"Oh, we will," Nanci said "We love Turquoise Valley Golf Course. Do you play?"

"Not no, but hell no. I have way to much self-regard."

Chapter 18

Early the next morning, we saddled up several of the winery's horses and set off on an estate tour.

Knowing I'd be astride a large animal for most of the next day, I drank several glasses of water between sips of wine the night before. Nothing worse than a hangover on horseback, even on the horse I drew. His name, appropriately, was Rocinante, for Don Quixote's skinny old nag. In a play on words, the slightly demented man from La Mancha dubbed his decrepit horse Rocinante, meaning reversed: a nag reborn as a gallant steed.

Picturing this Rocinante as a warhorse would indeed require the imagination of a Cervantes, but the horse's advanced age and docile temperament suited me to a tee. When I expressed doubts about my horse's stamina, Craig did a quick medical exam and rudely pronounced the horse fit for hazardous duty.

The guys led, while Nanci rode astride a spirited Arabian that was obviously miffed with having to keep pace with our sluggish company. Babycakes, the antithesis of his name, pranced, danced, and snorted in disgust at our lack of speed. Nanci ignored his antics, easily controlling him while pointing out various buildings, explaining their purpose, and which employees did what and why. I learned wine making is a complicated, sophisticated business, and she was an expert. I'll never uncork another bottle without appreciating what it takes to get it into my wine rack. But then, most of my wine comes with a screw top.

While taking a break at a vista point, I brought up something that bugged me. "Nanci, I have to ask you a question. It might sound silly, but I get the distinct impression that Sonrisa doesn't much like me."

"Don't take it personally. Her nickname certainly doesn't fit her nature, any more than this horse's does," she patted Babycakes, "but being a Mexican, I appreciate our national habit of playing with names. For instance, a really fat guy might be called Gordo, for fat one, but he also might have a moniker like Flaco, for Skinny."

I had a thought. "Say, what does the nickname, Nacho, stand for?"

"Oh, that's just the diminutive for Ignacio."

I smiled. Ignacio? Geez, no wonder Nacho chooses to go by his nickname. "I used to think sonrisa meant sunrise, but now I know it means smile. And you're right, the name doesn't suit. Does she ever smile?"

"Not in my presence. She is a little odd, but maybe she's not used to us yet. We cut her some slack because she showed up, out of the blue, just when our Rosa badly needed a friend. They are from the same area, with similar family backgrounds, just like Lupe was."

"Lupe?"

Nanci's perky mouth drooped. "Such a sad thing. Rosa's best friend, Guadalupe, they were like sisters, two orphans who found their way here via different, but similar roads. Rosa was teaching Lupe the ropes at the grape irradiation processing facility, and Lupe was a fast learner. Then, one day, she just disappeared. Gone. We contacted the police, anyone who knew her back home, everyone we could think of. Nothing. Rosa was devastated."

"I can imagine. How long ago did this happen?"

"Two months. Sonrisa showing up on our doorstep a week later, looking for work, was a godsend for our Rosa."

I pictured the hateful look on Sonrisa's face the night before and questioned her being God-sent to anyone, but maybe she just didn't like redheads. Or visitors. Whatever, she quickly regained her annoyingly bland countenance when I caught her out, but I'd witnessed that hate-filled look.

An unworldly bellow jolted me from mulling over Sonrisa's lack of grace. Startled, I sat straight in the saddle and snapped my head around. A jillion pounds of angry longhorn charged directly at me. Booger Red, I presume.

"Remember, Hetta, sit tight!" Nanci yelled. "He's a little short-sighted, but once he recognizes Rocinante, he'll stop. Whatever you do, stay in the saddle."

I got a death grip on the saddle horn and held my breath as the biggest damned longhorn on earth, or even Texas, barreled my way. Back on my granddad's ranch I'd hand-fed his longhorn stock, but this one looked like he was going to have me, and my horse, for lunch. Just ten feet away, he put on the brakes, and when he finally skidded to a full stop, one six-foot horn tip was within a few inches of my leg. Rocinante never even flinched, but I was within seconds of requiring a diaper change.

Booger Red snorted, pawed the ground once, albeit a little lamely after such a spectacular charge. Up close, and no longer a threat, his freckled face gave him a homely look and now he seemed downright embarrassed that it had taken him so long to recognize his horse friend. He swiveled his horn away from my leg, snuffled my jeans leg, touched noses with my horse, and gave me a look that said, "Okay, whoever you are, you're just damned lucky you're with my buddy."

I sat stock still. "Nice Booger Red. I think. Uh, folks, what now?"

Ted rode up alongside, gave me a handful of carrots, and told me to give them to the bull. Gingerly, I held one in my palm, Booger Red took it ever so gently, then nuzzled my hand for another, leaving a glob of bull snot for me to deal with.

"See," Nanci said, "he likes you."

"Oh, great," I said, wiping my hand on my jeans. "Ya know, he could do with a course in anger management. Or maybe glasses. What would have happened if he didn't recognize Rocinante?"

"You don't want to know," Ted and Nanci chorused. The ultimate house guest, in only twelve hours I'd managed to piss off at least one employee, and enrage a bull. Who says I'm not a charmer?

The thing about riding horses is that you either shouldn't do it at all, or more often. Anything in between is extremely painful.

Our mounts were sure-footed and gentle, but that didn't do a thing to save my thighs and butt from a serious ass whipping. Even on level ground, with a western saddle, inner thigh muscles take to screaming after awhile. Add trail riding up and down mountains, and you can multiply your muscle strain exponentially. By the time we returned to Hacienda de las Estrellas for a late lunch, I was sorely, no pun intended, in need of a medic. Not, of course, that I would admit it.

Since we were all a little horsey-smelling, everyone grabbed a shower before lunch. I unpacked a bottle of Aleve, restrained myself from swallowing all of them. I always carry industrial strength muscle cream, but even a generous dollop didn't soothe the deep aches. Even the two glasses of wine I had with lunch didn't make a dent in my misery, but did lull me into an afternoon nap. When I awoke, someone was tapping on my door.

Hobbling across the room, I found Nanci holding out a handful of small pills.

She gave them to me as I asked, "Arsenic, I hope?"

"Nope, just a muscle relaxant. They work wonders."

"You, my friend, are a saint."

"No problem. Drinks on the verandah in thirty minutes?"

"Can you send someone up to carry me down?"

She just laughed merrily and left. I'm such a crackup.

"I'm not kidding, here," I yelled at her back.

Chapter 19

Those muscle pills of Nanci's kicked in fast, allowing me to hitch downstairs for cocktails and dinner without screaming with each step.

After a glass of wine and a couple of hors d'oeuvres, I was feeling downright mahvelous, dahling.

Throughout the spicy tortilla soup course I kept 'em giddy with my clever repartee.

Halfway through the entrée, I opened my mouth to tell a story and nothing came out. Others might have considered this a good thing, but I wondered if I was having a stroke. Craig took note of the sudden lack of noise on my part. "Hetta, are you all right?"

"Ummph." My attempt to shake my head "no" ended up as a good imitation of a dashboard bobblehead. I slumped forward and was saved from a face plant into my enchiladas by Craig's strong grip. "Ank oo," I told him.

"Oh, dear," Nanci said. "I gave her a muscle relaxant this afternoon. I guess I should have warned her not to drink."

"How many did you take?" Craig asked, swiveling my head up so he could see my eyes.

I managed to raise one limp finger.

"Oh, well, you'll live. It's off to beddy-bye for you." He hoisted me out of the chair, threw me over his shoulder like a sack of cornmeal and footslogged, staggering a little under my dead weight, up the stairs. I really know how to make an exit.

Dumping me onto my bed, he covered me with a blanket and said, "I probably don't have to wish you sweet dreams. Night, night. I'll check on you later."

"Urk."

Through my drugged haze, I heard him return, twice. At some point during the night I woke up thirsty, wobbled to the bathroom, drank a liter of water, peeled off my clothes, and climbed between the crisply ironed sheets.

Church bells, twittering birds, and a strange scraping sound brought me to life. I was sleeping on my side, curled in my normal fetal position, arms wrapped around a pillow. My first mistake of the day was straightening out my legs, sending a wave of agony throughout the lower half of my body. Groaning, I then made another error: opening my eyes.

Something huge and black was three inches from my nose, its terrible pinchers grinding as it crept toward me. Shrieking, I propelled myself backward while shoving the pillow, complete with monster, onto the floor. The shock of my aching butt hitting the carpet on the opposite side momentarily overrode my fear. Folding over the bed, I bent my knees to relieve my searing calves and thighs. In the meantime, the thing had climbed back onto the bed and was inching my way again. Jackknifing erect, I screamed, "Fire!" figuring, "Bug!" wouldn't get nearly the rapid response required.

Carrying a bottle of water in each hand, Craig crashed through the door. "Where?"

"There," I pointed.

Craig laughed. "Cool. I've always wanted one of these." At that moment several others arrived, one man with a fire extinguisher.

"False alarm," Craig told them. "Hetta can't tell the difference between fire and a vinegarroon."

"A what?"

"Vinegarroon. Mastigoproctus giganteus. Some people call them whip scorpions, but they are totally harmless. I gotta admit, though, he sure doesn't look it."

I peered warily at the bug. "Looks like a squid with claws, if you ask me. How was I supposed to know he's harmless?"

Nanci arrived. "Oh, dear. Vinny," she said, shaking her finger at the monstrosity grinding away in the middle of my bed, "you know you're supposed to stay downstairs. Bad bug. Sorry, Hetta. He does look frightful, doesn't he?"

Rosa swooped in, picked up the six-inch insect, gave me a shrug, and took the thing away. It was then I realized I was dressed in an oversized tee that barely covered my butt. I sat on the bed, pulled a sheet around me, and asked, "Pew. What's that stink?"

Nanci sniffed the air. "That vinegary smell? That's Vinny. He emits the scent when he's frightened. Poor thing."

"*He*'s frightened? *He*'s the poor thing? He about scared the vinegar out of me. Are you telling me he's a pet?"

"Not a pet exactly," Nanci explained, pouring me a glass of water and shooing the others from the room. "Here, drink this. You'll feel better. I am so sorry about Vinny. He is actually a great asset to the household, because he eats roaches."

I lifted my glass and said, weakly, "Oh, well then. Anything that eats roaches can't be all bad, but man, is he butt ugly."

Craig stuck his head through the door. "You rang?"

I chuckled through my pain. "Naw, I was talking about Vinny."

"I've always wanted a Vinny for my bug collection. Does he have a dead brother around here by any chance, Nanci?"

"Nope, they are all alive and well, the whole family. If you'd like, I'll box him up for you, but you have to promise me he'll expire of natural causes."

Harmless or not, I didn't like the sound of that.

"Uh, Craig, you aren't taking that damned thing home with us are you? What's his, uh, lifespan?"

"I don't know how long they live, but I'll keep him in a terrarium until I go back to Oakland. You won't even know he's there. Okay?"

"I guess," I grumbled, recalling with a shiver a childhood pet tarantula the size of a dinner plate that escaped his terrarium one night to terrorize the household. If Vinny came to live under my roof, his longevity prospects had just suffered a turn for the worse.

"Great," Nanci chirped. "I have an old fish tank you can take with you. We kept a rat snake in it in the room next door, but he's been missing for a week or two, so you might as well take his cage."

I quickly, but painfully, jerked my feet from the floor. Snake? What is it with these people?

"Don't worry, he's non-poisonous," Nanci assured me. "We used to turn him loose anyhow every few days to clear out bugs, mice and the like, but now he's on the job twenty-four seven, I guess. Maybe poor Vinny crawled in bed with you for protection?"

"Then Vinny is a very bad judge of character," I growled.

Nanci guffawed. "Okay, everyone downstairs for breakfast in ten minutes," she announced as she bounded out the door. I could grow to hate that woman.

Limping around, I downed two more bottles of water, brushed my teeth and hair, and somehow pulled on clothes. Descending the stairs was an exercise in excruciation, but there was no way I was going to take another of those pills before the drive home. Plain old ibuprofen would have to suffice.

"There you are," Nanci chirped. "Good morning again. Feeling better?" She was drinking coffee and looking great.

Maybe hate is too mild a term. I duck-walked to the table, grimacing as I sat. "Better than what?"

Craig entered, heard me, and warned, "Watch it, Nanci, she bites before coffee."

A servant quickly filled my cup and scuttled out of reach. I loaded two heaping spoonfuls of raw sugar and a massive dollop of heavy cream into my cup, all the while glaring at Craig, mentally daring him to even mention Splenda and skimmed milk. Wisely, he did not.

Ted strode in, gave me a friendly pat on the shoulder, and plunked down next to me. "I heard you met Vinny. You okay?"

Caffeine had restored my manners. "Yes, thanks. Sorry about last night. I think that was the first time in my entire life I didn't finish an enchilada. Good grief, Nanci, what was that pill you gave me?"

"I really don't know. My doctor prescribed them to me after I pulled a ligament. Or was it when my horse pulled a ligament?"

That lightened the mood and we chatted while eating like lumberjacks preparing to decimate a forest.

If there is one thing I love, it's a Mexican breakfast. Give me corn tortillas, refried beans, eggs scrambled with chile peppers, and I've died and gone to heaven. "Did I hear church bells this morning?" I asked, recalling a moment of peace I'd experienced before being scared out of what little wits I have by our cousin, Vinny.

"Sorry, you missed mass," Nanci said. "If I'd known you wanted to attend, I would have wakened you earlier."

"Oh, I'm not Catholic, I just wondered if I was hearing things."

"We have our own chapel and a priest comes up from the village each Sunday. As you saw yesterday, we have over fifty people living up here, so it is easier to bring the church to us."

"I love your life, Nanci," I said. "You guys are living your dream, and helping others along the way. You even adopt *perros de calles*."

Ted laughed. "How'd ya know our dogs are strays?"

"I know a street dawg when I see one. Heck, I dated a few."

Craig nodded in mock grim agreement. "Actually," he told us, "left to their own, with no humans finagling their breeding, dogs revert to mostly looking alike. I did my doctorate on the subject. What I've seen here, though, is that once in awhile there's a coyote in the gene pool." Then he told them about Blue acting more dog than coyote.

Ted nodded. "We have our share of coydogs in these parts. What we need is a good vet in town to spay the strays. If you decide to relocate to Bisbee I'll fly you down here once in awhile for a spay and neuter clinic. The local authorities are forced to shoot dog packs on occasion, and unfortunately, so are we. They attacked our dogs and livestock, until, of course, we got old Booger Red. He makes short work of stray dogs, or coyotes. Well, he and Sancho, our attack donkey."

"My granddad had one of those donkeys," I told them. "Went after anything that even looked like a canine. He and my grandmother's Border collies got on fine, but Lord help a stray dog or a coyote. I guess between Sancho and Booger Red you don't have much need for guns around here? You did say, though, you shot some marauding dogs. I thought you couldn't own firearms in Mexico."

"We both have hunting licenses and shotguns. It's legal if you do it right. The trick is the transportation license. The feds get sticky on the movement of guns from, say, your house to town."

"So, only the narco thugs get a free license to kill, huh? They know pretty much no one has a gun except them, the military, and the cops. I read about the big shootout around here last fall."

Nanci said, "It was near Arizpe, just south of here, and very scary. We went on full defense mode when we heard some ranchers were kidnapped as hostages. The police tracked down the gang members, supposedly Zetas out of an east coast cartel with ties to Texas, and killed them. Good riddance, in my book, but we haven't really relaxed. There're too many places to hide in these hills, what with scores of abandoned ranches and few people."

"Speaking of ranches," I said, "do you know the people who own Rancho Sierra Coronado? Craig and I tried to stop by yesterday, but the gate was locked and posted. Maybe they are still spooked over the gang thing, as well."

"It's for sale and the owners are not around, only caretakers are there. The gate was locked? That's strange."

"I did see someone drive up on the other side as we were leaving, but by then we'd decided to move on. Those caretakers drive a fancy white SUV of some kind by any chance?"

"Hardly," Nanci said with a laugh. "Tomás has a decrepit flatbed. Why?"

"I saw a Jeep or SUV, a white one, behind the gate." I didn't mention my suspicion that it had followed us down to the river crossing .

"Who knows? Maybe they finally sold the place."

Craig stood. "We'd better get on the road, I guess." He grabbed my arm to help me up, which my screaming thighs greatly appreciated. "Hetta, you all packed?"

"You betcha. There's no way I am going up those stairs, so can you pretty please bring down my stuff?"

Craig left, Ted walked me out to the verandah, and asked, "I wonder if you could do us a favor?"

"Anything."

"Can you give Sonrisa a ride to Naco, Sonora? Her brother lives there, and she visits him every Sunday. It'll save her a long wait for the bus."

Why not? She and that vinegarroon should make perfectly sour company for each other, I thought, but I said, "Uh, well, I was thinking of stopping by my office in Cananea for a couple of hours."

Craig, who had returned with my suitcase, heard me and gave me a, say what? look.

Ted shook his head. "No way, not today. The news this morning said the mine is closed, complete lockdown. The miners have totally walked off the job. Matter of fact, you're lucky you don't even have to pass through town to get home. I guess things are a little tense."

Crappola. "Oh, well, then," I said meekly, "I guess we can give little Smiley a lift."

Chapter 20

With the stony facial expression of an Easter Island monolith, Sonrisa removed her bulky embroidered backpack, plunked it into the car's backseat, followed it in, then arranged her skirt and shawl neatly around her. While her mannerisms were in no way hostile, I wondered, once again, what lay beneath that stoic façade.

Craig and I chatted about friends, our plans, and the like during the drive from the winery to Naco, but our passenger never uttered a sound. As we entered the outskirts of town, I asked her, "*¿A donde*?"

"*Iglesia*." The church.

Two blocks later, I pulled to the curb in front of a church, she got out, and, without even a nod in our direction, crossed the street behind us and headed back in the direction from which we'd come.

"Gee you're sooo welcome, Sonrisa," Craig said, shaking his head. "What's with her?"

"Got me. Nanci says she's just shy, but the first night at the winery, when Sonrisa was serving dinner, I caught her looking at us with some serious hate in those little black eyes."

"Us? Or just you?"

"I think both of us, but not sure. Maybe she's got a bug up her ass over Gringos."

"On the bright side, she's slightly friendlier than that longhorn. How did you get so popular, Hetta? Must be that fabulous personality of yours."

"Very funny. I wonder if Booger Red has actually killed anyone."

"Nah, I don't think so, but he sure as heck scares the hell out of them. Ted told me he has to keep a sharp eye out for people making their way toward the border, set on an illegal crossing into the States. Sometimes they wander up the hill looking for food, and end up treed by the bull."

"Which means the only reason Booger Red hasn't actually done someone in is that they out-climb him?"

"That's my take."

There were only two cars in line at the border crossing. While we awaited our turn, I told Craig that the wait at Nogales, farther to the west, could take up to four hours, so Naco was a breeze. The customs agent, a woman I'd seen at the golf club restaurant, but who, if she recognized me didn't let on, asked us what we were bringing back from Mexico. We showed her our two bottles of wine, and were waved through with a, "Welcome home."

Only later did we learn we were international smugglers and could have incurred a hefty fine for not declaring Craig's vinegarroon. Jeez, what if a bug walks through on his own?

As soon as we got home, I called Jenks's hotel room and cell phone. No luck.

I checked my email. Nothing from Kuwait, but I did get two messages from Jan, dated Friday, the first one's subject: Help!

"Craig, come look at this."

He read Jan's email. "Can we call her?"

"It'd have to be on Chino's cell, and her second message says not to call."

"I guess that answers that."

"Okay, if, like she says, she caught the Friday night ferry, she arrived in Guaymas Saturday morning, so there's no use driving down there now. First off, it's a really bad idea to drive at night in Mexico, especially on the road from Cananea to Imuris, and we'd probably cross paths. We just have to sit tight and wait until we hear from her again."

"Maybe she called when you weren't in Guaymas to pick her up. She has your new cell number, right?"

"I haven't checked my messages yet." As I turned on the phone, I pondered aloud, "I wonder what's wrong now? Last time she bailed on Chino was because she felt uneasy with their age difference, but I thought they'd worked that out. Now she says she needs a place to stay and is headed here, but why?"

Craig stared at the computer as if demanding an answer. "I still think I should call Chino."

"Can't you read? Jan says *no*."

"Well then, what do we do?"

"We wait. No messages on my phone yet. Maybe the ferry was cancelled or late. Who knows? She has my address and she's a clever girl, so she'll find us, I'm sure."

Sure or not of Jan's abilities, it worried me that she was somewhere, alone, in Mexico. I don't like my friends or family unaccounted for, which is odd, considering I spend a lot of my life being unaccountable. With two of the most important people in my life amongst the missing, I was on edge, waiting for both Jan and Jenks to call. After tossing and turning most of the night, I was in a deep sleep a little before nine in the morning, which is, of course, when the phone jangled me awake.

Craig got to the phone first because, anticipating a call, I'd taken the phone to bed with me and it was now lost in the jumble of covers heaped up after a night of restlessness. By the time I found it, Craig was saying, "The bus station in Naco?"

Jan said yes, he said we'd be right there, and hung up.

I didn't even know there was a bus station in Naco, but we found it, and a bedraggled Jan, fifteen minutes after Craig hung up the phone. Dressed in a ragged gray hooded sweatshirt and even rattier pants, my friend carried her belongings in one of those colorful plastic mesh bags that serve as Mexican suitcases in one hand and, incongruously, a large designer purse in the other.

As we hugged, she broke into sobs and wailed, "Hetta, they shot him."

Craig and I exchanged a look of alarm. "Someone shot Chino?" I asked.

Between little gasps, she managed, "No, not Chino. The bus driver. Right on the main highway, in broad daylight. Saturday morning."

"Is he dead?"

"I don't think so. At least he was alive when the ambulance took him away. A car forced us off the road, and when we stopped this thug walked up to the driver's window and opened fire. I thought they were going to kill us all, but they jumped into this SUV and took off."

"My God, what is Mexico turning into? Colombia a few years ago? It's all about drugs and gang warfare. Oh, boy, wait until this hits the international news. Our parents will have a cat."

Jan's face went gray, then white. "Hetta, get me home. Now. I'm really sick."

We hustled her into the car.

"Sick, as in how?" Craig asked. He put his hand to her forehead. "No fever."

"Nope, the runs, cramps, and my chest is killing me. I don't know what's wrong, but it isn't good. Can't keep anything down, and only massive doses of Imodium got me here without embarrassing myself. That Montezuma's a vengeful bastard. What I need is a lot of sleep and a ton of water with, what a concept, actual ice cubes. In fact, I think I'll bathe in ice cubes. Better yet, just stick me in the freezer."

Something about Jan's bus story was bothering me. "Jan, seems to me you are lucky you're not on ice...as in a Mexican jail. You're a witness to attempted murder, and their method of making sure witnesses don't take a powder is to lock 'em up."

"The cops never showed, just an ambulance. I didn't wait for a new bus, I caught a ride as far as Imuris with a couple of guys on their way to Tucson, got a room in Imuris and the earliest bus here. It's been a hell of a trip. Are we there yet?"

Craig handed her a bottled water. "Almost. We'll get some aspirin in you, and after a little rest you'll be brand new. Uh, have you been keeping up with the news lately?"

"Hell, no. How could I, stuck in the middle of friggin' Baja nowhere. Why?"

"Guess you haven't heard of swine flu?"

"I don't care if pigs get sick. Or whales, for that matter. I've had it with animal life. Doctor Chino can take his friggin' job and shove it. I'm sick of whales, sick of living on fish tacos, sick of Doctor Chino Yee, and more importantly, just plain sick. What's swine flu?"

"Jan," Craig told her, "there is an epidemic, actually a pandemic, of this new flu strain. From your symptoms, I don't think you have it, but you'd best look sharp at the border."

"Naw, I don't think I have the flu, just amoebas, as they say in Mexico. That's their answer for everything."

"Think you can make it through the border crossing without throwing up? They might quarantine you if you barf in their booth."

"I'll do my best. Just get me to a hot shower and a bed. I think that alone will cure me."

"Sure, hon, comin' up. The house is only a hop, skip, and a jump from the border."

Jan moaned. "Please tell me there isn't a long line to cross, cuz I feel a heave coming on."

"I've never seen more than four cars, except after church lets out on Sunday. That's when everyone heads for the shopping mall at Sierra Vista.

Jan let out a sigh of relief, then asked, "Uh, you don't think anyone will recognize us, do you?"

"I've gone through several times and haven't seen a familiar face. More importantly, no one seems to know me. They must have rotated all our old buddies out of here."

Of course, Craig wanted to know what we were talking about, so I told him about a past adventure, when Jan and I ended up in deep caca with authorities, local and federal, on the U.S. side, and were accused of bird smuggling.

"So," he said, "let me get this straight. You two drove through the border fence, got arrested, then liberated a parrot that Fish and Game had in custody. Good for you. Were they really going to euthanize that bird? That's ridiculous, and if I had been here...whoa Nellie, lookee what we have here. What do you wanna bet neither one of them is her brother."

"What are you—" I was cut short by my own amazement. There was Sonrisa, all three feet something of her, riding down the main boulevard in the back seat of a tricked out Jeep Rubicon, actually smiling, and chatting away with the driver and passenger. At one point they all laughed.

The bright yellow Jeep, headed out of town, was driven by none other than the X-Boys. "Well, doodness dwacious, doesn't our little Miss Sonrisa have the knack for hitchhiking? I hope she doesn't end up dead in a ditch, cuz she shore ain't picky. I'll call

Ted soon, make sure she arrived home safely. Just because I don't like the little shit doesn't mean I want to see her harmed."

Craig nodded. "Not a bad idea, but looks to me like she's having a fine old time in the company of those Black Muslim dudes. Odd combo, to say the least."

Jan, curled up in the rear seat as best as her five-eleven frame allowed, popped up. "What? Where?" Evidently nosiness instantly overcomes nauseousness.

"Later," I told her. "First, let's get you home. You look like something the cat dragged in."

"Thanks, Hetta, I can always count on you to cheer me up."

"Hey, what are friends for?"

By late afternoon, it was obvious Jan needed more medical attention than a veterinarian and an engineer could administer. She'd spent the better part of the day making best friends with the toilet bowl and a bucket, and was badly dehydrated in spite of drinking glass after glass of water.

Since she'd let her American health insurance lapse, I decided she needed to do what the uninsured do: head for an emergency room. Craig offered to drive her there, but I didn't think showing up in a brand new Porsche with an indigent in tow was a great idea. My old VW was far more suited to the task.

Jan, doubled over in pain as we entered the Copper Queen Hospital, made for a chair in the reception area, while I went to the desk.

A sweet-faced woman whose desk nameplate identified her as Patricia Norquist, handed me a clipboard with a bunch of forms attached, and told me what she'd need from us. I took the forms back to where Jan slouched and moaned.

Rummaging through her handbag, I came up with her Mexican driver's license, then filled out the paperwork while she made a dash for the loo. She returned, pasty faced, just as I finished. I asked the few questions I didn't know the answer to and returned to the desk.

The woman perused my handiwork and sighed. "No insurance?"

"Nope."

"She lives in Mexico?"

This question piqued the interest of others in the waiting room, who stared suspiciously at poor Jan, since the swine flu outbreak had originated south of the border.

"Yes," I said loudly, "she arrived, sick, from Mexico. Today."

Several people quickly left, improving our odds of getting Jan in sooner by leaps and bounds.

The woman checked the list of Jan's symptoms again, seemed satisfied my buddy wasn't Piggy Mary, and gave me a wry grin. "I don't suppose you'd care to take responsibility for the bill?"

"Sorry, I'm broke. Uh, Sister Jan wouldn't want me to tell you this, but, well, she belongs to a religious order and has taken a vow of poverty. They would have helped her out in Mexico, but up here...." I let that hang.

The woman looked past me at Jan's gold handbag with its distinctive Fendi logo and drawled, "A designer order, no doubt?"

Dang, Ms. Patricia Norquist might work for a small hospital, but she knows her Fendi.

"Actually," I said, thinking fast, "it's The Sisters of Perpetual Poverty, a small convent headquartered in the Bay Area. So obscure that only the Pope knows about it.

"It's a refuge for nuns who have, shall we say, strayed into unabashed materialism. Kind of a nun rehab."

Ms. Norquist rolled her eyes at my unintended pun.

"They send them off to count whales and live on fish. You know, make them appreciate being nuns again. Anyway, they obviously have no medical insurance. And then there's the fact that the Sister is a, shall we say, fugitive from political oppression in her home country of...Cuba."

She fixed me with a cynical smile. "Okay, take a seat, we'll call you."

After another half hour went by, with only one person called into the inner sanctum, I mumbled a curse. A skeletal, scabby-faced woman leaned over the empty seat between us. Judging by the looks of several others in the waiting room, Meth is the drug of choice in these parts. "Your friend looks too good," she said, showing a mouthful of blackened, ragged teeth.

It took a great deal of control for me not to run away from her. "Excuse me?"

"She looks, like, healthy."

For my money Jan looked to be knocking on death's door, but compared to this meth head, she did look way too good to get fast attention. "Believe me, she's really, really, sick."

"I don't suppose your friend is also an addict?"

"Would it help move her up the line?"

"Only if she's suffering from severe withdrawal."

"Like if she hasn't had a fix in at least...."

The stringy haired woman, who could have been twenty-five or sixty-five, smiled that horrible smile and winked. "Forty-eight hours is the magic number."

If that woman hadn't looked so much like a Halloween ghoul, I would have kissed her. Instead, I slipped her a twenty. She took the money and left, no longer in need of meds, now that she could get right. I should have felt guilty, I guess, but desperate times and all.

I went back to the reception desk. "Uh, did I mention that Sister Jan is an addict, and hasn't had a fix in forty-eight hours?"

I was rewarded with an angelic smile. "My, but aren't you a fast study? And, thanks for making what promised to be my otherwise boring day. Someone will be out to fetch Sister soon."

Within minutes, Jan was hooked up to an IV, and a couple of hours later we were at home armed with a bagful of free meds, and a referral to a rehab counselor. While Sister Jan had vehemently denied dabbling in illicit drugs, I gave the doctor a meaningful look and took the stack of twelve-step literature offered.

Tests were done to rule out amoebic dysentery, giardia, and other stuff, but the doctor said it was likely just plain old Montezuma's revenge, which, because of her rundown state, was fairly fierce.

Chapter 21

Jan, after two days of mostly sleeping and watching TV in bed, was still pale but up to a cocktail or two on the verandah. Craig and I had waited until now to grill her like a red snapper for the down and dirty details of this latest fiasco, and why she was here in Bisbee, instead of with her amour, Doctor Brigido "Chino" Yee, at his campsite in the Baja.

While tossing dog biscuits to Blue, she got down to the good stuff. "I don't care if I ever see another whale, or Chino either, for that matter."

"But why, Jan? What did he do to you?"

"Nothing."

"Oh, well, that explains it. No wonder you slunk off in the dead of night. The bastard!"

Craig laughed and Jan looked sheepish. "Put that way," she said, "it does sound a little ridiculous. Call me self-centered, needy, whatever, but I would like, just once, to take precedence over a barnacle-encrusted behemoth."

"Hey," Craig protested, "I was a behemoth. What we lack in beauty, we make up for in cuddly."

"You men always stick together."

"Jan," he reasoned, "you knew Chino was a dedicated marine biologist when you met him. What did you expect him to do during peak whale calving season? Take you to the Four Seasons for dinner? Shower you with roses?"

"Ha! There isn't a flower within fifty miles of that friggin' shack we live in. And no, I don't expect the princess treatment, but a little attention on occasion would be nice. He needs an assistant, not a girlfriend. I'm tired of counting whales, talking whales, freakin' dreaming whales. I am whaled out."

"So," I asked, "I can rule out fish for dinner?"

"Whales ain't fish, but close enough. I may never eat fish again, ever. I've lived on fish tacos and refried beans for months now. If it wasn't for limes, I'd probably have scurvy to complement my runs."

Craig looked thoughtful, then told Jan, "I think you need a thorough physical. A real good going over."

"I ain't got no insurance, remember?"

"I've been thinking about that. I need a marine biologist on my staff."

"You want to hire Chino?"

"No, you."

"Oh, come on, you know damned well I'm no marine biologist."

"It's on your resume, you know," I chimed in, earning me a squinty frown.

"Oh, yeah, from another time I let you drag me into something smelly. You needed a marine biologist for a project, and presto chango, I was one."

"So versatile," Craig teased. "Never mind about that, I think your time on the Baja is qualification enough. First, though, you'll need a full checkup, as required by my insurance company. Actually, I've already called the Mayo Clinic in Scottsdale. I know someone there. They can take you."

We both stared at him. This was an incredibly generous offer, and one she couldn't turn down, but Jan looked stunned, and a little frightened. "You think I might have something really bad wrong with me?"

"No, sweetie, I'd just feel better if we ran you through the clinic. What do you say?"

"Well, heck, why not? I still feel puny, anyhow. When do we leave?"

"Day after tomorrow. We'll be in Scottsdale a couple of days, then back here before you know it."

We discussed this turn of events, then returned to the subject of Chino. Craig was especially interested in daily life at the whale camp, and the research they were doing. "You know, after the Mayo Clinic, I think I'll go over to the Baja and give Chino a hand, since his assistant's pitched a little Texas hissy and run off to Arizona."

"Hmph," said Jan. "You go right on ahead. I'll stay here with poor Hetta."

"Hey, what's this poor Hetta thing? You're the drug addict with no job and no health insurance. And, I might add, now you've even been kicked out of the convent."

When Jan and Craig returned from Scottsdale she was a mite frazzled from all her tests. She even had a nuclear stress test where they detected an anomaly in her heartbeat, but they didn't find anything serious. She started describing the details of the tests, but I cut her off. I hate needles and don't even want to hear about them. I did, however, comment on that new glow she had about her, especially in the dark.

She was deemed healthy, if a little anemic. Even though now on Craig's payroll, her salary of one dollar a year isn't going to go very far toward more designer bags.

While my friends were off getting Jan examined by the best, I needed something to take my mind off Jenks. To push away the almost physical pain of worry about him, I threw myself into stacks of drawings and operating manuals, pulling together a big fat report for mine management that I hoped would justify keeping me on the payroll, even though the shutdown dragged on.

Craig, upon their return, decided he would definitely visit Chino in the Baja, probably to get a break from living with two women, especially Jan and me. His thankless job of playing the highhanded drill sergeant, and our threats to mutiny, were taking a toll on him. He accused us, on more than one occasion when he'd been at the library all day, of having enchilada breath. Go figure.

Since Craig wanted to visit Chino, and I needed to check on my boat, we made plans for heading south.

I called Maria, who was one of the few people left in the skeleton crew at the mine.

"So," I asked, "any news on the strike settlement?"

"No, Café, but *Señor* Orozco is working with the unions in Mexico City. He took your last report with him and told me the union leader was pleased with your proposals."

"Good, that'll keep me on the payroll, right?"

"I do not know of such things, but he told me to continue sending you drawings and files, so I think so."

That was a relief. "I am going to San Carlos this weekend, so if you can get me through the gate, I'll drop off another report. Will you be there on Friday?"

"Oh, yes. I will notify security."

"I'll have two people with me. Is that okay?"

"No problem. What time will you be here?"

"Around nine. Uh, is El Ratón still around?"

Giggle. "Yes, *Señor* Racón is here."

"You know, I thought I saw him in Naco, Arizona, not long ago. Does he have friends over here?"

"I do not know. Do you want me to ask him?"

"No!" I shouted, not meaning to. Much quieter, I added, "It's not important. *Hasta* Friday."

"Hasta luego, Café."

Jan peeked around the door. "Who you yellin' at?"

"I overreacted when talking with Maria. That guy I told you about who works for the mining company, the one I call Rat Face? Craig and I saw him going into an RV over by the golf course, and guess who owns said RV?"

"The Xers?"

"What are you, clairvoyant?"

"Naw, Craig told me. Hetta, you aren't snooping where your nose can lead us into yet another mess, are you?"

"Who, me?"

She narrowed her eyes. "I swear, if you so much as get me a parking ticket, I will kill you. I mean it this time."

"Ya know, Sister Jan, drug withdrawal can make a person mighty cranky. You might want to consider a program."

I ducked, but not fast enough. The morning newspaper hit me in the chest. I grabbed it and was saying, "Temper, temper, Sister," when a headline caught my attention.

Cananea mine owners accused of negligence.

Mexico City

***Señor* Juan Orozco, Managing Director of Groupo Minera Cananea, denied allegations by miner union officials that the health of employees has been purposely jeopardized by management's failure to maintain safety equipment properly. For years, according to the unions, the concentrator unit has not been functioning properly, subjecting employees to dangerous levels of dust.**

One union official quoted a recent report on conditions at the mine. "The deliberate dismantling of dust collectors in the concentrator area processing plants by Grupo Mexico approximately two years ago means that workers in these areas have been subjected to high concentrations of dust containing 23% quartz silica, with 51% of sampled dust in the respirable particle size range, protected only by inadequate personal respirators. Occupational exposures to silica can lead to debilitating, fatal respiratory diseases including silicosis and lung cancer."

Admitting there might be room for improvement, Señor Orozco said they have hired the services of a world-renowned mining expert to analyze the situation and, if necessary, recommend repairs.

I quit reading and speed dialed the Trob, and since Jan loves eavesdropping on my conversations with Wontrobski, which she likens to me taking a knife to a gunfight, I put the speaker on for her infantile amusement.

"Good morning, Hetta."

"You know, Wontrobski, if you're gonna replace me, you might want to give me a heads up so I can make other plans."

"What are you talking about?"

I read him the article, then demanded, "So, just who is this so-called expert?"

"Well, Hetta, you."

"I beg your pardon?"

"You are the expert."

"I am no way an expert on concentrators, or mines." Or almost anything else, for that matter.

"Maybe so, but you are all they have."

"In that case, they're in deep doo doo."

"You underestimate yourself. I have to go now. Goodbye."

I held the phone in a chokehold at arm's length and screamed.

Jan gave me a devilish grin and shook her head. "You experts. Sooo temperamental."

"Big talk from a defrocked nun with a drug habit," I retorted, then we both howled at the pun.

Craig came into the office to see what all the commotion was about. "Hey, what's up? You two having a cat fight?"

"Nah, Hetta's just trying to strangle the phone." She filled him in on the latest expert stuff.

"Think how it'll look on your resume, Miss Coffey," he said. "Now, how about a nice brisk walk and some hot java at the golf course?"

"Say, Craig, you haven't, by any chance, taken note of that rancher hunk drinking coffee there about this time every day, have you?"

"Hunk?" Jan asked. "Rancher hunk? Take me to him."

"Oh," I drawled, winking at her, "I have a feeling this cow poke, you should excuse the expression, only has eyes for our hunk, Doctor Craig."

Craig tried to look indignant. "He's only interested in my tracking chip."

"So you say."

Jan grabbed her bag. "Well, rancher or no, I want coffee and a close up look at those Black Muslim dudes you guys are always talking about. I saw them in the Jeep the day I arrived, the one you said that gal, Sonrisa, was bumming a ride in, but I was too sick to pay much attention."

Craig frowned. "Speaking of, Hetta, did you call Ted and Nanci? Did Sonrisa get home safe and sound the other day?"

"Yep, but Nanci thinks Sonrisa must have taken the bus from Cananea, because she got home late. After dark, in fact. They were beginning to worry."

"Maybe our X-men went to visit their good buddy, El Ratón, in Cananea, and dropped her there."

"Maybe, who knows? I don't even know why I care, she's such a disagreeable little shit."

"Takes one to know one?" Craig suggested. "Okay, get on your walking shoes, we're headed out in search of exercise, breakfast, and caffeine."

"And cowboys?"

Chapter 22

Craig's dangling the caffeine and breakfast carrot helped me endure yet another forced march towards the golf club café via several miles of back desert roads. Of course, coffee and victuals would have sounded more promising had I not been flanked by a skinny blonde who could regain ten pounds, and a large black taskmaster determined that both he and I lose a few.

Jan, because she could, and without a soupçon of regard for my high degree of deprivation, ordered a huge, carb-and-fat-loaded cheese enchilada breakfast plate. Adding insult to injury, she slathered butter on a plate-sized tortilla while I sipped black coffee and nibbled a piece of dry rye toast. I wanted to strangle her and steal her food. Better yet, throttle Craig and end my misery permanently.

Only one thing might stay his execution. "Uh, Craig," I said as sweetly as possible while choking down rye-flavored sawdust, "when we get back to the house, I'll make your ferry reservations for Baja. You have definitely decided to go, right?"

Craig, who had unsuccessfully concealed his disappointment when the hunky rancher he'd befriended wasn't astride his usual barstool, waffled. "I'm still thinking about it. Can't I make reservations when we get to San Carlos?"

"Absolutely not," I lied, giving him one last chance to salvage his sorry carb-counting butt.

Jan looked up, ready to contradict me, but a mouthful of buttery tortilla saved her an ankle bash.

Luckily for Craig, he took the bait. "Okay, then, I guess I'll go for sure. I haven't seen my buddy Chino in years. I'm looking forward to it. I'll call him later today, make sure he'll be there."

Jan swallowed and daintily dabbed the corners of her mouth. I was gratified to see a big grease blob on her tee shirt. "Trust me, he'll be there," she said. "Nothing can tear him away from those damned whales."

"Kinda like you and that tortilla?" I grumbled.

"Hey, I've been sick. Oh, I think we have Xers, three o'clock."

Craig and I turned our heads to the right like marionettes. Hardly subtle. Sure enough, there they were, bow ties and all. They sat at the next table, ordered lunch since it was past eleven, and sat silently watching putters on the practice green.

"You're right, guys," Jan whispered, "they sure don't fit in." Then she giggled. "Like we do?"

She had a point. Her tall, slim, stunning blonde looks, along with Craig's sheer size set us apart from the lunch crowd of, well, average looking county residents, at least for this part of the county. I mean, this ain't exactly Scottsdale. However, next to my friends, I thought I fit in pretty well with the locals, but maybe I didn't blend as well as I thought.

"Hey, Red," one of the Xers said.

Startled at being addressed by the guys who, up until now, seemed to ignore everyone in the restaurant except the wait staff, I cleverly answered. "Who, me?"

"You see any other redheads in here?"

"Uh, no."

"Well, then, it must be you. We see you guys around," his eyes strayed to Jan, leaving me to believe he was not so interested in my irresistible little self, but using me as an entree to the new and lovely Jan. Eyes reluctantly back on me, he added, "You live close?"

"Sort of."

"You look like Californians," the other one said.

"Sort of," I repeated. For someone who loves drilling for info, I hate it when the tables are turned. "How about you? Not from Oakland by any chance are you?"

Craig nudged me under the table, probably to make sure I didn't mention the infamous Your Black Muslim Bakery.

"Naw, LA. So, since we're black you figured us for Oakland?"

The question was thrown like a gauntlet, a challenge to prove I wasn't some kind of racist. I'd dealt with this kind of shoulder chip before and had no intention of rising to the taunt, although it would have been fun to ask, "Watts?" just because he was being pissy.

"No, I asked because we're all based in Oakland."

That took a little attitude off him. "That so? What you doin' here?"

I wanted to say, none of your damned bidness, but then, if I did, I couldn't ask the same, could I? "We're...bird watchers. Well, I am. My colleagues are actually veterinarians. We're especially interested in the migration habits of the," Jan and Craig looked amused, waiting for my answer, "monk parrot." This was a subject I knew well, as my ex-pet parrot, Trouble, happened to be one of those pesky critters.

The Xer's exchanged a glance, then one asked, "What is a monk parrot?"

Jan, who also knew Trouble, piped up. "Monk parrots are feral birds that have migrated from South America and are not exactly welcomed up here. Truth is, they are illegal avians."

The two chuckled at our well-worn joke. "And you're counting them?" Somehow I don't think they believed us. "You get paid to do that?"

Craig finally spoke up, joining in the deception. "No, we're volunteers. What about you two? Why are you here?" His voice was controlled, but I detected a hint of his own challenge.

"Water."

"Like Humphrey Bogart in Casablanca?" I asked.

They looked confused, so Jan and I went into our act. Casablanca being our all-time favorite film, we had parts of the dialogue memorized. Doing my best imitation of Claude Rains as Captain Louis Renault, I cocked my head in a Gallic tilt and asked Jan, "'What in heaven's name brought you to Casablanca?'"

Jan, playing Bogart, growled, "'My health. I came to Casablanca for the waters.'"

"'The waters? What waters? We're in the desert.'"

"'I was misinformed.'"

Jan and I cracked ourselves up, but the Xers obviously had a limited sense of humor. Before they had a chance to clam up, though, I asked, "So, why are you here, really?"

"Believe it or not, we're doing a study on the San Pedro River. It runs, as you probably know, from Mexico into Arizona. There is some concern of contamination from the mining operation in Cananea."

Aha. Maybe that's what El Ratón was doing at their trailer? "So, you take water samples and send them off somewhere?"

"Exactly. We also have testing equipment in our RV." Hmmm. As the chief project consultant regarding contamination problems at the mine, shouldn't I have heard of a water study?

Something, probably the caffeine, jangled my calorie-starved brain. A picture of Sonrisa, jabbering away in the backseat of their Jeep flashed to the forefront. "So, I guess your Spanish must be pretty good, huh?"

Like bobbleheads, they both did a no shake. The taller one answered. "No, unfortunately, not a word. Well, maybe a word, but that's about it. Well, we have to get go—"

He was interrupted by a loud, cheerful voice. "Yoohoo, Sister Jan, I'm sooo glad to see you looking sooo well."

We were sooo busted.

It was Patricia Norquist, the receptionist from the Copper Queen hospital, where I'd taken Jan for treatment of her *tourista*. Just great.

The Xers exchanged a look, one of them mouthing silently at the other, "Sister?"

"What a wonderful coincidence to see you here. This is Father Harry, visiting from Holy Trinity Monastery in Saint David, just north of here. Sister Jan, surely you've heard of the Oblates of the Order of Saint Benedict? My memory fails me, what is your Order?"

The Farrakhan brothers, who'd been so intent on leaving, now sat back with smug smiles as Jan's cheeks flamed red and her pursed lips remained firmly clamped around a large forkful of refrieds she'd conveniently shoved into her pie hole.

I stood and stuck my hand out, as did Craig. "Hi, Father Harry, I'm Hetta, this is Doctor Washington," they shook, "and of course, our friend, Sister Jan."

Jan just nodded and made a mmmm sound.

"Well, I guess she's not really a Sister anymore since she, ah...." I let that pause hang heavy in the suddenly stifling air.

Jan took the clue and hung her head over her plate in what passed for disgrace. Father Harry, on the other hand, beamed a beatific smile, mumbled something about lost sheep and redemption, and quickly moved to a table.

We beat feet for the exit before we really looked stupid. As we passed the Xers, one of them smirked and waved. "Have a good day, Doctor, Sister Doctor, and of course, you, Red."

We were out the door before I realized I hadn't gotten the Xer's names. I must be slipping. A quick stop at the RV registration desk did the job though. Oh, yeah, Brother John Smith.

We went home, made ferry arrangements for Craig, and settled on the sun-drenched verandah to read the local paper and sip iced tea.

An announcement of a new Yoga class caught my eye. I need Yoga so I can kick myself in the butt when I screw up.

Jan reached over, rattled my paper, and whispered, "Company."

"Huh?"

"Don't look now, but we are found."

Of course, I looked. Sure enough, John Smith and his buddy rolled to a halt in front of the house. There were no golf clubs in their cart.

"Nice digs, bird watchers."

"Hello again, Mr. Smith," I returned, letting him know I'd checked up on him.

"Touché," he said, gave me a little salute, and rolled away. For some reason, his knowing where I lived bothered me, but then again, I knew where they lived, as well: too close.

Chapter 23

What with a couple of mysterious Black Muslims taking a sudden interest in us, we figured it was a good thing we were blowing town for San Carlos. Craig had a ferry to catch, I wanted to check on my boat, and Jan said she'd much rather slink out of Dodge than risk another awkward encounter like the one with that hospital receptionist and a monk the day before.

Jan, still chagrined by the Father Harry thing, took every opportunity to give me grief. I knew she'd see the humor in the situation soon, as she always does, and there's nothing like a road trip to cheer folks up and clear the air. As an added bonus, once we dumped our keeper, Craig, onto the ferry for Baja, Jan and I could hit the town like old times. Even she, who started out as his staunch ally, was chaffing at his Draconian exercise regimen, even though he let her eat and drink pretty much what she wanted.

We packed up my VW and left Craig's car in my garage, with promises, under penalty of death, not to drive it when we returned. As Craig so charmingly stated it, "You two are way too careless with stuff like cars."

We should never have shared with him our recent adventures, which, among other things, involved a burned up rental car, a pickup with a bent axle, and a totaled VW Thing. We were only directly responsible for one out of three of those incidents, but in Craig's mind, a wreck is a wreck.

I'd spotted a promising taco stand in Naco, Sonora, on my last trip south, so we decided to grab one or two for breakfast. This was after trying to convince Craig that, just as the Weather Channel map stops at the border, so does the existence of cholesterol and calories. Won over or not, he agreed to the tacos.

As we crossed the border, the usual flock of giggling school kids headed north, on their way to school in Naco, Arizona. I wondered aloud if they had any idea how lucky they were to be able to cross into the U.S. so easily, when others were dying, literally, to do the same thing.

"Hey," Craig said, "they're elementary school students. How aware were you as a kid that you were lucky to be an American?"

"Oh, trust me," I said, "very. We traveled extensively and I saw, first hand, kids sleeping in doorways and begging for food and money on the streets. I knew I was lucky. How about you, Jan?"

"Naw, I was just a stupid kid who didn't know I was poor. Mom forgot to tell me."

"You weren't poor poor. After your dad died, your mom had to make ends meet on a clerical salary. Craig, on the other hand, was a rich kid."

"I guess so, but my parents forgot to tell me."

I rolled to a stop in a cloud of wood smoke. The fragrant smell of grilling carne asada sent my stomach a-rumblin'. Mesquite grilled beef, topped with a dollop of fresh salsa, and then rolled in a steaming hot tortilla is a little piece of breakfast heaven.

As we savored our breakfast, a group of tired, hungry looking people gathered across the street. I clutched my third taco protectively.

Jan cocked her head in their direction. "Think they've just been dumped back in Mexico by the Border Patrol?"

I shook my head. "That sign says *Centro de Rehabilitacion y Recuperacion para Enfermos de Drogadiccion y Alcoholismo*. Rehab center for drugs and alcoholism. Maybe we should check you in, Sister, so you can ditch that habit."

Craig laughed, but Jan glowered. "Ya know, a pun can be overused."

"Oh, lighten up. I practically saved your life by moving you to the front of the sick line, and the only way to do it was tell them you needed a fix. Ungrateful wretch."

"Girls, girls," Craig held up his hands, "peace. Let's get on down the road before…well, well, look who's here. Or rather, there."

I looked where he nodded, and who should appear in front of that rehab building? Our little Miss Sonrisa. "For a tiny Indian from way down south, she sure gets around."

My voice carries. She spotted us and crossed the street. Walking straight to our table, she asked, "*¿Está usted va a la viña*?" No *good morning* or *how are you* from this one.

"And a good *dia* to you, as well. No, we are not going to the vineyard, *vamanos al* San Carlos."

She then made us understand she'd like a ride as far as the turnoff for the Ruta Rio Sonora, just north of Cananea. I reluctantly agreed, and she accepted with all the grace of a pit bull. She did, however, manage a crack of a smile and a nod when Craig offered her a taco.

Not another word passed Sonrisa's grim little lips as we finished our breakfast while chatting about our trip plans and schedule. When we let her off at her turnoff, she mumbled something that could have been thanks, or screw you. I'm betting on the latter.

"Charming little ingrate, huh?" I said, watching her stalk away.

"What is her problem?" Jan wanted to know.

Craig filled her in on what little we knew of Sonrisa's hard life before she ended up at the winery, and that Nanci said her reticence was due to shyness. As we pulled into Cananea, Craig and I were arguing over whether Miss Sonrisa was reticent or downright surly. Jan averred that Craig was probably right, and that I was being too hard on the poor little thing.

Mean old Hetta pulled into a Pemex station, topped off the tanks, and ended up paying five pesos each for the three of us to use the bathroom, even though I'd just overpaid by at least ten percent because all the pump counters are misset, and it ain't in your favor. Jenks calls it a *milagro*, a miracle, for only in Mexico can you get 22 liters in a 19 liter gas container.

Who says Mexicans aren't enterprising souls?

Things were quiet at the mine entrance. A few soldiers slumped about, but the former roadblocks and angry strikers were gone. The old man and dog once again guarded the gate, and even though they actually appeared awake, it was hard to tell, as the gate stood open and we rolled on through.

Maria greeted us outside, even though the temperature was in the low forties, and hustled us inside, where it wasn't much warmer.

"God, it's freezing in here, Maria. What'd they do, cut off your power?"

"Oh, no. *Señor* Racón requested we not use the heater. He says we must save *electricidad*."

"Oh, he does, does he. Where is the little *ratón*?"

She smiled. "In Mexico."

Craig looked puzzled. "I thought we were in Mexico."

I explained that Mexicans, when they say Mexico, mean Mexico City, then I asked Maria, "So, who's the boss today?"

She looked confused. "Boss?"

"Who is the *jefe*? Who tells you what to do when the bosses are gone?"

A frown crossed her pretty face as she thought about that. "I guess, today, that would be you?"

"Yes, I think so. When will Racón return?"

"Two weeks."

"Maria, will you type a letter for me?"

"Of course."

"Okay, here goes: To Miss Maria, uh, what's your last name?"

"Fuentes."

"To Miss Maria Fuentes. Until further notice, please keep my office at seventy-five degrees, Fahrenheit. Thank you, Engineer Hetta Coffey."

"Café, there is no heater in your office."

"Then leave the door open so heat can get in there."

"Yes, Café. Thank you."

"*De nada*. I'll be checking in at my office every day, so be sure it's warm, got that?"

"But, I thought you were on your way to San Carlos."

"Who told you that?"

"You did."

"I lied."

She smiled and gave me a kiss on the cheek.

Chapter 24

"Nice goin' back there, Hetta. Keep the heat on, indeed. You trying to get yourself canned?" Jan asked as we left the mine office and entered the main highway for San Carlos.

"Racón won't touch me for something as simple as turning up the heat in the office. Don't forget, I'm a world-class mining expert, he said so himself. Well, he didn't, Juan Orozco did, but they've painted themselves into a corner with the unions, touting me as the person who will fix everything."

"Boy, if they only knew," Craig said, then cranked his head toward Jan in the backseat. "Actually, I thought helping poor freezing Maria out was very thoughtful, and, after all, how often is Hetta thoughtful?"

"Hey, Doctor Washington, how's this for a thought?" I said with a show of teeth meant as a snarl. "You want to walk to Baja?"

"On second thought, Hetta Coffey is one of the most caring individuals I know. So, how long a drive to San Carlos?"

I shrugged. "Depends on how many slow trucks we get behind. Like that one up there. Hold on, we can take him."

"But what about that...Oh, crap."

We made it from Cananea to San Carlos in four-and-a-half hours, something of a record I was later told. I was given a great deal of help by Our Lady of Guadalupe; on the switchback curve where her shrine stands, one can see traffic coming down the mountain from the opposite direction for at least a quarter mile, so I managed to pass four trucks.

Craig swore he would never ride with me again, but I knew he'd get over it. Jan thought the trip miraculously uneventful, considering some of our past jaunts, and called Craig a wuss. They were still bickering over my driving skills when we skidded to a stop in front of the Captain's Club near Marina San Carlos.

"Last one to the bar gets a time out, and pays for the first round," I told them, launching myself from the driver's seat.

Craig, crammed into the back seat after insisting on a seat change, even if it turned him into a sardine, also got stuck with the bill. By the time we cranked down a few fish tacos and a couple of gallons of beer—even Craig, who I suspect was stuffing road fear—it was time to head for our rooms at the Adalai.

Small, family run, and off the beaten path, the Departmentos Adalai, as it is called, is a favorite with boaters. Rooms are cheap and clean, the owners friendly and accommodating. Luxurious, it is not, but it fits the bill for non-tourist types looking for a soft place to land.

We opted for two rooms, both with a small fridge and microwave. I'd packed a kit with coffee makings and healthy snacks, but Jan and I planned on grazing our way through town as soon as we dumped Der Carbmeister onto the ferry. Love the man, but he simply had to go. Maybe a few days of living on fish would give him a new attitude towards a good old greasy cheeseburger. His ferry didn't leave until Saturday night, so we were stuck with him for another day, but as soon as he was gone, we planned on a major fried shrimp scarf-down.

After breakfast at Barracuda Bob's the next morning, we headed for Marina Real to check on *Raymond Johnson*. In addition to her hull work, I wanted to have the engines serviced so when she launched we'd be ready to cruise. I was hoping that "we" would be me and Jenks.

In addition to checking on Mad Russ's progress with the blisters, I'd scheduled a meeting with my mechanic, Franky. Franky and I have a love-hate relationship; he loves working on boats, and I hate waiting for him to work on mine, even though he's worth the wait.

As we entered the work yard, I surmised the *work* part I was paying for got lost in translation, for while there seemed to be a lot of work going on, it just wasn't on my boat. Other boats bristled with ladders and men sanding, caulking, and painting. Nary a ladder nor man near the forlorn-looking *Raymond Johnson*.

"Uh, Hetta," Jan said, eyeing my poor boat, "what exactly did you say they are supposed to be doing here?"

"Not storing her, which is what it looks like. I at least expected to see the blisters fared out so they'll dry. I'm paying a premium to be in the work yard section, but *Raymond Johnson* looks exactly as I left her. Will you stay here and get one of the guys to call me on channel sixteen when Franky shows?" I waggled my handheld VHF at her.

Jan said yes, I asked Craig to accompany me and to put on a mean face, then we steamed toward the marina in search of *Tequila Mockingbird,* and her owner, Mad Russ.

Banging on *Tequila's* hull got no results, but just as we were ready to give up and walk away, Russ stuck his head out of the cockpit hatch. "Hetta?" he mumbled sleepily, "What are you doing here?" He glanced warily at the suitably menacing Craig.

"Checking the progress on my boat, Russ, which, I might say, is zero. Zip. Nada."

"I wouldn't exactly say that."

"What, pray tell, would you say, exactly?"

"It's drying out."

"How can the blisters dry if they aren't ground out so they can drain?"

He looked surprised. I'd done my homework since we last talked. I now knew what had to be done, and all the steps to get there. "Well, you know, I was getting to that. Soon."

"How about getting to this? You give me a bill for what you haven't done, and I'll pay for it by the hour."

"Aw, Hetta, you know how it is," he whined, but made no move to leave the safety of his boat.

"No, Russ, I don't. As the Donald would say, you're fired." I tramped back to the boat yard, where I tracked down Mario, the marina employee who'd discovered the blisters in the first place. He looked nervous, as though I'd somehow blame him for Mad Russ's lack of progress.

"Mario, who can I get to fix my boat?"

He smiled with relief and pointed to another man in the yard, one who was actually working on a boat. "Arturo."

Thirty minutes later, Arturo had a bunch of my money, and I had a schedule for the completion of *Raymond Johnson*'s bottom job. He also told me the blisters were much less severe than I'd been led to think and then, *milagro*: Franky showed. I was assured by my new guys that in no time my boat would be in her slip, shipshape, and ready to head for California. Franky even said if need be, he'd go along as chief mechanic.

Having a mechanic of his caliber on board for a trip north was mighty tempting, but his offer dampened my buoying spirits. Would Jenks be there to take her home, or would I indeed end up with a crew? Where was Jenks? Was he all right? It had been eight days since he said he was going to some mysterious location. In what country? He hadn't said when he would return, and, uncharacteristic for me, I hadn't asked. He did say he'd call when he could, but I had expected that would be by now.

Suddenly a devastating mental image of some wild-eyed, sword-brandishing, contractor-beheading terrorists loomed.

Jan, who was chatting with a couple of boaters she knew, broke away and grabbed my arm. "Hetta, you okay? You look like you're about to conk out."

I shook my head. "I'm not okay, I'm scared. What if Jenks is—"

"Don't even go there," she said. "Say goodbye to these nice folks. We are going to the motel, get our stuff, and head for the house in Bisbee, where, through the wonderful world of every resource we have, we are going to find Jenks Jenkins. Okay? Craig, you can take a taxi to your ferry tonight."

"No problem," he said. "You go do what you have to do. You'd better hustle, though, it's already pushing ten. I don't want you two out on Mexican roads after dark, and that's pretty early this time of year."

I didn't protest, for Jan was right. Action was needed and we were gonna do it. We drove to the motel, hurriedly packed up my VW, grabbed box lunches at Barracuda Bob's, and headed for the border. Just south of Hermosillo, I pulled over.

"Jan, hand me that map of Sonora from the glove compartment. I have an idea."

I spread the map out and traced a road with my finger. "See this? This road goes up the Rio Sonora, right by Ted and Nanci's vineyard."

"And?"

"And, Ted was in the Middle East with Jenks. They worked together. He started to talk about what they did over there once, but Nanci shut him down. If we go this way," I tapped the map, "instead of through Imuris and up Mex 2, we can stop by the winery.

Maybe Ted'll come up with a contact who'll track down Jenks. It's worth a try."

Jan studied the map. "Is this a good road? Can we make it to the winery before dark?"

"About the same distance as if we went through Cananea, looks like. Maybe even a little shorter. I can't tell you how good the road is from this map, but it is paved. When Craig and I went through...here," I showed her a spot on the same highway, just north of the winery, "we did have to ford the river. My guess is we'll have to do so a couple of times, but what the heck, it's not rainy season, so we should do all right."

She shrugged. "Okay by me, can we call Ted and Nanci, let them know we're on the way?"

"I'll try. They have HughesNet up there, therefore Internet, ergo, phone. Reach in my purse and get that little red book. Last name is Burns."

Rosa answered, said Nanci and Ted were out riding, but she'd let them know we were on the way. I hung up and told Jan, "I figured they'd be there. They told me they weren't going anywhere until next month. They're in the process of changing out cobalt rods and have to stick close to home until the exchange is made."

"Did you say cobalt rods? What the hell kind of wine are they making up there?"

I told her all about irradiated wine, now that I'm an expert on the subject. Maybe I'll add that to my resume, right along with internationally renowned mining consultant.

Chapter 25

The Rio Sonora Valley's villages are rustic, historic, and charming. Many of them are over four hundred years old and imbue a rural charm long lost to most of the United States and Mexico. Nary a stoplight, golden arch, or neon sign for miles. Just one sleepy, pristine pueblo after another, each anchored by a mission or church plaza at its center. Between villages, we rarely saw another vehicle.

The small colonial-style towns, which spread from central plazas worthy of a sit, are authentically colonial in style. The old houses, even those with peeling paint, looked homey and lived in. Rattling along on narrow cobblestone streets built well before automobiles were invented, we found friendly folks willing to while away time shooting the breeze with a couple of Gringas. We stopped briefly at each town, keeping a close watch on the hour and miles to go as we went.

Jan kept up a verbal travelogue, using a dog-eared guidebook I'd picked up at Barracuda Bob's a few months before. I never leave a map or guidebook lie, because you never know when you'll get a chance to check out a new spot, and here we were.

Touristing our way north, we hit Huépac and took a gander at their mammoth femur displayed like a hero statue, bought tiny but fiery chiltepin peppers in Baviacora, and gaped at Achonchi's black Christ figure. Jan wanted to hit the thermal springs reputed to have medicinal qualities, but we were running out of time and daylight.

Fording the Rio Sonora at night was not an option, so we reluctantly blasted by Arizpe's huge cottonwood trees teeming with great herons. The trip so far had been surprisingly relaxing, informative, and fun, so, of course, things had to hit the dumper.

We picked up a tail just north of Arizpe.

Charming as the pueblos were, we'd seen so few cars between towns that a tinge of unease niggled at their remoteness. Already on the alert because of reported *drogista* traffic in the area, my hands tightened on the wheel as we passed a white SUV parked on the side of the road. To make matters worse, two youngish men wearing baseball caps lounged in the front seat.

I didn't say anything to Jan, and was thinking maybe I was being paranoid when the SUV loomed in my rearview mirror. I moved over the centerline, hogging the road to prevent them from passing.

"Jan?" I said, "Tighten your seatbelt."

She did it without first asking why. She's been around me way too long.

I downshifted, hit the gas, and we were doing eighty in no time. The SUV stayed on my tail.

Jan craned her neck to take a look. "Where did they come from?"

"They were sitting on the side of the road, almost like they were waiting for us."

"Hetta, I know you have a suspicious nature, but are you sure they aren't just a couple of dudes on their way home in a hurry?"

"You saw them. What do you think?"

"Punks."

"Yep. How far to the next town?"

Jan studied our map. "I don't see anything. The winery turnoff is...what's the last kilometer number you saw?"

I told her. "Okay, then, we have about five miles to go. Think they'll follow us up the winery road?"

"Don't know, but I can surely outrun them for another few minutes. Dig my cell phone out of my purse. Ted's number is in memory." The SUV had dropped back some, but was still following us much closer than I liked. I frantically watched the countryside for a house, while praying we'd come upon a truck or bus going our way. If I could pass one and then really slow down, I'd have some cover. Where's a slow Mexican truck when you need one?

Jan tried the phone, but no service. Figures.

White knuckled, and in a cold sweat, I concentrated on keeping us on the road and the SUV in my mirror. On straightaways I pushed ninety. On curves, since I took up both lanes, I alternatively hoped for traffic, and prayed there wasn't any, because if we met, one of us was leaving the road.

"Hetta, remember how I threatened to murder you if you smuggled a gun into Mexico?"

"Yep."

"I was wrong, and anyhow, you never listen to me. So, where's the gun?"

"Sorry."

"The next time you listen to me, I really am going to kill you."

Even in my fearful state, I had to laugh. Howl, in fact. We both grew hysterical and I lost my concentration. When I looked into the rearview mirror, the SUV was no longer behind us.

My peripheral vision picked up a flash of white, and just like that, they drew alongside, staring at us with bewildered looks. Instead of being frightened by their move, their confusion only added to our cackles.

Tears blurred my vision so I had to slow down. If they intended to cut us off, this was the time, but they stayed a safe distance ahead. When I slowed, they slowed.

"Hetta," Jan hooted, gasping for air, "l-let's knock their dicks in the dirt."

"That's the best idea you've had all day. Hang on."

I hit the gas and was on their bumper in a flash. Now that the tables had turned, I felt, well, in the driver's seat. The biggest danger to us at this point was them hitting the brakes, but they didn't. I rode a foot off their bumper, trying to decide whether to, as Jan so charmingly suggested, try and knock their dicks in the dirt. At this speed, just a properly aimed tap on their left bumper should do the job.

We rounded a curve, and Jan yelled, "Hetta, the winery. I just saw a sign."

"How far?"

"Kilometer. Half a mile, more or less."

"I'm doing sixty miles an hour. Start counting, like, one one-thousand, two-one thousand. Out loud. This old car doesn't have a trip odometer."

"You got it." She counted, while I drafted the SUV and crossed mental fingers for what seemed forever. Finally, Jan hit four-hundred-forty, and I held my speed, but at four-hundred-forty-five, I hit the brakes, slowing to thirty miles per hour, hoping whoever made the winery sign knew how to calculate distance.

The SUV driver, seemingly unaware we'd suddenly slowed, disappeared around a curve just as we saw our road. I skidded onto it, then stopped. A brisk breeze instantly carried our dust away. Fighting the desire to sprint for the winery, I crept up the rocky incline at a dust-free speed. From my last trip, I recalled a dip where we could hide, a dry creek bed less than a quarter mile in. As soon as we got there, I killed the engine.

No longer visible from the main road, we sat, listened, and heard nothing but birds, and an ominous hiss denoting I'd possibly pushed my VW a mite hard.

"I think we lost them," Jan whispered.

"Let's wait another five minutes, and if we don't hear them we're probably home free."

It was an interminable five minutes until we agreed to forge ahead. The VW, however, had other ideas. After several tries, I gave up on starting her, we grabbed our overnight bags and trudged up the steep road. When we crossed over a cattle guard, I told Jan she'd better keep us a tree in mind as we walked, just in case Booger Red showed up.

Thankfully, just before dark fell in earnest, barking dogs led two armed, mounted ranch hands to us, and soon we were sitting in Ted and Nanci's living room, sipping excellent wine, telling of our road scare, and getting a scolding.

"Why didn't you call us before taking the Rio Sonora road?" Nanci wailed, visibly upset. "We would have told you not to, no matter what. There have been all kinds of problems along there, not the least of which have been roadblocks, set up by thugs. People have died."

"We did call. Rosa said you were out riding, but she'd tell you we were on the way."

"Well, she didn't. Rosa knew you were on the Rio Sonora highway?"

"Uh, I didn't tell her where we were. Taking that road was a spur of the moment thing, so I didn't ask any questions like I should have. I wasn't thinking, I guess."

Seeing my dismay at being so stupid, Ted said, "How could you know? I'll tell the staff to warn anyone who calls about that road until things get much safer around here. By the way, where in hell is Rosa?"

The question was directed at Nanci, who answered. "I haven't seen her since before we left for our ride. I can't believe she didn't tell us you were coming. When I do find her, we'll have a little talk." She stomped out of the room, fuming.

"She'll cool down," Ted told us, "but I wouldn't want to be in Rosa's *zapatas* right now."

"It's not Rosa's fault we took the scenic route."

"No, but at least we would have been expecting you. Anyway, all's well that ends well. You did the right thing, giving those guys the slip. No telling who they are." He asked me for my keys, and sent a couple of his ranch hands to tow my car to his shop.

Minutes later, Nanci returned, clearly distraught. Rosa was nowhere to be found.

The men sent to fetch my car also returned with bad news. Like Rosa, my beloved VW had vanished.

I would, in time, forget the fortune I'd spent having that car restored after an old enemy dumped her into the Oakland Estuary, but her sentimental value went deep. She was the only tangible thing I had left of my dog, RJ, since I'd bought the car for him. Okay, so maybe it was to save the leather in my BMW from dog drool, but it was still his car. And I could almost forgive someone taking her if they really needed a car, but those jerks, and I was positive it was the guys in the SUV, already had wheels. The question is, were they waiting for us on the highway and if so, why?

"So, who do you think these buttheads are?" I asked Ted. "And why would they chase us around and then steal my old junker?"

He shrugged. "Who knows? This is Mexico. If you leave it, it's fair game. Someone else might have taken it, you know."

I thought about that. Maybe so. It could be that the SUV guys were simply having a little fun on the road, nothing more. I mean, the world abounds in white cars, so I was probably being overly suspicious, thinking that white SUV was the same one Craig and I saw on my last trip to the winery. Even with my vivid imagination, it was a stretch. One thing for sure, though, I was out an automobile, and all I carried on it was Mexican liability insurance.

"Think we should call the cops?" Jan asked.

"We could," Nanci said dryly. Her answer and demeanor didn't exactly instill confidence in that plan.

"But?" I asked.

"Won't do much good. With your car permit, it can be out of Sonora in hours."

"What car permit?"

"The one required to drive here."

"I thought I didn't need one in Sonora."

Ted shook his head. "Not so. If you drive from Naco, through Cananea and on down to Imuris on Mex 2, you don't, but once you turn off on Ruta Rio Sonora, you are no longer in the so-called hassle-free zone. You have to get a permit."

"Well, fooey, I didn't. Not last time, either."

"Good thing the cops didn't get you. It's a big fine, and they can confiscate the car. Now, for sure, you do not want to report the car stolen because it is in Mexico illegally. Don't know what your car is worth, but it'll cost you big to get it back, even if you do find it. Sorry."

"It's just a car. No word from Rosa yet?"

"No," he said, "and it is so unlike her. She told no one she had plans to leave. We've searched every building on the place, thinking she might have fallen or something, but no luck. First Lupe walks off the job, now Rosa."

We were all in a bit of a funk when we sat down for a late dinner, but good company, great wine, and spicy food cheered us. Not so much that I didn't still wish a million painful deaths on the perps who took my car, but my practical side was already trying to figure out how we were going to get home, and where I'd get new wheels.

My worrywart gene, a gift from my mother, nagged that the garage door opener still clipped to my car's sun visor was going to cost me for a replacement. Also, someone could actually check the registration, find where I lived, and get into the house. Then, up popped another thing to worry about: Craig's car, sitting in the garage, keys in the ignition.

Nope, I thought with relief, my car was still registered to Jenks's apartment in California, and there isn't any mail with my Bisbee address in the VW, right? And what about—

"Earth to Hetta," Ted said, and I gave him an apologetic smile. "I'm flying to Sierra Vista in the next couple of days, so I'll drop you guys at the Bisbee airport, then you can call a cab, or maybe someone there will give you a lift, since your house is so close."

"That'll work. Craig's car is in my garage, so we'll use it until we come up with something else."

Jan shook her head. "Oh, no. Craig will have our heads if we touch that Porsche."

"Craig's in Baja and won't be back for days. He'll never know. I'll chalk mark the wheel location, then disconnect the odometer, just in case he checked it before he left."

All three had comical, quizzical looks on their faces, so I explained, “Misspent teenager-hood.”

Nanci laughed. “See, Ted, I knew there was a reason we never had kids.”

Chapter 26

The day after our daunting ride over the back roads of the Rio Sonora Valley, and my VW going walkabout, Ted mustered a posse and set off looking for Rosa, my car, and the winery van it turned out Rosa must have taken. At first there was speculation Rosa left a day early for her weekly shopping trip to Cananea, but she'd never done so in the past. Winery employees went to both Arizpe and Cananea, questioned Rosa's friends, and even the grocer she favored. No one had seen her since the week before.

Ted took to the air, then stomped in just at dusk, having flown a search pattern with no sightings. Rosa's disappearance, coupled with Lupe's weeks before, called for drastic measures, Ted told us. They were going to call the police. While this might seem logical in the States, cops are a last resort in Mexico.

"What about Sonrisa?" I asked my fellow diners. "Isn't she friends with Rosa? Maybe Rosa told her something that she thinks is unimportant, but isn't."

Ted looked at his head foreman, who said he'd questioned Sonrisa, and all other employees, at length, but no one knew anything. As if on cue, Sonrisa herself glided in with a fresh pitcher of ice water.

She circled the table, refilling glasses. When she got to me, I noticed her tense slightly. Never one to sit by and let the chance to annoy someone who annoys me go by, I asked, "Say, Sonrisa, seen your black buddies lately?" Her only reaction to my mention of her hitchhike with the Xer's was a noticeable straightening of her spine.

"She doesn't speak English," Nanci reminded me.

"Oh, right, I forgot. I was just wondering—"

Jan pretended to drop her napkin, leaned down, pinched my leg, and whispered, "Later. Let it go."

I did, but watched Sonrisa closely the rest of the evening. Her bland facial expression set my teeth on edge. Rosa, her supposedly new BFF and mentor, had vanished, so shouldn't she at least look worried? Or was I being too hard on her? After all, Nanci told me Sonrisa came from an area where not drawing attention to yourself is a matter of self-preservation. I wouldn't do well there.

After dinner, I cornered Ted about my own missing person: Jenks. He'd emailed and called Jenks, as I had, but gotten nowhere. The only thing we knew for sure was that Jenks was still registered at his hotel suite in Kuwait City, and Lars, his brother, was too. Neither, however, was in residence. We checked my home answering machine for messages, hoping Jenks left one, but only Craig called to say he was with Chino at the whale camp.

We all retired to our rooms early, worn down from a combination of concern and frustration. Jan came to my room and we popped a cork on Ted's finest.

"So, did, uh, Craig say anything else?" she asked casually, like she wasn't fishing for info.

"Oh, you mean, did Craig say something like, 'Chino says he simply cannot live without Jan and is contemplating throwing himself upon a sharpened whale bone'?"

She slapped my wrist. "Yeah, okay, I guess I was hoping for something like that."

"Sorry, all he said was Chino met him at the ferry in Santa Rosalia, and he was enjoying the beach. Besides, I thought you didn't care what Chino thought anymore."

"He could pretend to miss me. Oh, well, at least I know where he is. Not like Jenks."

"Jenks isn't being like Jenks. He's sorta disappeared before, but not for this long. I have a horrible feeling that something bad has happened. I can't help it, what with stories of contractors being beheaded and all."

"Surely CNN would have gotten wind of a kidnapped contractor. Besides, I don't recall anyone ever being nabbed in Kuwait City."

"How do we even know he isn't in Iraq? Ted told me himself that he and Jenks were no strangers to clandestine ops."

"Ops? You been reading Clancy again?"

I laughed, despite a hollow feeling in my gut.

Jan poured more wine. "I've got it!" she suddenly screeched, scaring the crap out of me. "Let's call the prince." Sometimes Jan is a friggin' genius. Why hadn't I thought of bringing Prince Faoud into the loop? He'd given us his private phone number after we'd weathered a hurricane together in Baja's Magdalena Bay, and he even contacted Jenks in Kuwait several months before, then lent him an airplane when Jan and I found ourselves up to our ears in bad guys down on the Baja.

"Brilliant, Jan. Think he's in Saudi Arabia?"

"I doubt it, since his relatives apparently pay him to stay away. Doesn't matter though, we have his cell number."

"We'll have to use Ted's house phone, my cell won't work here." I dug out my address book, thankful I hadn't left my stuff in the VW when she conked out on us. I also dug out a small flashlight and we tiptoed down the dark hall and stairs, into Ted's den. I eased the heavy French doors closed, then found a light switch.

The generator powering the entire complex shut down at ten, so the household was now running off battery power and inverter. I hoped the satellite system was connected to the battery grid, as it is on my boat. A series of blue lights on the router told me the good news. "We're in bidness, looks like. I'll call, you talk."

"Me? Why me?"

"Because, Miz Jan, old princey-poo has the hots for you."

"Yeah, but you wouldn't let me have anything to do with him, remember? You said I'd probably end up getting unveiled in his harem."

"Yeah, but that was before we needed him."

"Let me get this straight. It's okay if I end up in a harem, so long as you get what you want?"

"That about sums it up. Dialing."

As soon as I heard a ring I shoved the phone at Jan. She snatched it with a petulant huff. After a short while, she said, "Uh, Hetta, I don't thi—Prince Faoud? Oh, hi, this is Jan, I was on Hetta's boat at Mag Bay when we...fine, fine, and you?"

She listened, a crooked smile twitching one side of her mouth, and then cooed, "Oh, I'm sorry to hear that, but I'm sure you'll work it out. Say, the reason we called, Hetta and I, is we have a problem you might be able to help us with." She explained how Jenks was missing, we were worried, and was there anything he could do?

I waited impatiently until she gushed, "Oh, thank you. You still have his cell phone number?" She waited, mouthed, "Checking," to me, then into the phone she said, "Yes, that's it. He and Lars are registered at the Mövenpick, because Jenks likes the food. The front desk won't give us any information, so maybe you can pull strings. Hang on a minute, Hetta wants to talk to you."

With a feeling of overwhelming gratitude, I said, "Thank you, thank you, Prince Faoud. I can't tell you how much I appreciate your help. We're a little lost over here. My next move was to catch a plane to Kuwait City."

"No need for that. It is my pleasure to help. I trust you and the lovely Jan have been well?"

"Actually, the lovely Jan had a bad case of the *tourista*, but she is much better now." I ducked as Jan launched a couch pillow at me. "Matter of fact, she's downright feisty. Let me give you the number here, and my new home number. We're in Mexico right now, but we'll be in Arizona tomorrow. Uh, I have another favor. No big deal, but I thought maybe you could help."

"Anything within my power for ladies in distress."

Prince of a fella, that prince. "There is this Mexican guy with a family name of Hayat Racón," I spelled it. "He has hinted he's somehow related to the Carlos Slim clan of Mexico, and I would like to learn more about him."

"He is an Arab?"

"Lebanese, I think, like Slim."

"I guess, to you Americans, we all look alike."

"Oh, I didn't mean to—"

"I was jollying you, Hetta. I do not take offense."

"And none meant. More like I figure all you rich guys know each other, no matter what your ethnic origins, and since Slim is reportedly the richest man in the world these days, he qualifies for your exclusive club."

"I'll see what I can find out. What else do you know about Racón."

I didn't know much, but I told the prince how old I thought the Rat was, and that he worked for the mining group, sort of. Faoud then assured me he would find my Mr. Jenkins forthwith and get back to me. Just knowing someone with power and resources was on the job gave me a great deal of comfort.

We said our goodbyes, then I asked Jan, "So, what's the prince up to that you commiserated with when you first talked?"

"What's a prince to do? He's commissioned a new mega-yacht and his designer informed him that an on-board stable for his beloved Arabians is so much horse hockey."

For some reason this sent me into hysterics, something that happens often when Jan and I are together. We were trying to stifle giggles as we made our way upstairs, but not successfully, because we met Sonrisa checking us out. That impassive countenance, which normally drives me so nuts, only made me laugh harder.

Jan followed me into my room, reassuring me that all would be well with Jenks.

"I hope you're right. I'm to the point of, if he is alive and well, ending it all. I can't take this kind of relationship much longer. Maybe I'll cut him loose and let him go after some young, gorgeous type."

"Oh, Hetta don't be so dramatic. Jenks doesn't want someone young and gorgeous, he wants you."

Chapter 27

After the phone conversation with Prince Fauod I slept through the night for the first time in a week, perhaps because I now knew the prince's far-reaching feelers were in action, tracking down Jenks. I actually awoke to a moment of peace until I remembered with dismay that Jenks was not yet found. So many missing people and cars, and nothing I could do but wait.

Even a hot shower didn't help diminish a deep malaise that I finally identified as powerlessness. A self-admitted control freak, I am not one to normally let her boat drift with the tide, and I was adrift. Instead of doing things my way, I had somehow let others put me out to sea. This simply would not do.

While dressing, I jotted items on a list that I make out on those all too frequent occasions when my life heads for the rocks. These TO DO lists help me organize my feelings and identify those problems I need to get a handle on.

TO DO—AND I MEAN IT—LIST

1. Call daily for a progress report on *Raymond Johnson*, and demand those reports be backed up with photos.

Just getting that task on the list made me feel a little better, so I put on mascara.

2. Find my car.

Realistically, that was a tough one. Locating a stolen car in Mexico is damned near impossible, but I stubbornly refused to count my VW out. Yep, I would find that car. Thinking I looked a little peaked, I added a dollop of blush to my cheeks.

3. Job?

Actually that was one thing I seemed to be on top of, and now that the prince had agreed to look into El Ratón's background, maybe I'd dig up sufficient dirt to move him out of my way.

4. Trap the Rat.

I smiled, picturing him hightailing it to Mexico City, tail between his legs, chased after by Mexican secretaries armed with carving knives. This happy thought prompted me to put on a dab of lipstick.

5. Jenks. Decide if worth it, make pro vs. con list.

Just how long could we, should we, sustain pissing each other off from afar? When we were together, crazy in lust, we rarely argued, he treated me like a princess, and I treated him like...well, better than I treat anyone else. There are those who would argue I should work on my people skills, but Jenks actually seems to enjoy me, warts and all.

However, the longer we're apart, and the more he tells me what is good and bad for me, the more I resent him for being gone. My emotional status being dependent on actions of others makes me insecure, and when I'm unhappy, I like lots of company. Like moldy apples love spreading gunk.

I tried to remember my happiness scale, pre-Jenks. One thing for sure, I didn't need another to foist emotional distress upon me, I am a master of doing that to myself.

I was captain of my own fate when I met Jenks, but I was then operating under the Edna Ferber theory: Being an old maid is like death by drowning—a really delightful sensation after you have ceased struggling.

Simply put, before Jenks I had ceased struggling, and now here I was, treading water again. Jenks had to come home, or else.

6. Quit drinking, lose ten pounds.

Of course, this ain't gonna happen, but it always leaves me with something to strive for.

Somehow all this list and decision making empowered me. Or was it the hoarded Valium (I am not allowed to have more than one or two in my possession at a time, due to a terrible lack of self-control where these wonderful pills are concerned) I downed in anticipation of a bumpy small plane ride? Whatever it was, I descended, practically floated, to breakfast, suitcase in hand, smile on my face, ready to head home and tackle the world on my own terms.

Maybe, I rationalized, in some convoluted teaching moment, I owe those guys who took my car more than a swift kick in the balls. I mean, after being chased all over a Mexican highway, then having my car stolen, how much worse can things get?

But then again, as Humphrey Bogart once said, "Things are never so bad they can't be made worse."

Everyone was already seated around the breakfast table when I breezed in. From their glum looks, they were not in a state of grace such as I.

"Hetta, have you been into the wine already? It's a tad early, ya know," Jan said, after taking in the glide in my step and glow of contentment on my face.

"I am at peace."

"You found those guys who took your car, and dismembered them? Gosh, you have been a busy bee this morning."

That lightened the mood and brought smiles.

"*Au contraire*," I said airily. "I have forgiven them."

Jan dropped her fork. "No way."

"It's simple. I have decided not to let these offenses get under my skin. I can get another car."

"Who are you, and what have you done with the real Hetta Coffey?"

I beamed her a saintly smile and absolved her impudence. As Sonrisa filled my water glass, I greeted her warmly.

She scooted for the kitchen, obviously leery of the crazy Gringa's sudden benevolence toward her.

"Hetta may be onto something," Nanci said.

"More like *on* something," Jan mumbled.

"I mean it," Nanci said. "We have all worked ourselves into a froth here, and we don't know for sure any harm has come to either Lupe or Rosa. Maybe we're overreacting."

Jan, who had been watching me closely, smiled and mouthed, "Valium?"

I whispered, "Only a half."

Ted, not noticing our little exchange, answered Nanci by shaking his head. "We are right to worry. Rosa would never walk off the job, especially now. She removed the old rods a couple of days ago, and the new ones are ready to go in. We need to energize the system and not just anyone can do it. Rosa had Lupe trained before she vanished into thin air, but Sonrisa is nowhere near ready."

"You can't do it, Nanci?" Jan asked.

"Unfortunately, I inherited an arthritic condition." She held out her hands for us to see the noticeable swelling of her finger joints. "I don't think anyone around here wants me handling cobalt."

I bestowed upon her a beatific beam.

Jan rolled her eyes and asked Ted, "Rosa's training Sonrisa in the lab? I thought Sonrisa worked in the kitchen."

Nanci answered. "Rosa took her under her wing, grooming her for backup. I mean, it ain't rocket science, but it is somewhat delicate, and realistically takes two people, preferably three. With Rosa gone, now it'll be Ted and Sonrisa, with me as watchdog."

"Are you sure you have the time to fly us home?" Jan asked Ted. "We can take a bus, you know."

"I have to go north today for a meeting with the bank I can't miss. I was planning on staying over in Sierra Vista, but now I'll have to fly back so we can work into the night. And they might not show it much, but Rosa's disappearance has put a real strain on the entire staff, so I need to backtrack, pronto. If she's not here by the time I return, I'll make a police report. Not that it'll do any good."

"Love will overcome," I said, spreading my aura with wiggly fingers.

"Yeah, Maharishi Valium-hesh Hetta," Jan drawled. "Let's just do a little Hari Krishna conga line around the room, chant a few oms, and all will be well with the world."

"Cynic."

Ranch hands had already rolled Ted's plane, a twin engine Beech Baron, from its hangar when we arrived at the runway. While we chatted with Nanci, Ted bustled about the aircraft, checking this and that, hopefully very thoroughly.

As much as I hate to admit it, small planes make me nervous, thus the early morning Valium. I prefer my air transport complete with drink service and bathrooms, but getting home in a flash today held a great deal of appeal, especially after being pursued by shady characters on the roads of Mexico.

We were to land first at Douglas, where Ted made arrangements with officials there to enter the country. He explained the required rigmarole to us, said it was just part of flying these days, especially when entering the U.S. from Mexico. Once checked in and legal, he'd hop over to Bisbee Municipal, dump us off before heading for Sierra Vista.

"We better get to it," Ted told us. "Normally Rosa goes with me, we split up at the airport, she heads into town in a taxi and does the Walmart, Staples, that kind of shopping while I knock out the commissary list."

I asked, "So, Rosa has a green card?"

"Oh, yes. She's an employee of our corporation, and even though we're located in Mexico, we are also incorporated in the United States."

Jan and I volunteered to go to Sierra Vista with him, run Rosa's errands, but he said no thanks, he would have frozen food with him on his return, and since he had to check into Mexico at Nogales, he didn't want to backtrack in order to drop us off.

We waved goodbye to Nanci and strapped in while Ted taxied to the end of his runway. He handed us earphones with built-in microphones so we could hear and talk to each other over the engine noise.

When stopped at the end of the runway, he gave us a running commentary on what he was doing. "I have to do a runup. I'm cycling both engines to check the magnetos and props. Okay, now I'm setting the trim tabs, and here we go. Ready?"

No, I thought, but nodded a reluctant yes from the copilot's seat.

My heart stepped up a beat as we picked up speed on the bumpy runway. Another thing I like about real airplanes is that they taxi on real runways. I've spent plenty of time on puddle jumpers while traveling to remote jobsites, bounce-landing on dirt and grass fields successfully each time, but I can't say my confidence level has risen greatly just because I've survived.

We were rolling along at a pretty good clip when Ted suddenly cut the power and shouted, "What the hell?"

"My car!" I yelled, pointing as my VW caught up with, then passed us. "They've found her."

"Finally, some good news. Okay, I guess this changes your travel plans, so I'll let you two...what is with those guys? Dammit." He braked sharply.

My VW matched speed with the plane, keeping just far enough directly ahead in front of us to avoid pulverization by propellers. Now the brake lights pulsed on the car, making Ted follow suit.

My surprise and delight at seeing my car again quickly dried up, along with my mouth, when we damned near rear-ended her. It was thanks to Ted's piloting skills that we managed to keep squared behind the car, our nose centered just feet away from the VW's rear bumper. Jan and I let loose with a couple of wimpy eeeks, but Ted kept his cool.

He slowed us to a crawl so when the car abruptly stopped, Ted avoided hitting it, but just barely. We were all cursing the driver out in our own way when the car doors swung open and three men in black balaclavas and camouflage fatigues leapt out brandishing large weapons.

Ted muttered, "Crap, they've got automatics."

Jan whispered, "Oh, shit. Oh, dear."

"Urk," I cleverly articulated.

Chapter 28

When the men jumped from my VW, any benefit of my earlier Valium vanished. If Jan, and even battle-proven Ted, were any indication, we were all in a state of jaw dropping shock, unable to absorb that, like some action movie, masked, armed men were rushing our plane, obviously intent on a hijacking.

Or worse, hijacking the plane, and killing us.

I watched dumbly as my emptied VW rolled forward on her own for a few feet, then rocked to a stop, blocking the runway.

While Jan and I exchanged a look of pure horror, Ted went into a flurry of hitting switches on his console.

With great effort, I croaked, "So, Ted, you have a plan for this sort of thing?" even though it was pretty clear our options were nil to none. The men wanted the plane, and they were going to get it. At least I hoped that's all they wanted.

As if we weren't breathing our last, he calmly asked, "Hetta, does that car of yours have a manual or automatic transmission?"

"Manual." Was this really the time to talk cars? Men.

"Get into the backseat with Jan."

I unbuckled and inspected my high seat back with dismay. There was only about a foot of clearance above the headrest, and the split between the seats the same, both spaces way shy of my butt size. Somehow, though, I shinnied through with all the grace of a pole vaulting elephant, kicking Ted in the head before landing with a thump in Jan's lap.

She shoved me into the other seat, none too gently. "We're good," I told Ted, although I didn't know why. Good? Hell, we were screwed.

"Buckle in, and keep your heads down. These bastards are not taking my plane," Ted told us as he loosed the brakes and gave the engines power, all the while closing on the rear end of my car. With a gentle nudge, Ted centered on my VW's bumper and began pushing her.

Jan, who had been trying to keep an eye on the bad guys, shrieked as one of them materialized outside the window next to her. Ted hit the gas, and the masked man lost his wing perch and tumbled from sight.

While Jan and I stretched and craned our necks, trying to see what was happening, Ted concentrated on keeping the nose of the plane centered on the VW's bumper. If we slipped to one side, we would catch a prop and make mincemeat out of my car, and it probably wouldn't do us much good, either.

I wasn't exactly sure what the consequences would be, but I instinctively knew that one of us was unstoppable, and the other immovable.

For some reason, possibly because the men didn't want to harm the plane they were hell bent on stealing, no shots were fired. Yet. As a matter of fact, they now followed us at what seemed an insolently leisurely pace because they had the advantage, and they knew it. Unable to scoot the VW very fast, or very far, we would have no choice but to stop.

When Ted built his runway, he had to cut a big notch into the side of a mountain, leaving three sides with steep drop-offs. Okay, cliffs. He was now pushing my car, and us, toward one of those sheer drops where, in short order, we'd take a five-hundred foot plunge. The bad guys could afford to bide their time.

"Ted, we are going to stop, right?"

"We'd better, because this ain't no stinkin' glider. Right now, I'm buying time, giving the ranch hands and Nanci a chance to react to all the commotion. By now I should have buzzed the house, so they'll know something's wrong. Our people are armed, probably something these guys didn't plan on. See any of the good guys yet?"

"No, just those jerks. They've fallen back some, probably because they can see we're running out of runway. Wait a minute, there's someone crouched down behind them. I can't...yes! It's Sonrisa, so others can't be far behind. Uh, you don't happen to have any firepower on board, do you?"

"Not much. Reach under your seat. There's a latch release for a storage compartment."

I fumbled around and finally found an emergency flare gun case. Not the ideal weapon, but one I'd used to good effect in the past. I loaded a cartridge. "Got it. What do you want me to do?"

"Slow those bastards down. Jan, open your door so Hetta can get a bead on them."

"I'm on the move," I shouted as Jan worked on the door, and got it open. I wiggled over her, then she slid into my seat. "I ain't much of a wingwalker, but I'll do my best. Jan, hold my feet, make sure I don't end up head first in the dirt, okay?"

"I've got you."

Ted slowed more. "Okay, guys, this is it. We're at the end of this rope. Sorry about your car, Hetta."

I twisted around and caught a final glimpse of my bumper taking a swan dive into space. I gaped until Jan yelled, "Hetta! For God's sake, shoot someone!"

Pushing onto my knees, I launched forward, then slid my upper body out onto the wing. Jan, true to her word, not only held my legs, she sat on them.

"Okay, make my day," I growled.

I'd always wanted to say that.

Taking aim on the closest attacker, I was determined to take him out without blowing a hole in our own plane. It wasn't going to be easy, even though we were now fully stopped, because my firing angle was off.

"Shoot 'em, dammit," Jan demanded again.

"I'm tryin', dammit. Okay, okay, I've got him lined up." I braced my arm as best I could and was squeezing the trigger when the guy suddenly stopped in his tracks, spun, and sprinted away from us, toward the other end of the runway.

"Ha, I scared them off. They're turning tail."

Ted left the engines at idle and unbuckled. "Fantastic. Everyone out of the plane. If I have to, I'm going to push this baby over the side, because they are *not* getting it. Hetta, you first, then cover us. Go, go, go!"

We went, went, went.

Jan held onto my feet as long as she could, but when she let go, I still had a goodly headfirst drop. Luckily my fall was broken by a large bush, but then Jan knocked the air out of me when she landed on my back. We rolled aside just in time to avoid being flattened by Ted. All three of us scrambled behind that puny bush, as if it would stop a bullet.

Ted pried the flare gun from my clenched hand and knelt in a classic firing position. I closed my eyes, because everyone knows that keeping one's eyes clamped shut stops not only bullets, but also monsters that snatch you by the feet from under your bed. I missed my blankie.

Inappropriate laughter shoved me back to reality. Had Ted gone round the bend?

Opening my eyes I saw him standing, gun lowered, pointing with his other hand. "Oh, yeah, baby. It's my man, Booger Red, and he's got those assholes on the run. And, here comes the cavalry. Time for us to split, because those guys are way too busy to mess with us anymore. Hetta, you lead. Over the edge, for now."

We scrambled for the bluff and crouched on a ledge to watch the show. When I looked back and down, only a plume of dust marked where my car ended up. Sigh.

A brigade of farm trucks, tractors, Jeeps and an ATV or two had arrived, and armed ranch hands sped toward the center of the runway, while Booger Red charged from our end. Caught in the middle were the three assailants, who threw their guns down and hands up.

Booger Red, who evidently missed that class regarding the rules of the Geneva Convention, and the niceties of surrender, didn't even slow. Two thousand pounds of red-speckled fury mowed the kneeling, terrified men down with a bone-crunching wallop heard even above the airplane's engines.

Bodies flew, but not so far that six-foot horns couldn't reach them. Tossed over and over into the air like rag dolls, the would-be hijackers endured several more minutes of abuse so violent that Ted actually called for the brindle to stop.

Finally hearing Ted's voice above his rage, Booger Red went suddenly still. Standing over his victims, bull snot dripping on his foe, he bellowed a victory bawl or two, stomped a hoof, and was turning to leave when one of the men on the ground made a bad mistake. He moved. Once again, the bull head-butted that man, then bulldozed all three for several feet before giving their unconscious bodies a final toss. Stomping one last time, his hoof perilously close to an unconscious attacker's head, he then casually loped off, tail held high, bloody pieces of camouflage cloth streaming from his horns like Milady's scarf on her gallant knight's lance.

"Good bull," I cheered.

He stopped, turned his head my way, stuck his nose in the air and, I swear, took a bow.

Chapter 29

The wounded assailants, bound with rope, had been placed, none too gently, onto a wooden truck bed, then hauled off to the winery barn, since Nanci absolutely, positively refused the bastards a bed in her home.

She did, however, go along with rendering what first aid we could until a local doctor arrived, mainly because we all wanted them alive and explaining. When we went to check on the plane and get our belongings, all the battered men were still breathing and even letting out an occasional moan, but they were in sorry shape.

"What a freakin' mess," Ted lamented, pretty much summing up our day. "Well, at least the plane is undamaged, but can't say the same for your car, Hetta. And now we're gonna have to call the damned cops for sure, like it or not."

I know how much people hate sending for the law in Mexico, but it was unavoidable, whether the men who attacked us lived or died. If they live, what do you do with them? Likewise, if they die? Okay, you could bury them out in the desert, but in this case there were way too many witnesses.

"Since they tried to steal your plane," I said, "I doubt the police will be very sympathetic with them. Besides, it was Booger Red who attacked them, not us, and they did have automatic weapons."

"What automatic weapons?" Ted asked.

"The ones...oh, I see."

Jan didn't get it. "The ones they shot at us with."

Ted grinned. "Nope, never a shot fired. Not a hole anywhere on the plane, or elsewhere. We must have just imagined they had guns, right?"

Jan still looked puzzled. I think the shock of the incident left her unable to grasp subtleties. "Jan, Ted is right. No guns. There. Were. No. Guns."

Her frown finally relaxed. "Oh. Oh! Ted's keeping the guns, right?"

"Keeping what guns?"

A quick meeting was convened, all players in attendance except those guarding our captives and a couple of men posted along the road to guide the doctor, and make sure we didn't have any more unwelcome company.

Most of the Mexican workers looked to be in shock, none more than Sonrisa. She was literally quaking. I almost felt sorry for the tiny turd. Nanci put her arm around the little Indian and spoke softly in Spanish, reassuring her she was safe, the danger had passed.

Ted, having secured his plane in the hangar, joined us. He spoke in Spanish, with asides to Jan and me as necessary. The gist was that he was reluctantly calling in the law, so anyone who wanted to should scram before they arrived. He would stay put out of necessity, but Nanci, Jan, and I were to hightail it for Bisbee in Nanci's SUV, pronto. Anyone who chose to stay were not to answer questions from the authorities, but to refer all inquiries to him. From the looks of dismay on the workers' faces, Ted was going to be a very lonely guy for the next few days.

Sonrisa, once she understood that we three women were driving to the border, asked if we could drop her off in Naco to see her brother. Maybe she was smarter than I gave her credit for.

By the time we were loaded up and ready to roll, the doctor arrived. The would-be hijackers, conscious and belligerent, were pronounced by the doc fit enough to be beaten up by the police when they arrived. He then took a powder before the heat showed. Mexican police, it seems, are highly unpopular, avoided by both bad guys and the innocent alike.

Ted double-secured the hijackers with tie wraps and searched them. They carried no identification, and sullenly refused to talk, which, Ted assured us, would change with a little police brutality, Mexican style.

Before leaving for Bisbee, we drove to the end of the runway, peered over the bluff, and said a final farewell to what was left of my poor Volkswagen. Losing her was like losing my dog, RJ, all over again. Oh, how I longed for one more Sunday afternoon drive with him, his head hanging out the passenger window, splattering drool over cars behind us, and me with my window down in a futile attempt to dissipate seriously lethal dog farts, a direct result of our weekly Mexican food brunch.

We gals left Ted with the perps and a rapidly vaporizing employee pool.

We spoke little during the trip northward. I drove, because Nanci was too upset. We were almost to Cananea when we met two Mexican police cars, lights flashing, headed south, most likely for the winery. Sonrisa instinctively slid down in her seat, and Nanci ducked her head.

Nanci was rattled, worried about what would happen at the winery when the cops arrived, and fretting over the missing Rosa. Ted, as *patrón*, would be treated with more respect by the fuzz, but she also knew that others, the few men who loyally remained with Ted, would fall under a veil of suspicion in both Rosa's disappearance, and the attack by hijackers. In a country where everyone is considered guilty until proven innocent, is it any wonder witnesses are hard to come by?

On the other hand, justice is swift and evidence need not be too conclusive. For example, there was the case of the Canadian tourists who were robbed at gunpoint in a Puerto Vallarta park, and the perp was handily caught because he was "not from around here," and deemed guilty by virtue of the five-hundred peso note found in his pocket. Police were quick to point out that a man of his sort had no business with five hundred pesos. Case solved.

Sonrisa sat in the backseat with Nanci and never uttered a word the whole trip. I glanced at her in the rearview mirror a few times, sizing her up. Those eyes, black and, in my mind, snakelike, fit well with her pulled down lips and chiseled features. Stone carvings of her Mayan ancestors came to mind. Credit where credit is due, though, as shaken as she was immediately after witnessing the hijack attempt, she was now downright stoic, while I was still weak in the knees.

We dropped Sonrisa off near the church, then headed for the gateway to Heaven, or so the US border seemed to us. Eager to be on good old safe American soil, I pulled up next to the customs agent and was handing over our passports when all hell broke loose. Suddenly ordered from the car by yelling agents, we were quickly herded into that now all-too-familiar holding room and left, stunned, to puzzle out what went wrong.

"Damn, Hetta, think they realized who we are?"

Nanci tilted her head. "What the hell does that mean?"

"Oh, nothing, really. Jan and I had a little misunderstanding at this border before Christmas, but it was all cleared up."

"So you say," she said dryly, "I can't wait to hear this story."

I was recounting our bird smuggling incident when a female officer stuck her head in and told us we'd set off CBP'S PRD. In English, that's the Customs and Border Patrol officer's Personal Radiation Device, and we would be individually scanned. She left us more bumfuzzled than ever.

"Uh, Nanci, we did consume a lot of irradiated wine the past two days."

Nanci shook her head. "If that were the case, every baby in Mexico would set off the sensors. The milk is irradiated."

"Have you transported cobalt rods in your car?"

"Never."

The agents returned and escorted me to another room for further scanning, They were closemouthed, but since I didn't register as hot, I was taken outside. Nanci's SUV had been moved into an area normally reserved for trucks, so I assumed it, too, was being given a going-over on a larger scale.

Nanci was next to be released, but after another hour we still had not seen Jan. By now, Nanci's SUV was swarmed by all sorts of agents with mysterious instruments, then, as suddenly as we'd been detained, Jan appeared and we were all let go. Not ones to question freedom, we loaded up and hauled ass for my house.

Turns out, Jan forgot to get a note from her doctor.

"Let me get this straight, Jan," I said. "That nuclear stress test they gave you at the Mayo Clinic set off a Geiger counter, adding to our already impossibly crappy day?"

"Yep."

I rubbed my tired eyes. So far we'd been attacked by would-be hijackers, held as possible threats to national security, and then, to top it all off, locked out of my house. My garage door opener was still in my VW, now at the bottom of a cliff, and the front door key was inside the house, in a drawer, because I always entered through the garage. After a couple of false starts, however, I finally remembered the code for the garage door keypad and we got in.

Once in, Nanci placed calls to several high-ranking folks in Mexico City, apprised them of the hijacking attempt, and asked them to use their clout to help her and Ted out of this sticky situation. In Mexico, victims of crimes are held in high suspicion, no matter how innocent. If someone attacks you, they reason, you must have something to hide, otherwise, why would you be attacked?

We all took long hot showers, grabbed some wine and cheese, and headed for the verandah, where Nanci called Ted for an update. The police had, at first, bullied and hectored everyone in sight, but after a phone call originating from Mexico city, they turned downright solicitous. They hauled the bad guys off and promised to make inquiries about the missing Rosa.

Nanci laughed as she told us the story. "You know, I almost feel sorry for those thugs. They probably know nothing about Rosa, but by the time the cops get through with them, they'll make something up."

I had my own calls to make, namely to the prince and the Trob. Hmmm, sounds like the title to some new off-off-Broadway production. Maybe by now one of them knew where in hell Jenks got off to.

The Trob did not answer. In all the years I'd known him, this was a first.

I called Allison, his wife, my friend and sometimes lawyer. No answer.

I called the prince. Ditto.

Frustrated beyond belief, I let loose a primal scream, which of course scared the hell out of Nanci and Jan, who rushed in to find out what was wrong, then gave me a good cussing for the fright. I apologized and told them we all needed a good howl, so we headed for the verandah to do so.

Several late afternoon putters threatened us with great bodily harm, which we found hilarious.

Coyotes in the brush yipped answering calls. Neighborhood dogs responded in kind.

Blue trotted up for a treat, cocked his head at our howls, threw his bushy tail into the air, and sashayed off as if to say, "Someone around here needs a modicum of dignity."

We laughed, drank our wine, and howled ourselves silly in some kind of posttraumatic hysteria, until the cold drove us inside.

I turned on the fireplace, asked if anyone was hungry, but all agreed wine and more Brie was sufficient. Not a great idea, but by then we were way beyond good ideas.

The phone rang and I dove for it. "Hetta?"

"Trob?"

"Is she there yet?"

I tried to think, but wine overload has a way of making that difficult. She? Who?

"She? Who?"

"Allison."

"Your Allison?"

"Yes."

"Hang on for just a minute." I put down the phone, drank a large glass of water, thinking it might dilute some alcohol. Didn't work.

"Wontrobski, start over. Slowly, please."

"Is. Allison. There. Yet?"

This was beginning to have a who's on first Abbot and Costello flavor.

"You know, I can normally translate your language, no matter how esoteric, but help me out here. Where is Allison supposed to be?"

"She should be at your house by now."

"Why would—?"

The doorbell rang and Jan trilled, "Allison, what on earth are you doing here?"

"Ah've left Wontrobski."

"Trob?" I said into the phone.

"Yes."

"Yes," I said, leaving him with a good dose of his own cryptic medicine.

We hustled Allison before the fire for a grilling. Since she was several months preggers, she refrained from joining our quest to drink all the wine in the house, but she didn't seem to mind that we were half-past tipsy. I made her a cup of tea before we settled in to hear her story. More surprising to me than her marrying the Trob in the first place was that she'd now left him.

I waited until she took a sip of Earl Grey, then demanded, "Okay, what's wrong?"

"D-d-dubai," she blubbered.

Jan handed her a tissue. "*Gesundheit*."

"No, Dubai. He wants us to move there."

Now that was a shocker. Wontrobski, leave the city of San Francisco? My God, I can remember when he'd hardly leave the Baxter Brothers building. When I first met him, he worked eighteen hours a day, then walked a short distance to his hotel room. That was the sum total of his world. After he married Allison, however, he'd expanded his horizons slightly, but actually getting on an airplane? No way.

"Allison," I took her hand, "you can give us the details later, like when we're sober enough to remember them, but for now, I don't think you have a thing to worry about. Fidel Wontrobski will never, ever, board an airliner."

"You're right, he won't. They're gonna take us there on a big ship, along with everyone else. Baxter Brothers is moving their headquarters to Dubai." She suddenly looked alarmed. "Oh, crap. That's a major secret. You can't tell anyone, okay?"

Not tell anybody? She had to be kidding. I couldn't wait to get to the phone. First I'd go on line and buy all the stock I could afford, then call Dad and tell him to do the same. Then drop a dime to Fox, CNN, and all the rest. Delusions of riches garnered thanks to insider info danced in my head, and I counted my future fortune faster than you can say Martha Stewart. Okay, maybe that's not the best example, but I was calculating how much moola I could get my hands on to invest when Allison tapped my shoulder.

"Snap out of it, and forget what I said, okay?"

I crossed my fingers behind my back. "Sure, sure, Allison."

"I mean it, Hetta. I could go to jail for telling you about the move. And so could you if you do anything, like buy stock."

Is this woman a mind reader, or what? Rats. "I promise not to tell anyone or do anything to enrich myself. Is that good enough?"

"Uncross your fingers." Double rats.

I held out my hands. "All right, all right. I gather you do not wish to move to Dubai?"

"I told Fidel when I agreed to marry him that I never wanted to leave the Bay Area. I mean, I was even entertaining a run for mayor of San Francisco, until I got pregnant."

Jan took a sip and focused, with some difficulty, on Allison. "How did that happen?"

"Jan," I scolded, "don't you think that's just a little too personal?"

Jan spluttered a giggle. "Silly, I meant, how is it Allison almost ran for mayor?"

For that story, we decided to light a firepit and brave the chill to watch the last ray of the day fade behind the purple silhouetted Huachuca mountain range. Bundled into sweats, we crowded around the crackling firelog and listened as Allison gave a quick rundown on being approached by the local politicos who saw her as mayoral material, and she, flattered, almost went for it.

"Had they met your husband?" Somehow, I couldn't picture the Trob in a photo op, unless they were selling zoo tickets, since he closely resembles a buzzard. A loveable buzzard, but certainly not GQ material.

"Well, no. I kind of kept him under wraps. I think they thought, since he is a big wig at Baxter Brothers, I would appeal to both parties or something."

"Oh, gee, I didn't realize there was a Klingon Party in San Fran," I quipped, drawing appreciative cackles, even from Allison. "I thought they were all in Berkeley."

A golf cart skidded to a stop, and we, expecting to be shushed, were surprised to see the Xers gawking at us. They gave the new kid on the block, Allison, a look, but did not acknowledge our cockamamie greetings as they sped away.

"Who are they?" Allison asked.

"We're not sure, but Craig doesn't like them. Says they look like Black Muslims."

"Craig is right, they're creepy."

I stifled a yawn. Our day and too much wine was catching up with me. "Girls, I'm done. I'm going to get on the horn and try finding that damned Jenks one more time, then I'm hitting the hay."

Allison blinked. "Jenks? Didn't Fidel tell you?" Allison is probably the only person on the planet who calls the Trob by his first name.

"Tell me what?"

"Jenks won't answer his cell, because they worry about eavesdropping. God knows who might be listening. Hell, no one in Dubai can fart without some kind of electronic surveillance picking it up. Another reason not to go there."

"Dubai?"

"*Gesundheit.*"

"Shut up and drink your wine, Jan. Allison, are you telling me Jenks is in Dubai?"

"Oh, yes. He's front man for my husband. Since he's a private contractor, he can get stuff done without the Baxter Brothers thing getting out until they want it to. But if you ask me, it's a done deal."

"So, Jenks is safe and sound, in Dubai?" I punched a warning finger at Jan. She pouted.

Allison bobbed her head. "Yes, as far as I know."

"I am going to kill him. How dare he be safe."

Jan rose, slurred, "Atta girl, Hetta," and tottered into the house. I found her passed out in the very center of my bed, leaving me to bunk on the office daybed. Nanci and Allison took the guest room twins.

For such a big house, we were running low on bed space. Before I knew it, I'd be hanging out in the garage with Vinny, the vinegaroon. Craig's scary looking bug was evicted from the main house by popular demand, mainly mine, under threat of calling in the Critter Gitters. He now resided, on the loose, somewhere in the garage. Every time I parked, I expected a crunch and the smell of vinegar, but so far, so good, at least for Vinny.

Everyone drifted off to their rooms, and by the time I loaded the dishwasher with the day's collection of wine and water glasses, coffee and teacups, and various plates and flatware, my wine had worn off somewhat. I say somewhat, because I still had enough liquid courage left that I dared sending Jenks a scathing email threatening him with great bodily harm unless I heard from him, pronto.

I made up the daybed, got ready to get in it, checking email every few minutes to see if pronto had arrived. Nope. Finally I gave up and climbed between the sheets and was drifting off when I had a thought. Scrambling from the covers, I hopefully checked my SPAM file. Nothing from Jenks, but go figure, while my regular mail contained messages that I'd won the Irish Lottery and yet another Liberian wanted to marry me, it had slam-dunked an important message from someone with whom I was in constant contact into SPAM's file. I wanted to throttle SPAM, whoever he is.

The Trob's message, dated the day before, told me that Jenks was safe and sound in an undisclosed location, and he'd call me as soon as he could. Oh, and Allison was on her way to my house.

Ain't cyberland grand? Here we are, in an era of instant communication and my email goes walkabout?

Annoyed no end, I went back to bed, but my head hardly touched the pillow again before the phone rang. Untangling myself, then tripping on sheets in the process and falling onto the bed, I finally managed to corral the phone. Surely, if there is a God, She had Jenks on the line.

"Hetta?"

Not Jenks. Prince Faoud. "Hi, Prince."

"You are well?"

"Depends on how you look at things," I said, rubbing a place on my knee that collided with a desk corner during my dive for the phone. "Someone stole my car, then brought it back full of masked, armed, men who tried to hijack a plane I was on, then my car went off a bluff, and the car we drove home in was radioactive. How's everything with you?"

"Are you jesting me again?"

"I wish." Several pieces of information suddenly, like a Rubik's Cube, fell into place. "You aren't, by any chance, in Dubai, are you?"

"How did you know that? As a matter of fact, that is why I called. I am on a secure line and I have your friend, Jenks, with me."

"Oh, hell. Don't tell him what I just said."

"Too late, Hetta," Jenks said. "You're on speaker."

"I'm not speaking to you."

"You left a message for me to call."

"Prince Faoud, would you please tell Jenks I asked him to call so I could not speak to him. I am very angry with Mr. Jenkins. I've been worried sick about him while he's playing around in the lap of luxury in Dubai. He's probably at that big hotel that looks like a ship and costs a small fortune to stay in."

"Prince Faoud, would you please tell Hetta that I am indeed at the Buri Al Arab, but in your private suite. So what's with the armed masked guys? Hijacked airplanes? She promised to stay out of trouble."

"Prince Faoud, please cover your ears."

Chapter 30

Jan and I, the first ones up, drank coffee in the courtyard, letting Allison and Nanci sleep in. It was freezing outside, but we'd wrapped ourselves in blankets and lit a fire. Whoever built the house planned well, as both the south and north sides had fire pits, and the courtyard caught the morning sun, making it an ideal place to greet even the chilliest of days.

As the sun, fire, and coffee warmed us, Jan shook her head at me. "Ya know, Hetta, you've outdone yourself this time. If Jenks forgives you for that tongue lashing you gave him last night, it'll be a freakin' miracle. You should just be grateful he's safe. Nobody blows up anything in Dubai."

"You were supposed to be passed out, not eavesdropping."

"I needed a glass of water. God, will I never learn? I feel like crap, and will for the rest of the day."

"Soon as Allison and Nanci get up, we'll go have a big old Mexican breakfast that'll set you straight. I know a place where they serve menudo every day, instead of just weekends."

"Anyone for breakfast?" Allison chirped as she sauntered into the courtyard. "I'm starving."

"Think you can handle a bowl of menudo on the table, what with your delicate condition?"

"Menudo? Are you kidding? I love menudo. "

"Did I hear menudo?" Nanci asked, joining us. "Please, take me to it."

Four steaming bowls of tripe and hominy soup arrived at our table not a moment too soon for me. After dumping chopped onions, basil, and cilantro into the pungent concoction touted by Mexicans as the ultimate hangover cure, we chowed down as though we had not been fed for at least a month.

Conversation dropped to nil, superseded by slurping and moans of rapture. Nanci and Jan had a beer with theirs, but the idea of alcohol in any form made my stomach jump.

Also messing with my tummy was recollecting my rant at Jenks the night before. I simply have to learn not to spew when I'd had a few. Chewing on a tortilla wrapped around a delightfully rubbery piece of tripe, I tried to recall if I'd said anything I couldn't fix.

"Hetta, you look like a cow chewing cud," Jan said. "Don't look so worried, you probably didn't do any permanent damage. I think Jenks knew it was your fear for him driving that little hissy."

"Think so?"

"Yeah," Allison added, "he should be able to tell the difference by now."

"I've said much worse to Ted," Nanci chimed in. "I mean, at least you didn't insult his manhood or anything like that."

Was everyone listening in on my very private conversation last night? I had to get a bigger house, or fewer friends.

My cell phone rang. Hoping for Jenks, I snapped it up and answered without checking caller ID.

"Hetta? Hetta? Can you hear me?"

"Craig? Yes, I hear you, but you're breaking up."

"Bus, Naco around three. Okay?"

"What? Did you say—" the phone went dead.

"That was Craig? How's he liking the Baja?"

"Not. Best I can figure, he'll be in Naco this afternoon. Didn't we just get rid of him?"

"Yes, we did, like three days ago. What's up?"

"Not sure, but I'll drive to the border this afternoon, just in case he shows. I can't for the life of me figure out what he's doing back here so soon."

Jan stretched and patted her disgustingly flat stomach. "Who knows? What I do know is, I need an aspirin and a nap."

Nanci decided to go shopping in Sierra Vista while Jan took her nap. That left Allison and me with time to kill before fetching Craig.

"So Allison, want the big tour? We can check out a few shops in Historic Bisbee. Maybe you can score some Bisbee Blue for your hubby."

"He can get his own damned turquoise. I'm seriously angry with him and may never go back."

"You're pregnant, you have to go back."

"Some feminist you are."

This was a discussion I didn't want to get into, so I shooed her out to the garage after a warning for her to watch where she walked, lest she squash Craig's vinegarroon.

I figured, since Craig wanted me to pick him up, we'd use his car. It'd be a tight fit, but if push came to shove, I'd walk the two miles to the house from the border.

After hitting both sides of Main Street in Historic Bisbee, Allison dropped almost two grand on a painting, another five hundred on a piece of jewelry, and bought a case of killer bee honey. I trailed along, acting as pack mule.

A little before Craig was to arrive, we headed for downtown Naco, Arizona. All one block of it. We didn't have our passports with us, so we waited on the U.S. side for him. He'd only have a short walk from the bus station, which shouldn't be a big deal, what with that new healthy bod.

While we waited by the pedestrian crossing into Mexico so we could see Craig when he walked to the border, a stream of kids flooded the turnstile, headed into Mexico after their school day in the United States. Some came by bus from Bisbee's high school, others walked from the elementary school in Naco, Arizona.

"What's with this?" Allison wanted to know. "Don't they have schools in Mexico?"

"Yep, but a lot of these kids are actually American citizens, and prefer the educational system here. Why, I'll never know. Look, our friendly neighborhood Farrakhan brothers." I pointed out a yellow Jeep waiting in line on the Mexico side.

"Those guys from the golf cart last night?"

"That be them. Like I said, there's something shady about them."

Allison snorted. "What was your first clue, detective? That they were wearing bow ties on the golf course, with no clubs in the cart?"

The Jeep disappeared from view behind a Customs building, then emerged on the other side and rolled right past us. The men never looked in our direction.

"Hetta, Hetta, Hetta," Allison said with a disapproving look, and a shake of her head. "After all these years, you're still a Honky at heart."

"What? What did I say?"

"Ain't what you said, Grey Girl. For crap's sake, do you truly think we all look alike?"

I was totally confused. Did Allison believe I was prejudiced against these guys because they were black? I was trying to come up with an answer when she broke out laughing and I realized she was messing with me.

"Not funny, Mrs. Wontrobski. You know I'm not like that."

"Sorry, sweetie, I'm just yanking your chain. Truth is, anyone could make the same mistake."

"What mistake? What are you talking about?"

"Those guys. They are not the same two as in the golf cart last night. Both dressed alike, bowties, same haircut, and sunglasses. Close, but no cigar."

"Different men?"

"One of them was in that cart, but the other guy? No way. Hell, he's African."

"How do you know?"

"I'm African-American, remember? I know a real African when I see one. Don't ask me how, exactly, but I can tell the difference. It's a matter of posture, for one thing, and the shape of his head and his profile. He ain't homogenized, as I call it. Trust me, he is not from around here."

I started the car.

"Hey, where we going?" she asked. "Aren't we gonna wait for Craig?"

"He can hoof it. Do him good, and Jan is home to let him in. I want to see where this Jeep is headed."

"Why?"

"I don't know, exactly. Just nosy, I guess."

Within five minutes, we were in the RV park, but I didn't turn right, to where I knew the Xer's RV was. I circled slowly behind a line of oversized diesel pushers with enough slide outs to qualify as Transformers, and that would cover us from view. I got out and inched past an RV to check out the Jeep, but by then it was empty.

"I guess they went inside. So, if that guy is new, are there three of them now? When Craig gets here he won't be pleased with that news. Speaking of whom, I guess we can backtrack to the border, see if he's on his way to the house." I left the way we came, hopefully without getting spotted from the RV. As far as I knew, they didn't know Craig's car, but who knew anything by now? Why these men made my danger neurons jangle, I wasn't sure, but I'd somehow have to follow up on their claim of testing San Pedro river water.

We were halfway to the border when I spotted Craig walking alongside the highway, and he was not alone.

"Uh-oh," I mumbled.

"Uh-oh?"

"Yes, Allison, big uh-oh. See that guy with Craig?"

"What guy with Craig? I don't even see Craig."

"He's right...oh, I forgot. You haven't seen him in some time. There, my dear, is the new and improved hunk, Dr. Craig, no longer Craigousaurus."

"Wow. Ditto that wow. Who is that with him, speaking of hunks."

"That would be Doctor Brigido Comacho Yee. A.k.a. Chino."

"Jan's Doctor Chino?"

"The one and only. She's not gonna be happy with this house call."

I walked home with Chino so I could grill him, and Craig drove Allison.

Chino was anxious to have Jan back into his life, he said, even if it meant giving up his whales and getting a real job. He sounded genuinely sincere, if not enthused with riding a desk or heading a lab at some university. He made it sound as though earning big bucks instead of living on the beach was tantamount to jumping off the Golden Gate Bridge, but for her, he'd do it.

I took a neutral stance on the matter, neither taking her side, or his. Let them sort it out, I decided. I had my own troubles, which multiplied exponentially as we neared my house.

A shiny blue, 1997 Lincoln Town car with Texas plates was parked at a strange angle in the drive area. I knew the year and model, because I remembered when it was new. Cacophonous prattle, along with a whiff of bourbon, wafted over the courtyard wall, raking my already alcohol-shocked nerves worse than fingernails on a chalkboard. *No, please, don't let it be.*

But it was.

My least favorite aunt in the world, Lillian, held court in my courtyard, surrounded by my friends. Jan, who for some reason actually likes the old bag, shot me a smirk, but I got the last laugh when I pulled Chino through the gate. Jan's smirkiness vanished, replaced first by shock, then a menacing glower.

"There you are, Hetta darlin'," cawed Aunt Lil. "I've been enjoying your delightful new friends and, of course, it's always a pleasure to see little Jan."

"Aunt Lil," I said, dully.

Little Jan's face had turned a light shade of purple. Fists balled, she took two fierce steps toward Chino, who innocently held his arms wide. Disarmed, Jan dissolved in tears, whirled, and fled into the house.

Everyone except Aunt Lil, who was sucking on a flask and oblivious to anything else, gave the crestfallen Chino sympathetic looks. A heavy, embarrassed pall fell on the group until Auntie Lil broke the silence. "Oh, by the way, Hetta, you really shouldn't keep pets. First you lose my parrot, and now, well, your dog...." She raised a disapproving eyebrow.

"I did not lose your parrot. Trouble has a happy home on a ranch in Baja where...my what?"

"Your dog, dearie. You shouldn't let him run loose. After all, there are surely dangerous creatures in this godforsaken desert."

Auntie dear, I am the most dangerous creature in this godforsaken desert where you are concerned, I wanted to say, but then realized what she'd just said. "Dog?"

My aunt shook her head in disgust. "Really, niecey dear, I sometimes wonder about you. I mean, you are supposed to be such a smart girl, and then you…." Again, she let her sentence hang. My aunt is the queen of the dangling insult.

I wanted to hang her. No, that would be too fast. How about thirty years in the electric chair? Or perhaps tied to a railroad track? Or—

Lillian interrupted that train of thought. "Anyway, just so you know, I let the poor thing into the house."

Jan's bloodcurdling scream brought us all to our feet.

Blue, who left a trail of scat everywhere we chased him, was finally corralled in the office. I ran out another door onto the verandah, opened the gate to the golf course, then threw open the outside office door and made a wild leap for the top of the three-foot high pony wall. I barely made it before a snarling, snapping, crapping, Blue bolted onto the verandah, shot me what can only be interpreted as a furious glare, and headed for freedom.

I wanted to go with him.

Chapter 31

Soon after Blue's huffy departure, Ted called and said he was on his way up. Allison opted to go with Nanci to the Bisbee airport to get him.

Chino coaxed Jan from my bedroom, where she had taken refuge, and they went for a walk.

Aunt Lil passed out on a chaise lounge in the courtyard, leaving Craig and me to square away the mess of her making.

Craig was used to cleaning up animal crap, but I was hung over and had to take a couple of timeouts lest I toss last night's wine.

Finally done with poop, Craig and I collapsed on the verandah, me with a large glass of wine, he with a diet coke. Blue slinked up to his usual spot, looking as sheepish as a coyote can. I threw him a dog biscuit despite the mess he'd left us. After all it wasn't his fault he'd been trapped in the house.

As I recounted the runway terrorist story to Craig, Jan and Chino returned. Both were smiling.

Ted, Nanci and Allison arrived from the airport, Ted and Nanci looking like their dog died. "What's wrong now?" I wanted to know. "Somebody else disappear on you?"

Ted shook his head. "No, more like some*thing*. I hate to admit it, but it looks like Rosa took an entire container of cobalt rods with her when she left."

"Why on earth would she do that?"

"They are worth quite a bit of money to other farms that irradiate milk, fruit, and the like. She can sell them for enough to go home to Southern Mexico and buy a house. I guess we didn't realize she was unhappy."

Nanci huffed, "I just cannot believe Rosa would do something like this, Ted."

Ted shrugged. "You may have to. There doesn't seem to be any other explanation. She's gone, she was the last one with the rods."

Nanci sighed. "I still—"

The doorbell rang. I worked my way past the building pile of luggage and opened the door to find a scowling property manager.

"Oh, hi," I said, looking past him at my aunt sprawled in a lounge chair, arms wrapped around her flask, snoring like a trucker. I could smell the bourbon fumes from the doorway.

"Miss Coffey, may I come in for a minute?"

Reluctantly, I eased the door open. He wound his way through the duffel bags and suitcases, and followed me onto the verandah. I introduced him. Barely masking hostility, he asked if we could talk in private, so we moved to the office, where I noticed the lingering scent of coyote scat.

He sniffed the air and glared at me, not noticing that Allison had slipped into the hall behind him. "Miss Coffey, it has come to my attention that you have an inordinate amount of people living here."

"Oh, no. Not really. These are just friends from out of town who have dropped in. All at once."

"So they are all staying with you?"

"Is that a problem?"

"Your lease. You rented this place as a single woman, no pets. I came by earlier and heard the distinct howling of a dog, and now I count at least six other people."

"Oh, that wasn't a dog, it's my coyote."

He stood, shook his head, and said, "I suggest you find another place to live within the next two weeks."

"You're evicting me?"

"That's putting it a little harshly. I am requesting you find other accommodations."

"Yeah, well accommodate this. Get out of my house."

Allison sidled up beside him and shoved a business card into his hand. "Mr. Property Manager, we'll be looking over that lease this evening, and you can expect to hear from one of my Arizona associates no later than tomorrow afternoon. Meanwhile, you might want to reconsider threatening your tenant."

He looked at the card, huffed, "Lawyers," and slammed the door, unfortunately waking Aunt Lil. Not one to take her snoozing lightly, she let the fleeing agent have a hearty dose of Texas vitriol.

I almost liked her for a moment there.

It was decided Aunt Lillian, for what I insisted was a one-night only stay, have the single fold out couch in the office. Nanci and Ted moved into my bedroom, Craig got the living room couch, while Jan, Allison, and I grabbed the two twins and sofa in the guest room. Chino, accustomed to sleeping on beaches, opted for a bedroll on the dining room floor. Blue was not invited back in.

Something had to give. I've lived alone most of my adult life, and having anyone around other than Jan, and she for short spurts, puts me into a seriously grouchy mood. Jan knows this, and was warily tippytoeing around me the next morning as I sulked and sipped coffee in the courtyard sun.

"So," she ventured, "what're you gonna do?"

"Drink this coffee, get a gun, and murder everyone in their sleep. How's that sound?"

"Okay by me, since I'm up. Start with Chino."

I smiled, despite my ennui. "Let's go find breakfast before everyone wakes up. It could save their lives."

"Done."

We walked to the golf club, dead set on glomming onto breakfast enchiladas in peace, but it was not to be. We'd barely settled into our chairs in the dining room when the entirety of my household descended upon us.

Reluctantly shoving two tables together, I ordered a bloody Mary to calm my nerves, which was a mistake, as Aunt Lillian requested a double. Two sips later she was slurring her words.

As if my teeth weren't already on edge, halfway through our meal the Xer's sauntered in, gave our motley crew a once over, said, "Good morning Hetta, Doctor, Sister."

Allison looked puzzled. "Did he just call me Sister?" she whispered.

"No, that was Jan."

"Jan's no sister, she's white."

"It's a long story. Later."

Probably because I barely acknowledged the Xers, one of them sneered and said, "My, Red, your entourage just grows and grows."

"And yours changes," I shot back, drawing a look of alarm from Allison. Obviously startled by my reply, the Xer's exchanged a look, ordered sandwiches to go, and headed out, presumably to test river water.

"That wasn't real smart, Hetta," Allison said after they left.

Craig wanted to know what was up, Allison told him about one of the Xers coming across the border with what looked to be the other, but who wasn't.

"Interesting," he said. "Think they pulled a switcheroo on the border guys? That's pretty hard to do, but I guess we really do all look alike. This place is starting to get really small, with way too many coincidences. For instance, what about the Xers giving Sonrisa a lift the other day? And that guy from the mine, Rat Face, paying a visit to the Xers's RV. Curiouser and curiouser."

Ted looked up from his eggs at the mention of Sonrisa. "I don't know anything about someone named Rat Face, but I think I need to have a talk with Sonrisa. Her hitchhiking with just anyone could be damned dangerous. Matter of fact, when I called the winery this morning, the foreman reported she hasn't returned."

"Well, Ted," Nanci said, "she was pretty shaken up by the attempted hijacking. She's spending time with her brother. We can drive over the line and look for them if you like."

"Nah, we have to get home early, we have a replacement shipment for the rods we think Rosa took, but I won't need Sonrisa until the install. I'd just as soon she stay with her brother for now, what with all the excitement at the winery. And since we are flying back, please, Hetta, feel free to use our car since yours is, er, out of commission."

"That's an understatement," I growled. "That VW just flat ran out of lives. I've revived her for the last time, so don't even bother pulling her up the cliff. I would appreciate it, though, if someone could retrieve my papers and the garage door opener. I'm already in hot water with the rental agent, so he'll probably stick it to me for a new opener."

Allison chirped, "Should have left that VW dead the last time it took a plunge, but nooo, you had to spend a fortune on barnacle removal."

Ted, Nanci, and Aunt Lil knew nothing of my VW's dunk in the Oakland Estuary, so my so-called friend filled them in, adding rude comments on my folly. As soon as I could, I changed the topic to Ted and Nanci's winery, the beauty of its surroundings, and especially the fantastically stocked wine cellar, in an attempt to set a verbal trap.

Aunty Lil bit, hook, line, and sinker, and finagled an invite. Then, at my ever so clever suggestion, Craig and Chino volunteered to drive the threesome to the airport and then deliver Nanci's car to the winery.

Presto chango, back to only two guests, which improved my state of mind considerably.

"Pretty slick, Hetta," Jan said as we later watched the sun sink in the west. "Pretty slick, indeed. Now you just have to figure out how to get rid of Allison and me."

"Yeah," Allison agreed, "you missed your calling. You shoulda been a lawyer."

"And you shoulda used birth control," I grumbled.

"Hell, how was I to know my husband, and by the way, your boyfriend, would abandon us like this."

"Us? Oh, that's right, there's two of you there."

"No, *us*, as in you and me, Hetta. Let's face it, unless we move to Dubai, we are being left. Pure and simple."

"Can I take my boat?"

"I think not."

"Well, then, I ain't going."

"Ya know, Hetta," Jan drawled, "so far as I know, no one has asked you."

I seriously wanted to throttle her.

Chapter 32

Jan was, of course, annoyingly correct. No one, namely Jenks, asked me to move to Dubai. Not that I wanted to go, mind you, but giving me the chance to turn him down would reap untold satisfaction on my part. Men are *so* difficult.

"Hetta," Jan said, walking out into the dark courtyard where I brooded while stargazing, "truth is, you didn't give Jenks a chance to 'splain himself. I think you owe him an apology."

"Like you do Chino?"

"Truce. Let's face it, we're just not good at this man thing. Maybe we should join the Sisters of Perpetual Poverty."

"I made them up."

"Then let's start our own order. How about Sisters of Perpetual Indulgence? Oh, wait, that one is taken by those gay guys, dressed as pregnant nuns, wheeling around San Francisco on roller skates."

"Ah, San Francisco. You know, Old Bisbee has that sort of flare going for it, in an artsy way."

"Craig says he might move here. Evidently they need more local vets, and especially a large animal mobile unit."

"Ted said he'd stay busy on both sides of the border, so why not? Shoot, maybe he and Chino should set up shop together."

"Not unless they can find a whale up here in the desert. Chino will never give them up for anything, including me."

"Don't be so sure. Look, the man has money, so tell him to build you a suitable abode on the beach. One with electricity and hot water. Would that get you back? I love you dearly, but you cannot stay here forever, living off my largess."

"You don't have any largess, unless you count your butt."

"Hey, watch it, Sister."

"What's so funny? Allison asked, stretching and yawning as she emerged from an afternoon siesta. "And what's for dinner?"

"We're thinking Mexican, or Gus the Greek for pizza or gyros."

"You're thinking that, Hetta," Jan said. "I'm thinking a nice healthy salad. It'll be good for that large*ass* of yours."

Alison cocked her head. "Huh?"

"You had to be here. Hetta and I were just discussing how she's going to get rid of me. Us."

"Was not."

"Was too. And she's right, I need some direction."

"How about West?" I suggested. "As in, you and Allison get in her car and drive to the Bay Area?"

They exchanged a look. "Allison, I do believe we are being asked to leave Hetta's not-so-humble abode."

"No, I am simply suggesting a reality check. I am the only one here with a job, I need to get back to it, and you two, on the other hand, seem to be at loggerheads. Maybe if you go home you can both become useful members of society. How's that for a concept?"

"That gets rid of us, but what are you gonna do when auntie, Craig, and Chino return?"

"Chino can go count his whales, Craig'll get his own place, and Aunt Lil? I could just shoot the old bitch and feed her to the buzzards, but I value buzzards far too much."

"Such familial loyalty." Jan's voice dripped sarcasm. "That's our Hetta. We can always count on her when the chips are down."

"Yeah," Allison agreed. "And to think of all the times I've given her free legal advice."

Jan nodded. "And the tight spots I've helped her out of. All those Hetta-made man disasters. And where did she go when her dog died? My house, and for way too long. Does ungrateful wretch unkindly describe her?"

"Hey, you two. *Her* can hear you."

Allison and Jan made themselves scarce the next day, probably hoping for a reprieve on their upcoming eviction.

Enjoying my own company for a change, I made extra coffee, took it outside into the sunshine, determined to read my morning paper in peace. Sighing with contentment, I took a sip of dark, rich Colombian and spat it all over the morning's lead story. Moving quickly into the house, I locked the door and turned on the alarm. Only then did I sit down and finish reading the coffee-spattered news.

Cochise County Couple Assaulted by Mexican Gang

Bisbee: An elderly man called 9-1-1 Wednesday to report he and his wife had been the victims of a vicious home invasion.

The man, whose identity is being held for his own protection, said four hooded men, who spoke only Spanish to each other, broke down their front door, bound and gagged them, then carved Z's into both his and his wife's foreheads. After further terrorizing them with a machete, one man told them, in English, that they were never again to report activities on their land to the Border Patrol.

Just days earlier, the same couple had called authorities after spotting a group of a dozen or so suspected illegal immigrants crossing their pasture. Border Patrol responded and apprehended seven men, all Mexican citizens, and several bales of marijuana. The coyotes, or human smugglers, are still at large.

This incident raises new fears among border residents that the Mexican drug cartels, using gangs such as the Zetas as enforcers, are becoming emboldened by what many see as a serious lack of border protection.

The sheriff warned, in a CNN interview last month, "When aliens cross that fence, more likely than not, they're in someone's backyard. Now, it may be a two-thousand acre backyard, or maybe a two-hundred-square-foot backyard, but it's still *my* backyard, and you don't have a right to be there without my permission. There really is a cauldron here."

ter·ror·ism (tĕr'ə-rĭz'əm) n. The unlawful use or threatened use of force or violence by a person or an organized group against people or property with the intention of intimidating or coercing societies or governments, often for ideological or political reasons.

Or drugs and money?

Now that it was in *my* backyard, terrorism had a whole new meaning, and I was properly terrorized.

I unpacked my guns Craig brought me from Jenks's apartment in Oakland.

After cleaning and loading the weapons, I placed them strategically around the house, then finally settled down enough to get some work done. If I was going to have to leave the area for fear of retaliation by drug thugs, I wanted to get as much done as possible before I was forced to head for a hideout.

I put a chicken on to grill slowly, and by the time Jan and Allison returned with a load of goat cheese, fresh veggies, fruit and an apple pie, I was cheered a bit. We ate, drank, and discussed our futures. I didn't mention that mine might be a tad on the short side.

Allison wisely decided it was time to go home, after all, and face down the Trob over the move to the Middle East, but Jan was still unsure what she wanted to be when she grew up.

After a good night's sleep, Allison packed up and left for California, while Jan and I drove Craig's snazzy car to Sierra Vista so I could buy some wheels. I was thinking along the lines of a pickup with an extended cab, and a camper shell. Since becoming a boat owner, hauling stuff became a necessity, especially back and forth to Mexico. Also, I could sleep in it while on the lam.

We'd met the owner of a Sierra Vista car agency who keeps his boat in San Carlos. Love the yacht's name, *Deal Maker*. At the time I met Sean, it never occurred to me I'd need a car anytime soon, but now Jan and I headed for his lot.

We said our hellos, he fixed me up with a salesman, and after a couple of hours I zeroed in on a five-year-old Ford Ranger just like my dad's. The standard transmission adds enough zip to pass a Mexican truck, and there's plenty of room inside the camper shell for hauling the ubiquitous stuff. Or sleeping. Now came the hard part: paying for it.

The salesman eyed Craig's fancy wheels with admiration and asked, hopefully, "Got a trade-in?"

"Not unless you have a tow truck you can send to Mexico and drag my old car up a cliff."

He smiled uncertainly, wondering if he'd been wasting his time on some kind of nut case. Writing something down, he said, "So, no trade in."

"Nope. Look, I need transportation, this pickup will do the job, and if we can work together, I'd like to drive it home today. So, you think about your best offer while we go to lunch."

Not wanting to let a live one get away, he hastily offered to join us, but we demurred. Spending over ten grand on a used car needed a little thought, and a quick check of the Internet for Blue Book comps. He took a copy of my California driver's license, my social security number for a credit check, and promised to do the math before we returned.

We went to the Sierra Vista Library café for lunch, where I fired up my computer on their wi-fi and checked comps for the pickup while downing a feta cheese, sun-dried tomato, and Greek olive panini. The online Kelly Blue Book gave me more confidence in my impending purchase.

For all my other less than lovable idiosyncrasies, I do carefully maintain an excellent credit score, but not having a permanent residence in Arizona was bound to raise a red flag. Thinking it might help with the financing, we went to the DMV, where I intended to put in an application for an Arizona driver's license.

Miracle of miracles, I walked out twenty minutes later, slightly shell-shocked, with a new Arizona license in hand.

"Have we entered a new frontier of some sort?" Jan asked.

I waved my driver's license. "This would have taken a whole day in California. That's it. I am formally divorcing the Golden State, and embracing the Grand Canyon State. I hereby declare myself a full-fledged Zonie."

In another swift miracle, two hours later Jan was driving Craig's car while I followed in my brand new, to me, Ford Ranger extended cab pick-em-up truck. Red.

All it needed was a gun rack, which I fully intended to get, even though I'd remove it when crossing the border, lest the Mexicans get a bug up their ass, even sans the gun.

Jeez, the one place you really need a gun, and you can't take one.

Chapter 33

As the owner of new snazzy wheels, and a newly minted Arizona driver's license, I was pretty jazzed.

We stopped at the Second Amendment gun store in Bisbee, where I found the perfect truck accessory, a gun rack. I also bought more ammo, in case the five hundred rounds I had at the house were no match for drug cartel thugs.

Jan was in front of me as we entered the drive, and she suddenly slammed on the brakes. I almost rear-ended Craig's Porsche, but managed to stop inches from his extremely expensive bumper. Shaken, I made a mental note to get more insurance coverage, pronto.

We both got out of our cars and descended on the problem. Parked next to Aunt Lillian's blue tank, blocking the garage, was another leviathan, this one a shiny black Cadillac the size of Dallas and sporting Texas plates. A skinny dude about a hundred years old, wearing a hat bigger than the rest of him, sat on the fender. What now?

Closer up, the man's eyes sparkled like bright blue marbles, twinkling at me from a face resembling a cabbage patch doll that was left out in the sun too long. He whipped off his Stetson, revealing a surprisingly thick patch of curly white hair with that pink tinge suggesting he was a former redhead. He gave us a polite tip of his head and said, "I come fer Lil as soon as I got out."

Got out? Jan and I exchanged a glance. "And you would be? " I asked.

"Oh, pardon, ma'am. Name's Fred."

Ah, Mexico Man. I'd spent a little time trying to track him and my aunt down the year before, when the lovebirds headed south of the border and my mother was worried about them. I knew why she'd worry about poor ole Fred, but Aunt Lillian? Puh-leeze.

But, didn't mother tell me Fred dumped Aunt Lillian, then rechecked himself into rehab at the same Texas VA hospital where my aunt finds all of her prospective hubbies? As a retired nurse, she volunteers at what my dad calls the drunk tank, and there seems to be a cadre of over-indulged veterans who, to my mind, must be damned desperate for a wife. Or, in my aunt's case, dying for a wife.

Four of her five husbands called it taps after a short period of wedded bliss. My father said they sobered up, saw who they married, and died of fright. My mother, bless her kind heart, insists my aunt married men who needed a nurse in their last few months or years on earth. If you ask me, though, checking a guy out of rehab, then taking him on a drunken spree borders on manslaughter, at best.

This man seemed way too nice, and sober, for Lillian, but who am I to judge? Even though I just did.

Jan and I introduced ourselves.

"Oh, I'd know you anywhere, Hetta. Your aunt told me all about you." Fred's demeanor spoke volumes as to what he'd been told. I half expected him to whip out a crucifix and brandish it in my face.

"Aunt Lillian is not here," I told him, not planning to expand upon that statement.

Jan expanded for me. "She's in Mexico."

I thought about backhanding her, but then had an epiphany. "Yeah, Mexico. Come on in, and I'll draw you a map where you can find her. You can be there before dark if you leave now."

Jan gave me a look of admiration. We had worried for two days that the auntie from hell might return, but now we'd dump her on Fred, who actually seemed to want her. I felt a little guilty about sending him to his ultimate fate at the hands of my aunt, and for fobbing him off on Ted and Nanci unannounced, but Chino and Craig were still down there in case there was a ruckus, so where's the harm?

"Pure genius," Jan said as we watched the sun set. She tossed Blue a cookie.

"It's a gift."

She looked at her watch. "Fred should be there. Whaddya bet the phone rings right about," the phone rang, "now. You gonna answer it?"

"No way. I'll check caller ID later. Better yet, let's go listen to the answering machine."

We reached the office just in time to hear the end of a sentence that must have been a doozy. "...never see a cent of my money, you ungrateful little shit," caterwauled Auntie Lil.

"Looks like you're out of the will again, Hetta."

"I've been in and out of her will so many times I could qualify as an executioner in Imperial China."

"Huh?"

"Death of a thousand cuts. It was a form of slow torture."

"Kinda like creeping normalcy. You know, when something bad is slowly introduced so it isn't perceived as negative?"

"Yep, the frog in cold water analogy. He doesn't realize he's gonna get boiled because the heat is turned up gradually."

"I'd say you're, once again, boiled. Dang, looks like we'll have to keep working. I was counting on you becoming an heiress."

"Aunt Lil doesn't even have that much dough. She forgets that a few years ago, when she had just buried hubby number three, or was it four? Anyway, she asked me to help her with her finances. Of course, she had been on a two-week bender, so as soon as she sobered up she once again wrote me out of the will, this time for meddling in her affairs. She had maybe a hundred grand, and that little house on the lake. None of these guys she marries ever has any money, but they do have small insurance policies, so she sort of keeps an even keel, but my guess is she'll outlive her money."

"Not the way she puts away the booze."

"Amazing, isn't it? She's never really sick, except when she has the VO flu. Every time she ends up in the hospital it's because of overdosing on prescription drugs and booze. Being a nurse, she can always fake something else, and she keeps changing doctors, so no one ever calls her on it."

We fell into silence, sipping our wine. My thoughts turned dismal. Was this my future? An old drunk, so desperate for companionship that I'd marry every dude who expressed an interest? Not if I could help it. Unlike my aunt, I had no intention of making the same mistake over and over again, expecting a different outcome.

I stood suddenly, pitched my wine, glass and all, into the desert, marched into the office, and called Jenks.

I regretted throwing away my wine almost immediately because Jenks didn't answer. Not knowing what to say, I didn't leave a message.

Back on the verandah, Jan grinned and pointed to my wine glass on the cart path, which, by some miracle didn't break. Blue was lapping up Pinot Grigio with the gusto of a skid row bum.

"Wonder what PETA would say about you contributing to the delinquency of the wildlife?" Jan drawled. She'd already gotten me another wine.

"Or you contributing to my delinquency? I'm on the wagon."

She guffawed.

Reformation is not my long suit.

To my credit, I drank water with dinner, but I was on pins and needles, hoping for a call from Jenks.

"You're as jumpy as a prawn on a Teppanyaki griddle," Jan told me. "Simmer down and eat your lasagna. It is your last indulgence for at least a week."

"What do you mean?"

"South Beach Diet, remember? We start tomorrow."

"Crap. When did I agree to that?"

"You don't remember?"

"It must have slipped my mind."

She grinned and I wondered if I really had agreed to the diet. The woman can be sooo sneaky. I sighed and stared at the phone.

"What'd you say when you called him earlier?"

"Nothing. No answer."

"You didn't even leave a message?"

"Nope."

"Moron."

On that sweet note of encouragement, I loaded the dishwasher, set the alarm, and went to bed. Jan watched a documentary on Animal Planet, not about whales. I was still reading when she turned off the TV.

I doused my reading lamp, but lay awake, gazing at the stars and listening to coyotes sing. One of them crooned with a distinctive warble I recognized as Blue's. He was badly off-key, probably thanks to Pinot Grigio.

There's a lesson there.

As I lay awake listening to Blue's alcoholic croon, Jan's comment about creeping normalcy niggled at me. What about my life, my situation, whatever, had become so normal to me, when others saw it otherwise?

Living on a boat is unconventional, but hardly abnormal. I take on less than traditional projects, but someone has to do it. Some of those jobs involve off-beat characters, but does that make me an off-beat character?

I guess the big question is, am I a frog in the heating water, unaware of impending doom if I don't bail?

All of this profundity left me tossing long into the night, until I finally drifted off around two, which was five minutes before the burglar alarm shrieked a bajillion decibel warning.

I dove from the bed, grabbed my shotgun, flashlight, and cell phone that I always set up on the bedside table before going to sleep. I am not a graduate of the NRA's Basic Personal Protection in the Home course for nothing.

The house phone started ringing almost immediately, but I took time to lock my bedroom door before answering it. I gave ADT my name and code, told them I wasn't sure if there was an intruder, but that I was armed and prepared to defend myself if necessary. Meanwhile, I dialed 9-1-1 on the cell and said basically the same thing. Only then did I grab my remote, turn off the raucous alarm, and call Jan's cell phone. I knew for certain she would have locked her door when the alarm sounded. She answered immediately.

"H-hetta, what's happening?"

"Your door is locked, right?"

"Yes."

"Okay, stay on the phone. I'm locked in my room, the cops have been called, and I've got my shotgun. I won't come out unless you need me to. Do you hear anything?"

"No, nothing except Loca raising all Billy hell."

I cocked my head. Indeed Loca, the Rottweiler across the way was very agitated about something or someone. "I hear her. Did the security lights on your side of the house come on?"

"No."

"Mine either. Hang on, I'm going to hit the master. Every one of the outdoor lights should light up at the same time." I scooted to the bank of switches on my bedroom wall and, as the instructions said, flipped two of them off, then immediately back on. The desert and golf course lit up like a shopping mall parking lot.

"Are spots lit on your side? "

"Oh, yeah. Like the city of New York."

"Good. Go into your closet and shut the door. I'm going to do the same in my room. Again, if you hear someone messing with your bedroom door, I will come out blasting. Do not get in my line of fire, you hear me?"

"Okay, I'm in the closet. Now what?"

"We wait. I gotta call someone. Put your phone on vibrate and I'll call you right back, okay?"

Living in the middle of nowhere has its drawbacks, one of which is a lag in response time by the authorities. The old saying, 'When seconds count, the cops are just minutes away' would certainly apply. I had no idea how long that delay would be, so I picked up my cell and hit speed dial for Tim Ramos's personal number, hoping the Border Patrol agent was hunting down illegals in a nearby pasture. He didn't answer, so I left a message, then hit the number the homeowner had programmed into the house phone for the local Border Patrol office. Of course, I got a recording, so left yet another message.

Later I would wonder at the wisdom of renting a home with the Border Patrol in phone memory, but for now I was glad to have it. One can never have too many heavily armed good guys around.

I slid to the floor with my back against the wall and called Jan back.

Even though the temperature outside was in the mid-forties, the closet felt like a sauna. My trigger finger was slimy with sweat, so I pulled a tee shirt off a hanger and wiped my palms. Sitting in the pitch dark of that closet, straining to hear danger, I was comforted by Jan's breathing on the phone. Silly, I know, but one takes comfort where one can.

"Hetta," she rasped, "someone's jiggling my bedroom doorknob."

"Shit." I moved from the closet. One thing the NRA teaches you is to never stand on the other side of a door, so I leaned on the wall next to the doorframe and strained my ears, but any sound on the other side of the house was drowned out by blood pounding my eardrums.

"Jan?"

Her reply was a sob, followed by, "Oh, no. They're trying to break the door." I heard a pounding noise, but no splintering, then a curse.

"You stay put, I'm coming out."

"No. No, you can't."

"I can and I will. Sorry, honey, I have to hang up now. Stay in that closet so I don't shoot you." With that, I dialed 9-1-1, put the phone on SPEAKER and chucked it onto the bed.

When the operator asked, "What is your emergency?" I yelled, "Whoever you are in my house, leave. Now! I am armed and will defend myself."

I was now on record as fearing for my life, and warning whoever was scaring me that I was armed. In Arizona, a woman's home is her castle, as it is in Texas, and she has a right to self-defense, and that of her friends and family within. But was the intruder armed? At that moment, it hardly mattered. He had broken into my home, and was battering down a bedroom door behind which a defenseless woman hid. I had to remember that for the judge.

Another loud crash, this time with the distinct sound of splintering wood, told me time was up.

Easing my bedroom door open with the gun barrel, taking a quick peek around the door frame, I spotted the outline of a large figure in the hall across the living room, in front of the guestroom. Ducking to safety, I once again yelled a verbal warning, this time accompanied by a sound that usually sends any sane person running away: the pchk pchk—this is the best onomatopoeia I can come up with, but it doesn't do that chilling sound justice—of a pump action shotgun being chambered prior to some serious badassery.

I hadn't spent much time practicing with this particular gun. My father gave it to me after a little run-in with an unsavory character back in San Francisco. That time I'd used my grandmother's old 12-gauge, loaded with rock salt and dried bacon rind. My father, being a practical sort, decided this was not good enough and, for my birthday, bestowed upon me a 20Ga Remington 870 Wingmaster JR, with an 18.5-inch barrel. It's the thought that counts.

Don't let that *junior* thing fool you. While many consider this a starter gun for youngsters, I deem it the perfect weapon of home, or boat, defense because of its smooth action, and shortened butt stock. When I left for Mexico I had to leave it in Oakland, but thanks to Craig, that baby was back in my hands and ready for action.

In the nick of time, it seems.

When racking the slide, I prayed the intruder recognized that ominous sound and would head for the hills while dumping his own load, but the bastard turned and ran at me. "Stop or I will shoot!" I yelled, but the idiot never broke stride.

I fired and instantly re-chambered, even though he screamed, let loose a string of f-bombs, and disappeared through the open front door of the house.

Standing my ground, ready in case he was a complete moron and doubled back, I tried a little unsuccessful breath control. Shooting indoors is much louder than out in a cow pasture, but I keep a pair of earplugs attached to the gun, and had the good sense to use them. Even so, my ears rang, but not much louder than the roar of pumping blood. In spite of all that inner noise, I still heard the Rottweiler going nuts, then the blessed growl of high-powered engines. A lovely glow of flashing red and blue lights washed the living room walls.

Backing into my bedroom, I shut the door, told the 9-1-1 dispatcher the cops had arrived, where both

Jan and I were in the house, and hung up. The phone rang instantly.

Thinking it was Jan, I said, "Stay where you are for now. Everything's all right. I nailed the bastard and the cops are here."

"What?" Jenks squawked.

Crap.

"Uh, Jenks, I'm just a little busy right now. Can I call you back?"

Not waiting for his reply, I cut him off and called Jan, who wanted to know, "Hetta, who'd you shoot? I heard him yell. Is he really gone?"

"Yep. I sure hope the cops got him."

"Can I come out of the bedroom now?"

"Absolutely not. Lay down on the bed with your hands on your head, and the lights on. Bye."

I hung up, called 9-1-1 once again, affirmed we were both unharmed, and staying put. The dispatcher connected me directly to an officer outside my house. As I answered his questions, I slid to the floor and leaned against the bed, opened the breech on the gun, put it on the floor, and kicked it away.

Suddenly exhausted, I crawled on the bed and pulled the covers up to my chin.

My meltdown began with teeth chatters, then crying. A female officer bristling with firepower entered, spotted pitiful me on the bed, asked if I was injured, and then if I could stand. She was still taking no chances, wanted my hands on display, so I had to let go of my blankie.

Getting out of bed, with my hands held high and legs rubbery wasn't the easiest of feats, but I managed. "I'd move faster, if I could," I sniveled. "My legs feel like jelly. Did, uh, I kill someone?"

The officer lowered her gun and smiled. "Not with bacon and salt, you didn't, but you sure put a dent in his pride, hit him right in the nu…uh, groin."

Jan came up behind her and smirked. "Yeah, Hetta, they don't call you a ballbuster for nothin'. Thank God it's over. The bastard walked, well, limped, right into their arms. You did good."

"Yeah?" I snuffled.

"Yeah. And I have even better news. Here," she shoved her cell phone into my hand, "Jenks wants to talk to you."

Could this night get much worse?

I gave Jenks a quick rundown on what just happened, swearing on my saintly grandmother's grave that I had done absolutely nothing to bring the nutcase to my doorstep. Jenks, while sympathetic, didn't come across as convinced of my innocence, but did say he loved me and missed me and that counted for a lot. Our conversation was cut short by the arrival of yet another law officer.

Topaz Sawyer, a diminutive deputy with a head of hair which closely resembled that of a shaggy German Shepherd, led me to a dining room chair, asked if I'd like some water, and calmly began asking me questions. What I really wanted was a stiff shot of anything but water.

Jan had been escorted by a second officer into my office. My guess is they separated us to see if our stories of the night's events matched.

After another round of questioning, some of it repetitious, Ms. Topaz asked, “Do you make it a practice to leave your garage door open, Hetta?” We were practically bosom buddies after a half-hour in each other’s company.

“Absolutely not. It was closed, and I locked the door into the pantry, as well. I am very security conscious.”

Another deputy approached. “Looks like he tried that door, didn’t work, so he bumped the front door.”

“Bumped?”

“As in bump locked it.”

“Bump locked? What the heck is that?”

Topaz wrote something on the growing incident report. “It’s a master-type key you can buy on the Internet that, inserted into the lock and then bumped with a special tool, allows the key to turn. Takes a few seconds. We’ve seen a few break-ins we suspected were bumps, but this is the first time we caught the guy with the key.”

“Yeah,” another said. “Not only that, he evidently had your garage door opener, but thanks to a better locking system on the fire door into the house, he couldn’t bump the lock. We found the opener next to his SUV.”

“Was it white? His car?”

“Yes, why? Do you know someone with a white SUV?”

“I saw one earlier today when I was sitting in the courtyard. I heard a car, and the neighbor’s dog was barking, so I looked out. She only barks at strangers, so I knew it wasn't her owner or his family. A white car was leaving, headed down the road. We don't get much traffic, since it's a dead end."

Jan, who'd joined me at the dining table, opened her mouth, but slammed it shut at my warning look. She'd give me hell later for not telling her about the white SUV, especially in light of the one that chased us. On top of that, I thought we owed Ted a call before giving away the fact that my garage door opener was last seen on my VW's visor at his winery, so for now we needed to clam up.

"Well, the dude must be a moron," I said, "or can't read. There is an ADT sign outside, and stickers on all the windows."

"Truth is, a lot of folks have fake security signs. Maybe he thought no one was home, so even if the alarm went off, he'd have time to grab some stuff before police arrived. One thing for sure, I don't think he was expecting you to be armed."

Jan grinned. "Hetta's almost always armed. It's one of the reasons I hang out with her."

I shrugged. "Hey, my daddy always said some folks'll think you're paranoid if you carry a gun, but if you have a gun, what the hell do you need to be paranoid about?"

Topaz smiled. "So we can assume you have other firearms in the house?"

"Only a .38 revolver, which is in the office, a 30-30 in the hall closet, a .22 automatic in my bedroom, and a pellet pistol in the garage, for pigeons. I hate pigeons. Oh, and, uh, a .9mm Springfield XDM." I was reluctant to admit owning the semi-automatic with nineteen in the clip and one in the chamber, but figured I'd better come clean since they'd probably find it anyway.

"An XDM? Why didn't you use it, instead of a shotgun?"

"Truthfully? I figured XDM's were banned here, like in California." I also didn't want to admit I'd acquired it illegally in California. I have friends in low places.

"Nope. Hell, I wish I had one." Her smile widened. "Why rock salt and bacon rind in the shotgun? It works very effectively at close range, but won't do much otherwise."

"The second round is a double aught, and the last three are slugs. My grandmother says that's the way to load, you know, just in case."

"In case of what? That the guy is still in one piece? You must have some family," Topaz said, but again, there was a note of humor. "I'd say the guy got very lucky the first round nailed him, and even luckier he got out the door. If you can call stumbling right into the loving arms of a border patrol agent lucky. You called the Border Patrol after you dialed 9-1-1?"

"A gal cannot have too many armed men about. I called everyone I could think of. There is almost always a Border Patrol vehicle close by, so I figured they might respond first. Looks like I was right."

"They were Johnny on the spot. Any idea who this guy is?"

"Since I still haven't seen him, nope. I've only lived here for a few weeks, and I don't know a lot of people yet. You think he might have actually been after me?"

She shrugged. "It's a possibility."

"More like a probability," Jan mumbled under her breath.

"Excuse me?" Topaz asked.

Jan, cowed by my glare, said, "Nothin'."

After everyone left, we jammed a chair under the doorknob, even though the dead bolt was working fine again after being bumped. The next day, I planned to replace it with a new bump-proof model and charge the cost to the owner.

Jan and I had a glass of wine to calm our nerves and went back to bed for what was left of the night. I couldn't sleep, and gave up at six, even though it was still dark. Jan didn't fare any better in the sleep department, so morning found us jangled with caffeine, and generally grumpy. It was into this atmosphere that the hapless property manager bungled. Evidently, bad news passes fast in this small community.

When I opened the door, he was inspecting the door lock. Luckily I'd already mopped up the blood spatters in the hall and out in the courtyard.

"What now?" I growled.

"May I come in?"

I threw the door open, he stepped inside as though entering a viper pit.

Jan moved between us, whispering out of the side of her mouth, "The man is just doing his job, Hetta." To him, she asked, "You want some coffee?"

He eyed me warily. "Uh, that would be nice."

"We're out on the verandah. Go on out, Hetta will bring your coffee, won't you, dear? Cream and sugar?"

"Black."

I couldn't find any rat poison, so I left his coffee black and joined them outside. A foursome was on the green already, enjoying a morning that dawned surprisingly warm for their tournament. Little could they guess that just a few hours ago my house was the scene of crime, fear, and violence. My stomach did its twentieth flip-flop of the morning as the night's events rushed back.

"Are you all right, Miss Coffey?

"Yeah, Hetta, you look awful pale."

"I'm fine, or as fine as someone can be after being terrorized in the dark of night."

The property manager put his cup down. "Understandable that you are upset. After all, you shot a man."

Jan's eyes bugged out and she scooted her chair away from him, as though dodging the line of fire.

"Listen to me, you twerp. I am not upset because I blasted a piece of vermin who broke into my house in the middle of the night. I am upset because I didn't kill the bastard. And I am very upset that you rented me a house with unsafe locks on the doors."

The poor dude leapt to his feet, mouth hanging open in shock. "Now look, you can't possibly blame me, er, the owner, for this."

Jan read where I was headed and joined the fray. She hasn't studied at the side of the master for nothing. "Yeah, if it hadn't been for Hetta being here, your owner's stuff would probably be in Mexico by now. You should give poor Hetta a freakin' reward."

Atta girl, Jan.

"However, I'll settle for new locks. And not being evicted," I told him, doing my best to sound wronged. I would have added a sniffle, but thought that was overdoing it.

Scurrying for the front door, he said, "Someone will be here today to change the locks, and I've already informed your lawyer that she was correct, and you can have as many short-term visitors as you like. Sorry for your trouble." With this, he escaped.

We dissolved into giggles, drawing a frown from a golfer trying to sink a putt.

"Miss Coffey, I am Sergeant MaGee from the Cochise County Sheriff's department, Investigations Division. Do you mind if I come in and ask a few questions?"

I sized up the tall blonde dude at my front door. Covering most of his hair was a woolen cap, with, of all things, two blue earflaps. He was handsome, in an Irish Wheaton terrier sort of way. "Please. Want some iced tea?" *Or a dog biscuit*?

"No thank you, ma'am."

Jan tittered softly. She knows I loathe being addressed as ma'am. Every woman in the world probably remembers when it first happens, because from that day forward you are no longer a girl.

I bit my tongue and asked, "You gonna tell us who that jerk was last night?"

"First, I have a few questions."

That didn't sound good. I looked past him. He seemed to be alone, a good sign, as I doubt he'd come solo with intent to arrest. After all, they knew there were guns in the house. Still, my heart sped up.

I guided the investigator out onto the verandah, where brilliant sunshine superheated the concrete. He removed his cap, explaining he wore it to protect ears prone to both sunburn and chill. We made small talk about the golf course, where he played regularly, how we liked the area, stuff like that. I was relaxing a bit, taking a sip of tea, when he dropped the bomb. "Miss Coffey, what exactly is your association with known Mexican gang members?"

I spewed iced tea—luckily not all over the officer—and simultaneously managed to suck some down the wrong pipe. I was gasping for air and Jan rose to whack me on the back when I managed a breath and waved her off. Remembering to breathe through my nose, it was still three or four minutes before I regained control. "Sorry. What was the question?" As if I didn't know.

He repeated the question and I did what all guilty people do; I answered with a lame, "Why do you ask?"

"Because you shot one of the them last night, and even though he's not talking, we don't think he was here to steal the flat screen."

"Oh, shit," Jan groaned, "was it Paco?"

It's a good thing for her I'd put the guns away.

"...then this other guy," I told the riveted MaGee, "who we think might either be a drug lord or a US undercover agent of some kind, shot Paco, and we left them on the beach. Haven't seen either of them since."

The investigator never interrupted, but his head swayed as if watching a tennis match as Jan and I team-tagged our story. Our sentences tumbled into each other as we recounted our Mexican adventure, meeting Nacho and his fellow homies, then saving a village on the Baja from some druggies running a meth super lab, which Nacho blew up. We left out a few minor details, like our stealing Nacho's truck, Nacho subsequently kidnapping us, and what we considered his involvement in a huge border drug bust and a shootout between the Mexican federal police and a bunch of Zetas.

"So, as you can see, to answer your question, yes, we did sort of meet a gang member, a guy named Paco, but Nacho said he was ex MS-13, and we thought Nacho killed him," I explained, thinking I sounded quite logical.

At the mention of MS-13, the cop, who was glazing over a bit, sat bolt upright. "MS-13?"

"Yeah, but I think he switched to the Zetas at some point. I don't know much about gangs, just what I read in the paper. Anyhow, that's what Nacho told me. If you want some backup on my story, I can put you in touch with Marty Martinez, a retired Oakland homicide cop who was with us for part of the showdown."

He rubbed his forehead. "I think I'll have that tea now." Barely had those words been uttered when the front door burst open and Craig rushed in, with Chino right on his heels. He spotted MaGee and said, "Oh, looks like you've already heard."

"Heard what?" we all asked in unison.

"Those guys that stole your car and tried to hijack the plane? They are friggin' Zetas!" he bellowed.

Oops, I guess Jan and I forgot to tell Deputy Dawg that part of the story.

The afternoon became a virtual marathon of interviewers, who chugged down pitcher after pitcher of tea and gallons of coffee while talking with all of us. Seems the Sheriff of Cochise County has a keen interest in anything related to Mexican drug cartels. Craig knew little of interest to the various cops, but Chino was on scene for the Christmas Eve debacle. It was, after all, a search for his missing grandmother—whom, it turned out, was simply shacked up with a villager—that lead us to our fateful encounter with Paco.

Jan and I, of course, were grilled like salmon fillets. Cell phones aplenty stayed busy as agencies exchanged information with their home bases, and each other. Ted and Nanci were called again and again, probably tiring of repeating the same story to different people. Marty Martinez, my retired cop buddy, got a call or two at his home in Baja. I also picked up on enough of one conversation in Spanish to know the caller was conversing about some shadowy liaisons on both sides of the border.

As the hours dragged on and more information surfaced, one thing became abundantly clear; the common denominator in the whole complicated mess was none other than Miss Hetta Coffey.

It also became clear that no one knew why, including *moi*.

This probably would have been an ideal time for me to share that cryptic message from Nacho to mind my own business and stay away, but why open yet another can of worms? I was the only one, aside from a marina employee, who knew about that email, and for now I planned to keep it that way.

As soon as everyone left, though, I'd call the marina, see if by chance Nacho left a contact number they forgot about? Oh, sure, he probably left a business card reading:

Lamont "Nacho" Cranston
Shady undertakings our specialty
www.nachomuchomacho.com
Se Habla Espanol

Yeah, *Quando* pigs fly.

Chapter 34

When all the cops finally left, I called San Carlos.

The gal at the marina office wasn't the one who was there when Nacho showed up, but miracle of miracles, she told me my boat would be ready to launch in a week or ten days.

Shocked at such rapid progress, I called Arturo, my new boat blister guru and, second miracle of the day, he answered. Turns out my blisters were superficial and in a week he would have *Raymond Johnson* ready to splash. I hung up and did a victory dance. It was about time I got some good news.

Chino, Craig, and Jan went out to dinner, but I opted to stay put, grateful for time alone to ponder what in the hell was happening, and why.

After checking, then re-checking that all windows and doors were locked, and setting the alarm—which, like any borderline OCDer, I re-re-checked—I then bump-key proofed exterior doors, all five of them, by jamming chairs under the knobs.

Satisfied that Fort Knox had nothing on me, I then barricaded myself in my bedroom with my computer, a ream of paper, all five guns, a bottle of wine, and two family sized bags of potato chips. Hetta's last stand.

Sitting in the middle of the bed, I compiled a chronology of events, people, and places, beginning with the last time I saw Nacho.

Agua Fria, Baja, December 24: Nacho gunned down that psychopath, Paco, who was intent on slitting my throat. Saved from a nasty end, I returned to my boat where Jenks and I made a hasty exit. Since then, had I not received that *stay away* message, I wouldn't have put Nacho into this latest mix, but now he could be a major player. But how? Nacho warning me to stay away: What did it mean, and from where?

The mine: I took a job at the mine. Okay, but how on earth was that connected to Nacho, and thereby gang activity? Was my job at the mine somehow stomping on gang toes? Seemed a stretch, but if so, how does old Rat Face figure in? I didn't like him, but the only suspicious activity I could pin on him was some kind of relationship with the Xers, and the Xers reeked of dirty.

The Xer's: How dirty, and in what capacity? Other than my gut feeling, I had nothing on them, but they *are* here, and there *is* trouble. I don't believe in coincidence.

White SUV: First spotted at Rancho Sierra Coronado, then at the river ford. Same one that chased us up the Ruta Rio Sonora, and then brought the thug to my house? Another stretch.

The winery: Almost hijacked, car stolen. Again, my intuition screamed that two such insults upon my sweet self must be joined at the hip, but were they?

Paco: If he is indeed dead, as we assumed when we left his sorry bullet-ridden bod on the beach, then who would hold enough of a grudge, or have a motive, to come after me? Paco, dead or alive, kept popping up as my prime suspect. Even dead, he could be the problem. Nacho told me Paco had ties to MS-13, and no slight to one of theirs was ever forgiven. MS-13 wipes out entire families in brutal revenge for a simple insult to a member of their gang, so I suppose getting him killed might be construed as a dis, as they say in gang slang? As a bare bone fact, Paco might be alive today had I not been involved, peripherally as I was, in his demise.

So, if not revenge, then what? What had I bungled into this time?

Was it simply that I dialed 9-1-1, ratted out a group of human smugglers I encountered on my road and that set off this whole chain of events? Nah, too extreme.

My head ached from more questions than answers.

I read somewhere that some proponents of spiritual teachings insist there is absolutely no coincidence in the world, and everything that occurs can be related to a prior association, no matter how vast, minute, or trivial. Hmmm. That wasn't going to help me sleep any better, so I downed an Excedrin P.M.

I slept well, and long, never even hearing my friends return. They entered through the garage-to-pantry door, using their key for that deadbolt. I can only imagine their amusement at seeing all the other doors jammed with chairs.

When I awoke at nine the next morning, it was with a start and a moment of crystal clear clarity. Nacho was the key, and I had to find him.

Calling a meeting of the minds, I told everyone my theory that Nacho was somehow involved in this mess, and was the one person who might explain all events. He was the common denominator, not me, I reasoned.

"How do you figure that? So far, Miss Hetta, I do not recall seeing Nacho being hijacked, nor his home invaded by Zetas. That would be you."

"However, Jan," Craig said, "you were there in both cases, as well. How do we know it's not you they're after?"

"History. No one is ever after me, it's always Hetta. For the past twenty damned years—"

I cut her off. "Let's get on track here. Chino, you got any ideas?"

He shook his head. "No. I think Jan and I should return to the Baja. Craig, you must come, as well."

"What am I? Shark chum?" I demanded. "Sure, throw me under the bus, run off to the safety of those damned whales, all of you."

Jan shot Chino a dirty look and stuck out her chin. "You go hide amongst your whales, Chino. Even if Hetta is the screw up here, I'm not abandoning her."

"Hey, why am I the screw up?"

"You let them find you. I told you, after that Baja debacle, to get yourself and your boat out of Mexico, but nooo, you never listen."

"I had no reason to leave. Nacho took care of Paco."

"Did he, now? I wasn't invited to a funeral, were you?"

"Back to my original premise. We have to find Nacho and ask him if that pervert really died."

Jan flipped her hands into the air. "Like we could possibly track down a guy who thinks he's The Shadow, and is either a dope dealer or a federal agent of some kind for who knows what country? Plus, if you had any common sense at all, which you don't, you'd stay the hell out of Mexico."

Chino, obviously stung by Jan's practically calling him a coward, quietly said, "I can find him. No one is looking for me. I'm Mexican, I blend in. I'll go in search of this Nacho. I saw him on the beach Christmas eve, so I know what he looks like."

We all stared at him, then Jan batted her eyelashes. "Really?"

Chino blushed and nodded.

"I'll go with you, Chino," Craig volunteered.

"Sorry, my friend, but you cannot. No offense, but you would seem writ large in Mexico."

Writ large? I love it when Chino's British education surfaces.

We were still discussing our next move when the phone rang. I answered, talked a couple of minutes, and returned to the group.

"Okay, I want everyone out of my house. Pronto."

"Oh, come on, Hetta, we're just trying to help."

"And I appreciate it. Forget Nacho, forget everything. Pack up and hit the road, all of you."

Jan’s eye’s narrowed. “Who was that on the phone?”

I couldn’t hold back a grin any longer. “Jenks. He’s hitched a ride on a private jet that’ll dump him in Tucson, and he’ll be here tonight. I don’t care why, I just know I’m a very happy camper, so scram. I’ll spring for your hotel bills.”

Chapter 35

A CPA, a veterinarian, and a marine biologist head for Mexico in search of a mystery man; stop me if you've heard this one.

Within two hours of Jenks's call, my friends were packed up and ready to go.

Chino was to lead the search for Nacho, and Jan agreed to go along on his word that he would buy a fully equipped RV, with satellite TV, for the beach camp. Rather than put them on a bus, I generously lent them my new pickup because they wouldn't all fit into Craig's money machine, nor was it the ideal vehicle for inconspicuously stalking Nacho. That still left me with Aunt Lillian's tank, and a shiny red Porsche I promised not to drive.

Waving them a fond farewell, I did a little jig. I was a free woman, with my house my own for the first time in what seemed like ages. At first I reveled in my solitude, spending the first few hours piling everyone's leftover stuff into the garage and house cleaning. Finally, I took a break on the verandah, enjoying the quiet, waving to a few golfers. A sense of unease, however, rose as the bright Arizona sun began to set, and I fled into the safety of the house, within easy reach of firepower.

After all, Jenks was on his way, but not yet here.

Jenks called from Tucson, sounding tired, but said he couldn't wait to see me.

I'd already set the table and readied all his favorites: meatloaf, real mashed potatoes, corn on the cob, peas, and ice cream. Okay, not very romantic, but it is what he loves. I remember returning to the States after long stays overseas, looking forward to good old American fare.

After an extra long, hot shower, I laid my clothes out for the evening. First I unpacked a pair of Eff-me pumps with six-inch heels I hadn't worn in months, since they'd been stored, along with my guns and other clothes, at Jenks's apartment in Oakland. I sent Craig an ESP *thank you* for bringing them to me.

Thanks to Craig's no white stuff and exercise regime, an emerald green silk cheongsam I'd had custom made in Hong Kong fit better than ever. The prim Mandarin collar, and side slits to you-know-where, balanced a nice-and-naughty gal look guaranteed to snag and keep a guy's attention. With it, I wore only the ruby pendant Jenks gave me, dangly earrings to match, and those high, high, heels.

I hadn't gussied up in a dog's age, and narrowly avoided blinding myself with the mascara wand. Living on a boat had taken its toll, but two hours of primping covered a multitude of sins. After painting my nails what Jan referred to as Floozie Red, I impatiently waved them in the air to dry while checking the clock.

Poofing my hair one last time, I gave myself a boob boost, tugged at my hem, and dabbed on a little more Joy. Oh, yes, I was sooo ready for Jenks.

A last glance in the mirror almost had me undo the whole getup. It was too much. I looked like a Hong Kong street walker. Way too eager, too desperate, too—the doorbell rang and I flew through the house, damned near taking a header, unaccustomed as I was to heels.

So much for playing hard to get.

Throwing open the door I said, "You made good—oh, hell."

"*Quierda*, you are not glad to see me?"

"Nacho? What are you doing here?"

"Café, you never call, you never write."

He gently pushed the door open, stepped in, locked it behind him.

I stood there like the idiot I am while he checked out the room's low lighting and crackling fire, then gave me and my outfit a long slow look, raising his eyebrows in approval. The table was set for two, a bottle of Viña de las Estrellas champagne chilling in a silver bucket, candles flickering everywhere, and flamenco guitar music played low. Taking a step closer, he half-whispered, around that lazy, sexy smile of his, "So, you *were* expecting me?"

I found my voice. "You are the last person I reckoned on. Did you come to tell me what that ridiculous message you sent me means? I've got people out looking for you, so just tell me and get lost." I didn't know whether to be frightened or annoyed, and was doing a fair job of being both.

Nacho ignored my rudeness. "Café, you are actually beautiful."

The surprised tone in his statement pissed me off. I inched toward the granite bar, where my .9mm semi-automatic lay in plain sight.

He glanced at the gun, moved between me and it. "Chica, is that an XDM, or are you just glad to see me?"

"Very funny. Now, either start talking, or beat it."

"No hug, after all we've been through together?"

"Ya know, Nacho, a wise man once said, 'I learned long ago, never to wrestle with a pig. You get dirty, and besides, the pig likes it.'"

"George Bernard Shaw."

Nacho never ceases to amaze me. "Look, I'm expecting company, so whatever it is, make it fast, *Ignacio*."

His jillion-watt grin made him even more handsome, if that's possible. "So you *have* been thinking of me. Do you know what my name, Ignacio, means?"

I shook my head.

"Fiery."

Despite the fact that Jenks was on his way, I felt a little tingle way down low. Nacho has a way of making that happen. I gulped. "Just talk."

He shrugged. "Okay, okay. Those little problems you've been having with, shall we say, undesirable types? It is done."

"Done?"

"Done. *Termino*. You made a grievous error in judgment when you challenged those men from the RV park."

How did he know about that? I played dumb. "What are you talking about?"

"Let me refresh your memory. You and your friends were having breakfast at the golf club and the men you refer to as the Xers were there. One of them said to you, 'My, your entourage just grows and grows, and you said, 'And yours changes.' This was not smart on your part, Café, as your friend, Allison, told you. Also, it forced our hand. We had to move up our operation."

I was dumbfounded. Did they, whoever they were, have the tables bugged? If not, someone was right there, listening and reporting verbatim. "Oh, yeah? Well what did I have for breakfast?"

"Enchiladas. Look, you can be angry later, I just want you to know you are safe. It is over." He handed me a newspaper. "Tomorrow's edition. You will find it interesting."

We both heard the pop and growl of a car pulling into my gravel driveway.

"I must, reluctantly, leave you, but first," he handed me a card, "take this. Memorize the number, destroy the card. Ask for me, Lamont. *Adios, mija, y vaya con Dios*." He gave me the faintest lip brush just below my ear, then, just like that he was gone, letting himself out through the French doors facing the golf course.

I stood transfixed, staring into the darkened glass. A hot spot burned where his lips touched my skin. The doorbell jangled me, I whirled, and this time looked out before opening the door.

Jenks wrapped me in his long, strong arms, and I immediately forgot Nacho.

Jenks forgot he was tired.

Chapter 36

It wasn't until the next morning that I read the card and newspaper Nacho gave me. They were both lying under a jumble of emerald silk and six-inch heels. The card read:

L. Cranston Pest Control
1-800-gotbads?
We get what's bugging you.

A quiet hiccup of laughter escaped as I opened the newspaper and read the headlines in the *Sierra Vista Observer*:

Human Smuggling and Drug Ring Busted in Southeast Arizona, Dozens Others arrested in Both Arizona and California

Bisbee: On Friday, the Cochise County Sheriff's office announced the arrests of Muhammed Yusef Ali, 35, and Malik Aylousa, 38, both from the Los Angeles area, along with eight East African illegals from Tanzania, on Highway 92. An undisclosed amount of illegal drugs were also confiscated.

The two Americans were allegedly transporting East African illegals from Mexico to Los Angeles in a luxury RV reported stolen in the Los Angeles area several months prior. The arrests are a result of an incident last December, when U.S. Border Patrol agents stopped a vehicle for speeding in Bisbee and discovered it was being driven by an East African without proper documentation. This led to an extensive investigation leading back to Naco, and a Black Muslim group in Los Angeles with ties to a Mexican cartel. Two of the members, Ali and

Aylousa, had been residing in the stolen recreational vehicle at a local RV park, and both have extensive criminal records that include money laundering and drug charges.

Police and federal agencies say many more arrests on both sides of the border are imminent. The *Los Angeles Times* reports that smugglers get up to forty thousand dollars a head for East Africans, and that Muslim groups in the United States are cashing in on helping their fellow Muslims gain entry into the US.

In recent years, Mexican drug cartels have largely taken over the human smuggling trade out of Mexico, and officials suspect the American smugglers are working with gang members to transport East African and other Muslims through Mexico into the United States. The cartels, that in the past used Mexican illegals to transport drugs, have turned to lucrative human smuggling.

A U.S. Border Patrol spokesman told the *Observer*: "The drug cartels have determined this is big business. Drug cartels control these corridors. Just like we're watching them here, they're watching us. It used to be, 'Get across the fence and run.' Now it's a lot more organized."

The involvement of the cartels in the human smuggling trade has made life even more dangerous for our Border Patrol agents. Often, when agents encounter a so-called coyote, they are attacked. As Homeland Security steps up its war on drugs and smuggling, the cartels find new venues for their drugs and money.

Recently, airplanes and ultralights have been used to move drugs. Most are stolen in Northern Mexico, loaded with drugs, flown across the border to remote landing sites, then abandoned. Two recent incidents involving a daring daylight hijacking of a Cessna 206 in the state of Baja California Norte, and an attempted hijacking in northern Sonora indicate an escalation in cartel methods, and boldness, as both planes were occupied by American citizens. No Americans were harmed in either incident, but Mexican authorities report three men killed in the attempted hijack in Sonora.

Illustrating just how ingrained the human smuggling business has become in Arizona, is the announcement by Immigrations and Customs Enforcement that they discovered a record 163 drop houses last year in the Phoenix area.

In a small box on the same page, another article:

Mexican Marines Raid Ranch in Sonora, At least 20 Dead

HERMOSILLO, Mexico: Mexican marines and other authorities raided a ranch in the northern border state of Sonora and rescued six people who were allegedly kidnapped by an organized crime gang. The Department of the Navy said the people were kidnapped in separate incidents over the past few weeks, but declined to say why.

The ranch, once a resort visited by the likes of Ronald Reagan, had fallen into the hands of the drug cartel, and was allegedly being used as a staging area for both human and drug smuggling. More disturbing are unconfirmed reports that some of the dead included members of Fatah al-Islam, a radical Palestinian Islamist faction said to be linked to al-Qaeda, and operating out of Lebanon. The US State Department declined to comment.

Whoa there, Nelly. Were the two incidents related? Good grief, I had really stumbled into it this time but, like Nacho said, my troubles were at an end. It somehow seemed too easy, all the loose ends tied up like that, but there it was in black and white. I reread the articles.

"Three Mexicans killed in the Sonora plane-jacking incident? No way," I said aloud. "Old Booger Red messed 'em up some, but my guess is the police finished them off." I threw the *Observer* down, hitting Jenks's arm.

Jenks jerked awake. "Who? Up to what?" he asked hoarsely. He'd slept in, jet lag messing with his habit of getting up at four most mornings.

"Sorry, I thought you were awake. Some guys at the RV park I call the Xers. Craig said they were up to no good and," I shook the paper at him, "he was right. Looks like you came to save me for nothing. Not that I mind, mind you."

He grabbed me and pulled me onto the bed. "Well I'm good and awake now."

Much, much, later we went to the golf club for breakfast so I could get the inside lowdown on the Xer bust, which was the biggest happening in Naco since it was bombed in 1929.

It was then that an Irish Catholic by the name of Patrick Murphy, after steadily imbibing in Bisbee's famous Brewery Gulch, had an epiphany: he'd lend a hand to the poor Mexican Catholics who were waging war against their government for their anti-church activities.

The Cristero Rebellion, as it was called, had been going way too long, with its fellow Catholics losing ground.

Murphy kept an airplane in Cananea, and fueled with booze and religious fervor, he decided it was time to bomb the Mexican troops in Naco, Sonora. His aim failed him, and instead he dropped a bomb on Naco, Arizona, making that town the only place on the continental United States to suffer an aerial bombing.

An American movie operator was injured, the Naco Pharmacy lost it's windows, and several other stores were shattered. To make matters worse, Murphy did it again four days later, this time blowing up the car of an Mexican army general who kept it parked on the American side for safekeeping.

Murphy was eventually shot down by the Mexicans, but neither country bothered filing charges.

Times, they have a-changed.

Now the Xers were looking at major jail time, and over a hundred more Tanzanians and a few Chinese illegals were rounded up in LA, with the investigation ongoing. Homeland Security hinted it was just the tip of a very profitable iceberg. "So, I wonder, what were these Tanzanians gonna do here in the states?"

Tim Ramos, the agent I was grilling shrugged. "We hear they work in Muslim-owned businesses, for one thing."

"How can they ever pay back forty grand that way?"

"Not so hard to do. If you figure what they'd have to pay legal employees, what with a minimum wage, overtime and the like—they work these guys twelve, fourteen hours a day, six, seven days a week—illegals are a bargain. They are virtual slaves for a few years, then they can begin sending money home."

Jenks, with his quick head for math, calculated that a minimum wage employee, working forty hours a week, plus more in overtime, could pull down over thirty thousand a year if all were legal. Businesses using willing slaves made economic sense. And if, on the way into the country, the illegals pack in some drugs to boot, it didn't take a Harvard Bidness School grad to see why so many risked so much.

"Not only do I now understand the problem, I also see how this is a war that needs serious attention. If Mexico isn't going to become Colombia, Washington better get it's head out of it's ass and give Mexico a whole bunch of support," Jenks said as we rode home in the golf cart.

"Not money. It will just disappear into politician's pockets. What a mess."

"You think it's bad over here, you should be where I've been."

Was that an invite? So far Jenks had avoided the subject of Dubai. We parked the cart in the garage, and as we were getting out, he said, "Let's go down to San Carlos for a few days before I have to head for San Francisco."

"Oh, jes." I called the marina and they told me my boat was ready, they'd splash her that afternoon on the high tide and send in a clean up squad to have her ready for us by the time we arrived the next day.

Ted called. Both Rosa and Lupe were home, and yes, they were kidnapped and held at Rancho Sierra Coronado until freed by the Marine raid, but they didn't know why they were taken. The missing cobalt rods were still a mystery, but all he cared about was they were home safe and sound. However, Sonrisa had not returned since we dropped her off the week before in Naco, and he feared she'd been scared off permanently. I tried to sound sympathetic.

I called Maria at the mine, asked if she'd be in the next morning so I could drop off some paperwork for her to forward to Mexico City.

"Oh, yes, Café, I will be here, but please address your correspondence to *Señor* Orozco. *Señor* Racón was called back to Lebanon on an urgent family business matter."

Man, oh man, my day was getting better by the minute.

"I want to make us legal," I declared as Jenks and I packed the car for our trip south.

He almost dropped a suitcase, probably thinking I was about to propose marriage. I let him stew for a three-count, then let him off the hook. "If we're gonna stop by Ted and Nanci's on the way back, now that the world is a safer place, we're actually gonna get a car permit for the drive up the Rio Sonora Valley."

Was that vast relief washing over his tanned and handsome face? "Uh," he stammered, "I thought you didn't need one anymore."

"Not for San Carlos, or on the main roads to get there, but when we go to Ted and Nanci's winery we'll be outside of what the Mexicans so charmingly call the Hassle Free Zone, and after the last trip I took through there, hassled doesn't sound like fun."

"We can get the permit at the Naco border?"

"You know, I'm not sure, but I'm going to give it a shot. Damned if I'm going to drive out of my way to Agua Prieta to get one, so if that's the case, we'll travel on good intentions and a fair smattering of Gringo denseness should we get pulled over. Besides, we're driving Aunt Lillian's car, so if it gets confiscated, so what?"

"I love your ability to make a situation work to your best intentions. Or your worst."

"It's a gift."

Chapter 37

We rolled through the border just as the usual gaggle of school kids, hauling backpacks, chatting, laughing, and jostling each other, headed into Arizona. Once again I went through the explanation of the border school situation. Jenks wondered if there was traffic the other way, for kids whose families wanted them to attend school in Naco, Sonora.

"Hmmm, good question, but I don't recall seeing uniformed kids heading south, and as you will see, the ones in Mexico are wearing the plaid. Crap."

"What?"

"Red light. We have to go through customs. No big deal, all we have is some food and our clothes. I locked all the guns in a closet back at the house."

Jenks grinned at this. "Most people, Hetta, do not carry arsenals in their vehicles."

"The events of the past few weeks have made me touchy. And as old Thomas Jefferson said, 'Those who hammer their guns into plows will plow for those who do not.' I hate to plow."

Jenks was still chuckling when we pulled into the Aduana inspection bay. A very attractive young lady in a tight uniform leaned over Jenks and opened the glove compartment, flashing cleavage in his face. Lucky for her I left the guns at home.

She asked me to pop the trunk, and took interest in my brief case, which she asked me to open.

Since I planned to stop by my office at the mine on the way to San Carlos, I'd thrown my latest work into the case. Not finding reams of drug money in my Halliburton case, she bid us a good trip and sashayed back to her office. Every Mexican man within viewing distance watched her swaying rear with avid appreciation. Jenks, however, did not, bless his little soul.

I moved the car into the first parking spot I found, in front of a *farmacia*, and told Jenks, "You gotta walk across the street, right there where we crossed the border. That's where you get your tourist visa. Mine's still good." I pointed to the *Migracion* office. "Get the one that's good for a week. It's free, and no sense spending twenty bucks, since we're coming back anyhow. You can spend that twenty on my precious self."

He smiled, promised me a few precious Margaritas, and I watched him walk away, thinking how wonderful it was to have him home, no matter how briefly. No matter the reason. Which, by the way, he'd been pretty vague about, but I suspected my friend Allison had put more than a quiet word in the Trob's ear about our situation. Whatever it was, I didn't care. He was here, and I was glad. More like thrilled.

I gathered Aunt Lillian's car papers, along with my passport and purse, and was exiting the car to find out about a sticker so we could travel legally to Ted and Nanci's for a change, when I spotted a lone child, headed for the border crossing. Bundled up like Nanook of the North, she struggled, head down, with a heavy backpack, but kept up a purposeful stride seldom seen in children on the way to school.

Smiling to myself, I remembered another little girl, back in grade school, foot-dragging it alone instead of with other kids, already marching to a different drummer. I'd have to analyze that trait some day, because it seemed to carry through all too often into my present life.

Sighing, I was locking the door when my hand froze on the handle. The forty-degree temperature was nothing compared to the chill that ran through my entire being.

In a flash, I knew. I *knew*.

Everything that had happened during the past few weeks fell into place with a crash that made my knees weak. *Everything*.

Through the window at Immigration, I saw Jenks sitting at the official's desk, studiously filling out forms. Two young soldiers lounged against the wall at the Aduana on my side of the street. No cars waited at the border to cross into the United States.

Only the lone child strode toward the pedestrian crossing.

One lone child with a Huipil backpack.

I, like many, have had moments of knowing. Like the time, when I let go of a plastic loop at a county fair, I *knew* it would perfectly ring the bottle and win me a huge Teddy bear. Once, in Vegas, I *knew*, when I placed a stack of chips on 14, that it would win. It was a combination of déjà vu, because I saw myself winning before I acted, and premonition. Whatever, both times, when I thought about them later, were a little frightening.

This moment, however, was not one of clairvoyance, but more like one that a safecracker must experience when the tumblers all fall into place.

Sonrisa's constant meanderings along the highway and into Naco.

Sonrisa's barely disguised contempt for Americans.

Sonrisa at Ted's airport during the hijacking attempt, eyes wide with surprise and fear. She had expected to get into that plane after the men took it from us.

Sonrisa sitting quietly in Nanci's car on the way back to the border after the attempted hijack, then the radiation detector going off at the border. Not because of Jan's stress test, but because of stolen cobalt pencils from the winery that Sonrisa carried in that Huipil pack.

A terrorist had been in the car with us, transporting what was needed to construct a dirty bomb: cobalt pencils.

I. Just. Knew.

I jumped into the car, started it, backed out into the empty street, and hooked a U-turn back toward the border. As I picked up speed, everything else seemed to move in slow-mo time, even my breathing.

Calculating distance and timing, I also knew what I had to do.

How ironic that Sonrisa and I should be destined to share a fate.

The first person to notice me was Jenks.

He was standing by the immigration officer's desk, half-turned to leave, as my aunt's car streaked by in the wrong direction, going almost airborne on steep speed bumps. His expression, as I registered it in my peripheral vision, went from quizzical to alarmed. Then he was gone from my field of vision, and only one thing remained, much like when you reverse a telescope.

My hands, freezing and sweating at the same time, lost all feeling. As I sailed over the speed bumps on the Mexican side of the border and landed with a rib-jarring, axel-threatening whomp, I floored the accelerator.

A US border guard who was looking my way, reached toward his weapon. His mouth opened to sound a warning. Another ran to his side, dropped to one knee, and aimed in my direction just as my bumper connected with Sonrisa.

With a sickening thud, Sonrisa went airborne. I stomped the brakes, but skidded under her. She fell onto the hood and my forward momentum sent her head crashing through the windshield, which imploded into a million tiny nuggets. Wide dead eyes stared at me from where the glass used to be, and her tiny body was twisted at an odd angle so I could see both her hands. They were empty. Her Huipil backpack lay in the crosswalk.

Looking into those cold, and truly dead eyes, I had a sudden moment of clarity: I had to get the hell out of Mexico. To the Mexican's thinking, I had just run down one of their children like they would a stray dog.

Jumping from the car onto lead legs, I smacked right into Jenks, who grabbed me by the shoulders. "Jesus, Hetta, what in the hell just happened here? What is wrong with you?"

Pounding feet and rattling weapons heralded Mexican soldiers, but the US border officials wisely stayed put on American soil. I didn't blame them, because that was damned sure where I wanted to be.

I pointed at the backpack and yelled, "Jenks, bomb! We have to get across the border."

He didn't hesitate for an instant. Yelling out, "American citizens," he held both hands high, one with his passport in clear view. Following his lead, I threw my hands onto my head, and we both ran, quite literally, for our lives. Problem was, we had a good chance of getting cut down by friendly fire before I had a chance to explain.

Come to think of it, how would I explain? Sonrisa lay dead on the Mexican side of the border, and I had, in front of probably twenty witnesses, killed her in cold blood.

It was at that moment I spotted agent Tim Ramos, crouched, weapon drawn. "Tim!" I screamed, "bomb! In the backpack!" I headed straight for my fellow Texan, praying his knowing me would count for something.

Within seconds Jenks and I were at the bottom of a pile of uniformed agents, every one of them with a gun or two. Through a break in human limbs, I saw the Mexicans stop and drop, their guns aimed at our pileup.

Although I was pinned like a quarterback with a bad defensive line, I managed to yell, once more, "Bomb! Dirty bomb! In that backpack! She's a suicide bomber!"

Something very solid, maybe a boot belonging to a fleeing member of Homeland Security, whacked me solidly in the head and I literally saw stars.

Then the world exploded.

Chapter 38

From the sounds and smell, I knew I was in a hospital and hoped it wasn't one affiliated with a federal prison on either side of the border.

A hand rested on my arm, and I instinctively knew it was Jenks's. Okay, two for two. I was alive, and so was Jenks. However, I resisted opening my eyes, because I feared some part of me was missing. Not my arm, at least.

On the bad side, however, was I facing life in a Mexican jail for vehicular manslaughter, or life in an American prison for the same? Nope, I'd just as soon go back to sleep.

"Hetta, I know you can hear me," Jenks whispered.

"No, I can't," I mumbled, surprised how much that small effort hurt. Oh, yes, sleep was definitely better, so I went back out. This time though, I actually dreamed.

I was back on the boat in the Sea of Cortez, lying on the warm deck, naked, hand in hand with Jenks. Bright sunlight warmed my eyelids, washed my svelte (hey, this is *my* dream here) body. The boat rocked gently in a slight, cooling breeze. Wavelets slapped the bow, sea gulls skreighed, a fish splashed.

Then somehow Nacho pulled alongside in a fishing panga. "...and the authorities on both sides of the border, at the highest level, want this kept under wraps. Hetta need not worry," I heard him say.

Jenks asked, "But what about the, uh, bad guys?"

Bad guys? Come on, let's call a spade a spade. "Terrorists," I croaked, and opened my eyes.

Both men stared at me, then Nacho glanced back over his shoulder at the closed door to my hospital room. "Ah, Café, you are awake, after all. Jenks and I were discussing the, er, situation."

"Is she dead?"

"Who?" Nacho pulled an innocent smile.

"Sonrisa, with the bomb."

"We know of no one named Sonrisa, and no bomb. That bump on the head has stirred your overly vivid imagination."

"But—"

Jenks cut me off. "No buts. Never happened."

Okay, I can be a little dense at times, but I finally got it. "What never happened?"

They both smiled.

Epilogue

The boat rocked gently in a slight, cooling breeze.

Wavelets slapped the bow, sea gulls shrieked, a fish splashed. We were back on the boat in the Sea of Cortez, lying on the warm deck, naked, hand in hand. Jenks snored softly as bright sunlight warmed my eyelids, washed my body.

This time though, it was real, not some hospital drug dream, and Nacho was not in the picture. In fact, we had not seen him since that day in the hospital. My guess is he had a whole heap of covering up to do. We will probably never know who Nacho is, or who he works for, but two-to-one his employer goes by a well-known acronym. Maybe it's better we don't know, for he'd most likely have to kill us. I still have his card, even though he told me to memorize the phone number and tear it up, just in case I need to be sprung from another fine mess involving dope dealers, smugglers, and suicide bombers.

No report ever surfaced about Sonrisa's attempt to detonate herself at a US Border crossing. It was as though she did not exist, therefore she could not die. Jenks and I put our heads together and came up with a theory that Sonrisa was meant to take a kamikaze dive out of Ted's plane after it was hijacked, most likely into Fort Huachuca.

Who was she, and why would she do it? The only hard evidence of her was an embroidered shawl Rosa found in her room. The Arabic writing, when transcribed, read Safiyya. I looked up that name and learned that Safiyya was Muhammad's aunt who saved Muslims from destruction in the battle of the Trench when she heroically killed a Jewish spy. Muhammad's eleventh wife was also named Safiyya.

I Googled Muslims in Mexico and was astonished to find a site claiming Muslim extremists were actively converting poor Mexican Indians to their religion, then recruiting them to do their dirty work. Perhaps Sonrisa found a home with them, one she had never had as an outcast in her own country. I gave Border Patrol agent Ted Ramos the photo I'd snapped of Rosa and Sonrisa on the road the first day we met them. Maybe the government types could figure out who she really was.

Ted and Nanci Burns learned more details of the raid at Rancho Sierra Coronado. Rosa and Lupe were held hostage in a storage shed, but never knew why. I knew, but was not allowed to tell them, that Sonrisa was sent to their winery on a mission to steal the cobalt rods.

Newspapers reported the roundup of more East African Muslims in a San Diego INS raid. A human smuggling ring, linked to a local mosque, and a group of Lebanese-born Mexican citizens had been operating out of an undisclosed location in northern Sonora. The Africans were deported, smugglers jailed.

The strike in Cananea is nearing its end, as is my contract. The office scuttlebutt is less about strikes and more about the mysterious disappearance of El Ratón. No one but me knew of his connection to a smuggling ring and a terrorist group. Too bad he escaped to Lebanon before my buddy Nacho could get his hands on him. Or did he?

Doctor Brigido "Chino" Yee and Doctor Sister Jan Sims are still counting whales in the Baja, but now they live in a fancy RV complete with satellite TV, high speed Internet, and, best of all, indoor plumbing. Chino's love life has taken a turn for the better.

My new Uncle Fred called from Mazatlan, where he and Aunt Lillian have rented a house on the beach. Although I'd last seen my aunt's car in Mexico, engine running, body sprawled across the hood, I reported it stolen from a side street in old Bisbee. Auntie collected the insurance money, and the car probably has a new and happy home with some Mexican who is less than squeamish about a few bloodstains.

Dr. Craig Washington bought a restored miner's shack in Bisbee, and has opened a mobile large animal practice operating on both sides of the border. His new partner, in more ways than one, is the cattle rancher we'd met at the golf club. Turns out he owns a huge spread near Bisbee. For the first time ever, Craig is with someone who has more money than he has, and who actually treats him well. Of course, they are deep in the closet, but for them it is a good and comfortable closet. Vinny enjoys the run of Craig's new digs and is actively seeking a partner of his own.

Booger Red was the extremely reluctant recipient of Craig's implanted tracking chip, and I would have dearly loved to watch that operation. I heard there were only a few injuries. At least Ted and Nanci can rest easy the big bull won't surprise them, or any of the many Europeans who flock by the bus load to sample their wine, now that they won another prestigious international award for their Bull Nose Burgundy.

Jenks got over being displeased with me, but not before declaring I could give Jimmy Carter lessons on creating international disasters. He will return to Dubai for a few weeks, but until then he is all mine, and when my contract ends, I'll meet him in Paris. *Oh, là à!*

A seagull landed on a rail and awked for a treat, waking Jenks. He turned onto his side, pulled me close, and made me very happy.

My Jenks is a man of few words, but very, very, good deeds.

~The end~

About the Author

Raised in the jungles of Haiti and Thailand, with returns to Texas in-between, Jinx followed her father's steel-toed footsteps into the Construction and Engineering industry in hopes of building dams. Finding all the good rivers taken, she traveled the world defacing other landscapes with mega-projects in Alaska, Japan, New Zealand, Puerto Rico and Mexico.

Like the protagonist in her mystery series, Hetta Coffey, Jinx was a woman with a yacht—and she's not afraid to use it—when she met her husband, Robert "Mad Dog" Schwartz. They opted to become cash-poor cruisers rather than continue chasing the rat, sailed under the Golden Gate Bridge, turned left, and headed for Mexico. They now divide their time between Arizona and Mexico's Sea of Cortez.

Her other books include a YA fictography of her childhood in Haiti (*Land of Mountains*), an adventure in the Sea of Cortez (*Troubled Sea*) and an epic novel of the thirty years leading to the fall of the Alamo (*The Texicans*).

From the author

Thank you for taking time to read my book. If you enjoyed it, consider telling your friends about

Hetta, or posting a short review on Amazon. Word of mouth is an author's best friend, and is much appreciated.

I have editors, but boo-boos do manage to creep into a book, no matter how many people look at it before publication, and if there are errors, they are all on me. Should you come upon one of these culprits, please let me know and I shall smite it with my mighty keyboard!

You can email me at jinxschwartz@yahoo.com

And if you want to be alerted when I have a free, discounted, or new book, you can go to http://jinxschwartz.com and sign up for my newsletter. I promised not to deluge you with pictures of puppies and kittens.

BookBub is another way to learn of my free or new books. You can follow my author page there and they will alert you when my books are featured. https://www.bookbub.com/authors/jinx-schwartz

Also, you can find me on Facebook at https://www.facebook.com/jinxschwartz That puppy and kitten thing? No promises on FB posts :-)

Just the Pits (Book 5 in the Hetta Coffey series).

Hetta is hired for what sounds like an unusually legitimate mining project in Mexico's Baja, so it looks like smooth sailing ahead...until she discovers that people and pesos are disappearing faster than you can say, "This job is the pits!"

And Hetta Coffey as sleuth? Goodness knows she's nosy enough, but her detective skills leave a lot to be desired. Luckily for her she gets help from her best friend, Jan, and a mysterious Velveeta thief.

Amazon link: **http://bit.ly/jtpits**

Made in the USA
Middletown, DE
10 August 2018